CONTEN

Introduction	v
Prologue	1
Chapter 1 *Greer*	9
Chapter 2 *Ryder*	31
Chapter 3 *Greer*	45
Chapter 4 *Greer*	59
Chapter 5 *Ryder*	73
Chapter 6 *Greer*	93
Chapter 7 *Greer*	109
Chapter 8 *Ryder*	125
Chapter 9 *Ryder*	141
Chapter 10 *Greer*	159
Chapter 11 *Greer*	171
Chapter 12 *Ryder*	185
Chapter 13 *Greer*	203
Chapter 14 *Greer*	217
Chapter 15 *Ryder*	235
Chapter 16 *Greer*	249

Chapter 17 *Ryder*	263
Chapter 18 *Greer*	275
Epilogue	293
Hello lovelies,	299
Also by M.L. Broome	301
Connect with M.L. Broome	303
About the Author	305

COPYRIGHT

Hook Up

Copyright © J.E. Soper 2021

All rights reserved.

This book is a work of fiction. References to real people, events, establishments, organizations, or locales are intended only to provide a sense of authenticity and are used fictitiously. Names, characters, dialogue and incidents depicted in this book are products of the author's imagination and are not to be construed as real.

No part of this publication may be reproduced, downloaded, transmitted, decompiled, reverse-engineered, or stored into any information storage and retrieval system, in any form or by any means, whether electronic or mechanical, now known or hereafter invented, without the express written permission of J.E. Soper and TerraCotta Dragon Arts.

Cover Design

Suzana Stankovic, LSDesign

Cover Images by: Adobe Stock Images

Editing by: TerraCotta Dragon Arts

Formatting by: TerraCotta Dragon Arts

Published in the United States of America

INTRODUCTION

Dear Reader,

Hook Up was originally published as part of *K. Bromberg's Driven World* but the rights have since reverted back to TerraCotta Dragon Arts.

The story is essentially the same, save for a few name and character changes.

Best,

M.L. Broome

For my mother, Mary, who taught me that you accomplish anything, so long as you lead with your heart.

Thanks for believing in my scribbles.

PROLOGUE
RYDER

I love two things in this world: racing and Greer Hammond.

Racing because of the adrenaline rush as I fly around the kart track and Greer, because she's perfect. According to my best friend, Greg, I have a better chance of becoming the next Michael Schumacher than dating his big sister. Not that he understands why I would want her to begin with.

"She's old and ugly," Greg would argue, his nose scrunching in distaste.

"She is not. Take that back. Greer is the most beautiful woman in the world."

And so it went with the two of us, although his observations never swayed my affections. In my eyes, she's the ideal woman, and one day, she will be mine.

My other goal? An F1 world championship.

I may only be ten, but I have goals. No, they're not dreams, because I plan on making them my reality, and that's what I've told my parents since I was seven. My mother claims I was born old, whatever that means.

I've always known what I wanted, and what I could live without.

It's a fairly easy breakdown.

Unfortunately, my life is not so easy at the moment. My father has the big C, the dreaded cancer. My folks hid it from me for a while, thinking I couldn't figure out something was wrong. Suddenly my tough-as-nails father couldn't move from the bed and was too weak to attend my races.

He never missed a race before.

It wasn't a difficult deduction.

Now, he spends his days in the cancer ward of Memorial Sloan Kettering. I didn't know any hospital names before Dad's cancer. I'd have been happy to keep it that way.

Mom didn't want to leave Dad alone during his treatments, but she knew a hospital was no place for a boy my age. Besides, how would I get to the track every Friday and Saturday? Dad had one request after he discovered he was sick—that my life change as little as possible.

Lucky for me, my best friend is also into racing, and Greg's parents were more than willing to let me spend the summer with them, trucking us both back and forth to the kart track. When I say parents, I mean Greg's mom. His dad is rarely around anymore, spending every evening working late at the office.

A huge work project, or something.

But Mrs. Hammond? She drives us to the track without fail, ensuring she keeps the promise my father made to me when I started racing.

See, I'm good. Really good. I win almost every race and after the last one, I heard people—total strangers—claiming I'm the next big thing.

So, I know I'm going to make it. That's why I can't miss a single race or practice.

I miss my dad being at the races, though. He always supported me, even though he hoped I would change my mind about racing and become a doctor. I have the IQ, but medicine never interested me.

He doesn't want me wasting my big brain, but I'm not. Racing encompasses all sorts of math and science, my two favorite subjects in school.

Mainly, Dad wants me happy.

For the most part, I am, especially when I have a front-row seat to Greer as she lounges by the pool. It doesn't matter that she only sees me as her younger brother's friend.

One day, she'll see me for who I really am.

"Stop staring at my sister," Greg hisses, tossing a wet towel in my direction.

I flip him the bird, but my gaze never falters. How can it? She's the perfect woman—well, almost woman. She's eighteen, with tan legs and long, dark hair that swings against her hips when she walks. Plus, she has a smile that lights up her face and freckles dusting her nose. I could stare at her forever and never tire of the view.

"Dude, are you listening?"

With a sigh, I shift my attention to Greg. "Yeah, I heard you, but it won't work."

"Why not?" Greg stares at the racing magazine, his hands forming the imaginary parts in the air. "The more air the engine gets, the faster it moves. You know that."

"It's a torque issue."

A look of understanding passes over my friend's face, and he begins scribbling furiously in his notebook. Greg loves racing as much as I do, but his passion isn't the wind whipping past your face as you take the inside corner. It's the idea of building a car to generate that feeling.

We're a perfect team.

"What are you two doing?"

I shoot a smile in Mrs. Hammond's direction. She's an older version of her daughter, and she's been super nice to me this entire summer, even that one time when the nightmares got a bit too real.

That night, she and Greer sat me on the couch, one on either side of me, as we watched Mortal Kombat, per my request. I was so embarrassed Greer saw me cry, but she was totally cool with it. She never brought it up once, not even to Greg.

See? Told you she was perfect.

"Stuff, Mom," Greg grumbles. That's his standard greeting where his mother is concerned.

I don't get it.

"Greg, Ryder, I'm going out for a bit. Greer is in charge."

"I hate when Greer watches us." Greg may not like the idea of his big sister being the boss, but I'm thrilled.

Jabbing him in the arm, I shoot him a reassuring smile. "She's not that bad. It'll be cool."

"That's because you love her and want to marry her. Yuck."

"I think it's sweet," Mrs. Hammond retorts, shooting Greg a dark-eyed gaze. I know that look. She's had enough of his lip, and unless he wants to spend the evening in his room, he'd better quit. "But, I'm afraid Greer is too old for you, honey."

I've heard this argument before. It never deters me. "Maybe now, but it won't always be that way."

She chuckles, shaking her head. "You are such a precocious child. An old soul, Ryder Gray."

Another one using that term to describe me. "What does that mean?"

"It means you're not a pain in the ass like my brother."

A grin splits my face as Greer enters the conversation. "I'm way cooler than him."

She laughs, and it's as beautiful a sound as an engine purring. Maybe more so. "Isn't everyone?"

Greg lobs a pool noodle at Greer, but she sidesteps it easily. "Can everyone be quiet? I'm working."

Greer rolls her eyes at her brother before meeting my gaze, nodding toward the house. "Want some dinner?"

"Sure. I'll help you cook."

"I want dinner. I'm hungry." *Now* Greg is all too eager to enter the conversation.

"I thought you wanted peace and quiet, Greg."

"Nah. Dinner sounds way better."

Greer plants a hand on her hip, sending him a glare. "You're not two. You're ten. Make yourself some mac and cheese."

"Come on. Can't you do it?"

Greer shakes her head, her lips pursed in a thin line. But she's not mad. She's trying to hold back the laughter. Despite appearances, she adores her little brother. Sometimes, I think she even adores me. "What are you going to do when I'm gone?"

Greg shrugs, unaffected by the question, but it's a topic I hate to consider. This is Greer's last summer at home. She leaves for college this weekend. She wants to be a doctor, and I know she's smart enough. She's the smartest woman I know.

But her college is hours away, and she'll only be home for holidays. That's why this summer was so important. I got to spend time with her. At first, she barely spoke to me. A quick wave or smile was the extent of our friendship. But then Greg had to go to the dentist, and they left me alone with Greer.

I found her lounging in her usual poolside haunt, headphones in her ears as she rocked out to whatever obscure music she had discovered. Normally, I kept my distance, but that day I sat next to her, asking about the music and bands and why she loved them.

Before I knew it, we were sharing her headphones, so I could experience the sound firsthand.

After that, I tagged along with her to the record store, though I'm not sure what's so exciting about the pieces of vinyl. I like music, but I prefer black on tires. But Greer? She adores the music of the sixties and seventies, even though it's technically not cool by teenage standards. The best part about her is she doesn't care what others define as cool; she follows her own path.

Slowly, over those couple of months, I morphed from being another pain in the butt kid to someone she talked to. Confided in, even. We spoke about college and how she was worried to leave home. She sensed something was wrong between her parents, and I couldn't deny she was probably right.

I told her about my big dreams, and she made me pinky promise I wouldn't give up on them. The only dream I didn't mention? That one day she would be mine.

But our greatest moment? The night she played an Otis Redding tune and told me how she couldn't wait to fall in love and dance to this exact song. I didn't understand all the lyrics, but I knew one thing—I'd play that song for her one day.

Now, there's only two days before the coolest, most beautiful woman in my world leaves, and I'm not going to be there to say goodbye. I have a race this weekend, and it's one I can't miss.

"I wish you could see me race, Gigi," I mutter, my gaze glued to the floor.

She's Greer to strangers, but her friends and family always call her Gigi. After that day by the pool, she told me I could call her that, too.

I was in.

"I'm sorry, Ryder. I know you're going to win, though."

"I know."

Another chuckle flies from her lips as she ruffles my hair. "Your ego is certainly intact."

"What does that mean?"

"Nothing. Never change, Ryder Gray."

Greg huffs out a breath. He's grown tired of my friendship with his sister. It takes time away from our plans to conquer the world of racing.

I'm not worried. I plan to do both.

"He has a crush on you, Gigi. I think it's gross."

Greg did not just say that in front of her. I focus my blue-eyed glare on my best friend—*former* best friend—as he spills the beans about my feelings for his sister. "Shut up, Greg, or I'll tell everyone how you ate your own snot at the last race."

Greer's face contorts in disgust. "That's nasty, Greg." Planting her hands on her hips, she directs her attention to me. "Is that true, Ryder? Do you have a crush on me?"

Now my entire body is awash in embarrassment. Staring at the floor, I scuff my shoe at the edge of the tile. "Yes."

She tips up my chin, making me meet those dark, luminous eyes. "That's really sweet, and I think *you're* really sweet, but I'm way too old for you."

"One day you won't be, though," I argue. "One day we'll all be grown-ups."

A grin flashes across her face, lighting her up. "I suppose you're right. But I bet when you're a grownup, you won't have a crush on me anymore. You'll become a famous F1 racer and forget all about me."

"Never." I mean it, too. I'll never forget Greer.

"Hmm, we'll see." She smiles, releasing a soft sigh. "How about this, then? Many years from now, when we're both grownups, you come find me. Do we have a deal, Ryder?"

Greer extends her hand, and I waste no time sealing my future. "I'll never forget you, Gigi. I will find you again."

CHAPTER 1
GREER

TWELVE YEARS LATER...

"Want to dance?" Austin, my date for the evening, leans toward me, damn near bowling me over with his alcohol-infused breath. I hate when Austin drinks. When he drinks, he gets grabby.

Not a good look.

"I'm good." I manage a smile, even as I plot various ways to kill him without the police catching on.

The last sentiment is a joke, although I suppose it is one perk of being a nurse practitioner. Not an *advertised* perk, mind you.

Under normal circumstances, Austin is personable and handsome. We met at work, and for the first month, it was fun, despite him being a complete flop between the sheets.

I figured I could teach him, show him the proverbial sexual ropes, so I kept dating him. But he kept sucking, and not in a good way. So, after a few months of less than stellar sex, we split up, opting to remain friends.

That's the upside of breaking things off the right way. You don't hate each other. If only my father had taken that lesson to heart, he might still be a part of my life. But he didn't, and he isn't. Water under the bridge at this point.

It's maddening how most people don't communicate, assuming the other understands what they're thinking or feeling. I've spent the last decade studying the human condition and I guarantee one thing. Humans are clueless, particularly where emotions are concerned.

Throw the *L* word around and people lose every ounce of their common sense.

That's why I never throw the *L* word around.

"Didn't I tell you it would be a good party?" Austin sags against the wall, staring into his empty cup. I wonder if he thinks it might refill itself.

"It is a good party." It's not a lie. The guest list is a who's who of young and elite Manhattanites—all beautiful, tailored and totally soused.

Too bad I don't enjoy parties. I prefer small, intimate gatherings where I don't have to pretend I can understand what anyone is saying over the din of noise.

I get enough excitement at work. In my downtime, I crave solace. Not that there's any to be found here. Might as well get a drink. "I'll be back."

Austin waves his cup at me, but I fade into the crowd without acknowledging his request. The last thing the man needs is more alcohol. Shimmying up to the bar, I squeeze in, offering an apologetic smile to the man next to me. "A whiskey sour, please," I request from the bartender, noting how the stranger to my right is staring at me.

Not a down-low, inconspicuous stare, either. He's openly brazen about it.

What is his deal? It's not like I stepped on his foot or spilled a drink down his shirt. Although, if he keeps leering at me, I might be tempted to do both. Simultaneously.

After another few seconds of his intense gaze, I realize I'm going to have to deal with this ass.

Nothing like starting the new year off with a drunken buffoon.

I pivot in his direction, my hand planted on my hip. "See something you like? Take a picture. It'll last longer." I turn back to the bar, wishing like hell the bartender would hurry.

"Glad to see the sauciness is still there, Gigi."

Whirling around, I lock gazes with the stranger, realizing he isn't a stranger at all.

I haven't seen him since he was ten. Not in person, anyway, although it's impossible to miss the photos of him circling social media. He's quickly becoming the next big thing in the world of racing, and as my gaze drifts across his wide shoulders, chiseled jaw, and piercing blue eyes, I realize he's a big deal in *many* ways.

"Ryder Gray."

A smile breaks across his face and the dimple that was adorable when he was a kid is pure sex on a stick now. Leaning in, he presses his lips to my cheek, pausing to whisper in my ear. "It's been a long time."

Ignoring the sparks lighting up all over my body, I accept the drink from the bartender, taking a greedy sip. Time to regain my balance. "The last time I saw you—"

"I was a kid." He glides his fingers over his jaw, his eyes roving the length of my body. "I'm not a kid anymore."

That's putting it mildly.

"I see that. You look good. You grew up right, Ryder." I

sound like a blooming idiot, complete with a stupid grin plastered on my face as I try to appear nonchalant.

"You look amazing, but you always did."

"The last time you saw me, I was eighteen. I've changed quite a bit."

His fingers glide through the ends of my hair, barely dusting my shoulders. It's a recent change and one I'm none too fond of. Figures he'd point it out without saying a word. "Don't ask. It was a moment of weakness." I motion to my hair, swallowing some more of my drink. Did the bartender put any alcohol in the damn thing?

"You're incredibly beautiful, Greer." There's something about the way Ryder compliments me. Even as a kid, he used to spout the most romantic and fanciful things.

I laughed them off then. They're harder to laugh off now.

Clearing my throat, I back up, giving myself a bit of breathing room. What is my issue? I don't get flustered around men. I always have the upper hand, likely because the last thing I'm looking for is a commitment. Do I want them to put a ring on it?

God, no. Just no.

It's not that I don't relish the idea of romance and happily ever after. Who doesn't? But work is my focus. My only focus, considering the stack of student loans I have from my multiple degrees.

Get a higher education, they said. It'll be worth it, they said.

I'd like to have a word with whomever *they* are.

"How are you?" I manage, my back to the bar.

There's that dimple again, his smile showcasing even white teeth. "Living the high life."

That's an understatement. Ryder Gray is riding high on his talent and looks, and there isn't an end in sight.

"So I've heard. Read, really."

"You read about me?"

I could play coy, but I lack those flirtatious skills. "Of course. You're a celebrity. I can say I knew you when. I can also say I remember when you fell off your bike, skinned your knee, and cried for about twenty minutes."

Ryder laughs, running his hand through his dark locks. "Let's not talk about that day. There are so many more memorable ones."

"It was cute. You were cute. A very sensitive boy who loved fast cars."

"I still love fast cars." He leans in, determined to impede any space I put between us. "Want to go somewhere quieter? I can hardly hear you over all these people."

Doesn't that sound wonderful? Unfortunately, I didn't come to this party stag—technically, at least. "I should check on my date."

The smile falls from Ryder's face as he carefully nods. "Is it serious?"

I sputter my drink, shaking my head. "Heavens, no. We aren't dating. We were, but now it's... complicated. That sounds like I'm still sleeping with him, which I'm not. Austin and I are friends... in a weird way." With a sigh, I offer him a smile, desperate to shut myself up. "I'm not built for relationships."

His brows raise as a look of surprise stamps across his face. "You're every man's dream, Greer, saying things like that."

"So they say," I reply with a shrug, a sick feeling settling over me at his observation.

Every man's dream. That's me, all right. The woman who's a hell of a good time in the sack, a blast at any football game, and one who can hold a debate on basically anything.

I'm not the woman you open doors for or pick up the tab. I'm the tomboy type in a very feminine wrapping. The friend, sometimes with benefits.

I've heard so many men use Ryder's exact words about my low-maintenance approach to dating, but hearing him utter that statement makes me feel like a bit of a loser.

"I think it's bullshit, though."

Now it's my turn to be surprised, as Ryder's voice cuts into my internal monologue. "What is?"

"You claim you're not built for relationships, but you haven't found the right guy yet. When you do, all those things you swore off will be the only things that matter."

Damn him for being so perceptive. I want to pop off with a smart retort, but he's right. All my bravado is just that—armor to protect myself from winding up like my mother, alone and bitter at fifty. Oh, and broke to boot.

But unlike the other men who pass through my life, Ryder knows my family. The good, the bad, and the positively sordid.

In other words, the guy sees right through the excuses I toss around like confetti, and in true Ryder fashion, he isn't afraid to state the obvious. He was always that way—such an old soul, even at the age of ten. Now, he's an old soul in a delicious package.

What is wrong with you, Greer? You used to babysit Ryder. Snap out of it.

Granted, he is only eight years younger. An eternity when you're a teenager but hardly a blip when you're both adults.

Tearing my gaze from those intense blue eyes, I focus on my drink, as if I might find the answer in its depths. "I don't want to end up like my mother."

Ryder shoots me a reassuring smile as he grasps my

hand, his fingers warm against my skin. "Greg told me she had a rough time after the divorce."

"She never saw it coming. My father packed his things and snuck out in the middle of the night. He'd been fooling around with his co-worker for years. Hell, you probably met her at one of their parties. She was sleeping with my father while pretending to be my mother's friend. I pity my mother for how they treated her, and I never want to end up like her."

His fingers stroke along my palm, and I'm shocked by how his simple caress calms my nerves. Granted, it's also firing up other parts of my body, but I'm choosing to ignore that fact.

"Don't pity her. Your mother can look at herself in the mirror every day. Can't say the same for your old man. Besides, didn't his new wife up and leave him, taking half of everything?" Ryder swigs back his drink, a knowing expression on his handsome face. "That's karma."

"True, but his karma affected us all. Look at what happened with Greg. He had to quit racing. He loved racing."

Those baby blues darken. "He told me he didn't want to do it anymore. He claimed to be tired of the constant practices and travel."

"He would tell you that. He was embarrassed. When my dad left, my mother couldn't afford any of the niceties. Racing was a luxury." Finishing my drink, I motion for another. Talk about a downer of a conversation. "Enough of our trip down my memory lane. Let's lighten the mood." Grabbing my refill, I raise the drink in his direction. "To reconnecting with old friends."

Our gazes hold as we clink glasses and for the first time in years, I feel like my old self. That teenage girl, ready to take the world by storm, until the storm arrived, and I realized I wasn't nearly as tough as I once believed. Storms can really knock the sails out of your dreams.

"It's about damn time. It seemed every time I was on the island, you were off at school. Again. How long did you attend college? Forever?"

I chuckle, although Ryder isn't far off, and I have the stack of debts to prove it. "Eight years, so a good chunk of my life."

"You're a doctor, right?"

"Nurse practitioner."

"So, you're like a doctor?"

I giggle, grasping his arm. "Don't let a doctor hear you say that. They'll have a conniption."

"I can handle them."

"You can run them over in your race car."

Ryder laughs, and I'm mesmerized at how it lights up his face. Damn, but he grew up fine. I'm fairly certain with his easy grace and effortless good looks, he's had more than his share of ladies at this point. I'm also certain he's not the type to leave a woman with anything less than total satisfaction. "I try to play by the rules in my ride, but for you, I'll make an exception."

"There you are. I wondered where the hell you went."

Austin's snarky voice cuts into our conversation, and I turn, forcing a smile. Lovely. Judging by his red-rimmed eyes and belligerent expression, he's now deeper in the sauce.

"Hi, Austin. This is my brother's best friend, Ryder."

Ryder's gaze locks with mine, but despite his neutral expression, I notice the muscle jumping in his jaw. He's none too happy at the interruption. "I was your friend, too, Gigi. Don't forget all those trips to the record store."

"We had fun." Unlike Greg, who believed giving me a hard time was a rite of passage, Ryder always seemed interested in me. I even recall him claiming he had a crush on me all those years ago.

Austin throws out his hand, flashing Ryder a smile. "An old friend of Greer's? Wow, maybe you understand what makes this woman tick. Damned if I know. I dated her for months and she never opened up. Not emotionally, anyway." He winks, no doubt a drunken attempt at camaraderie, but his statement feels like a punch in the gut.

Even though I've already admitted my lackluster relationship skills to Ryder, I don't need my ex to bring up my shortcomings. Unless he wants me to bring up his... which I highly doubt. Leaning in, I hiss out a whisper. "Stop being an asshole."

"I love it when you talk dirty. Come on, let's go dance." Austin grips my arm, his clammy fingers the antithesis of inviting.

I have no plans to go anywhere with Austin. He's in his toxic drunken phase, meaning his personality vacillates like a pendulum. I witnessed that hell enough times during our brief dating period. "I'm staying here."

Austin's expression turns sour, his grip firm. "Let's go, Greer."

Ryder wraps an arm around my shoulder, pulling me flush to his chest. Talk about a difference. His embrace is warm and intoxicating. For the first time in forever, I feel safe. "She said no, buddy. Back off."

"Who the fuck do you think you are?" There's the asshole I know and hate. He needs to cease and desist, considering he's a head shorter than Ryder and barely able to stand of his own volition.

Ryder, for his part, is hardly intimidated. "Someone who's going to wipe the floor with your ass if you don't walk away now."

Volleying his gaze between us, Austin releases a huff. "Screw you both. I'm out of here."

After watching Austin stomp off, I turn to Ryder, flashing a rueful smile. "Thank you. You didn't have to do that."

"He's an asshole, Gigi. No man should ever speak to you that way."

"That's why we aren't dating anymore. One of many reasons."

"No wonder you don't believe in relationships. Let's change it up. Date a real man. One who appreciates how spectacular you are."

Those azure eyes—beyond intense as they focus on my face, dare me to disagree.

My heart pounds as I hold his gaze, realizing Ryder has an effect on me I've never experienced with another man. An out-of-control, unable to tear myself away feeling. With a sigh—and a great deal of effort—I avert my eyes, willing my body to settle.

I'm not entirely certain I'm a fan of this feeling Ryder stirs within me.

He must sense my apprehension as he grasps my elbow, leading me into the melee of people commingling about the Manhattan loft.

"Where are we going?"

"Somewhere quiet. I haven't seen you in over a decade, Greer, and I don't want to share you with a roomful of strangers."

Ryder must know the owner of the penthouse suite because he sure knows his way around. Pushing open a door, he leads us onto a rooftop patio.

I shiver against the New York chill, smiling as Ryder slips his jacket around my shoulders. "I can't take your coat. What will you wear?"

Backing me against the brick wall, he cages me in, his muscular forearms resting on either side of my head. "I have you to keep me warm."

"You're a natural with the pickup lines. Perfect delivery."

If my comment bothers him, he doesn't let on. "Do you prefer Austin's behavior?"

"Definitely not. The man is a waste of oxygen. When he's drunk, at least. I owe you, Ryder."

"I have so many ways for you to make it up to me." There's that sexy smirk again, even if I suspect he's only joking.

Too bad for him. I could do all manner of naughty things to a man like Ryder Gray, particularly since the years between us are now a non-issue.

Ryder leads us to a sheltered alcove, decorated with couches, a minibar, and an outdoor heater.

Perfect.

Settling back against the cushions, I drink in his dark good looks. Ryder was always adorable. One of those kids you knew would grow up to be a heartbreaker.

I wasn't wrong.

Staring out over the Manhattan skyline, I wonder what it must be like for this level of luxury to be your reality, instead of a cramped studio on Long Island. "This settles it. I need to become insanely wealthy, so I can buy my very own rooftop hangout."

"Stick with me and I'll buy you anything you want."

"You'll buy me a rooftop?"

"Among other things."

What a flirt. The man certainly knows how to woo women. Giggling, I clink glasses with him, breathing in the night air. It feels good to laugh. Sometimes, I worry I've forgotten how.

"I missed your laugh, Gigi. I missed everything about you."

His words settle over me like a warm blanket, even if I know he's spouting a line. "It's been twelve years. You remember nothing about me."

Shaking his head, Ryder drapes an arm around my shoulder, pulling me close. "Want to bet? You love Elvis and David Bowie. Actually, you like all the music of the 60s and 70s. Pistachio is your favorite flavor of ice cream, even if I can't for the life of me figure out why. You adore Practical Magic and made me watch it so many times, I *still* have passages memorized. You claim not to be built for relationships, but I know you dream of being in love."

With every word, I fall deeper under his spell, enthralled by the idea he never forgot me. "You do remember me."

"You're unforgettable, Gigi." He slides his fingers along the column of my throat, letting them drift down to my collarbone. "You still wear the same perfume."

"I can't believe you remember that." With a laugh, I hold out my wrist for him to smell. "Honey and amber."

But Ryder has other ideas as he leans in, sliding his nose along my neck. "You always smelled so good."

My heart threatens to beat out of my chest when I feel the soft warmth of his tongue against my skin. His caress is tender. Seductive. And lighting up every cell in my body.

Pulling back, Ryder cups my face, resting his forehead against mine. "I told you I missed you."

Tracing his lower lip, I hold his gaze, feeling more like a schoolgirl at thirty than I did at eighteen. "They don't make men like you anymore, Ryder. You must have women clamoring for you."

Ryder leans back with a sigh, a thin smile playing on his lips. "Promise me something."

"What?"

"Stop throwing up walls, at least where I'm concerned. I'm not some random guy, and I'm certainly not going to hurt you. So," he taps the end of my nose, "let's avoid the topic of me and any other women. That's the last thing I want to discuss."

"Ever?"

"Where you're concerned? Yes."

He has a point. It's not a road I care to traverse, either. "Deal. I don't want to know, anyway. But, I do want to know everything else about you. We have a ton of years to catch up on."

"Where do I start?" Ryder asks, running a hand through his dark waves. Damn, but it's longer than mine now.

Propping my legs across his lap, I snuggle closer, warding off the winter chill. It's also a perfect excuse to bask in Ryder's warmth, and the man doesn't seem to mind my advances. "The last time I saw you was twelve years ago. So, age ten until now."

"Most of my life is not that interesting. I'll bore you to death."

"I beg to differ. You were a fixture in my family for years. I'm your unofficial big sister."

Ryder's eyes widen as he shakes his head vehemently. "Take that back. You are *not* my sister."

"I said unofficially."

"Would I do this with my sister?"

I don't have time to respond before Ryder claims my mouth, his tongue gliding along the seam of my lips. With a soft moan, I grant him access, feeling every cell in my body spark as he pulls me onto his lap, his hands sliding along my spine.

The man's mouth is magical, my pulse racing as the kiss

deepens, his tongue sliding against mine in the most seductive of battles. I feel his hunger bubbling beneath the surface as he kisses me, his mouth making promises I pray he keeps.

The rooftop door slams as partygoers invade our private sanctuary. But this moment? This beautiful moment, our breath mingling as our hearts settle, belongs to us.

The brisk night air fogs our breath, but I'm not cold anymore. Not with my body pressed against Ryder's, his hands refusing to pause in their exploration of my curves.

I'm not sure who taught Ryder to kiss, but they deserve an award. I can't feel my legs after our lip lock. Hell, I can't feel anything beyond the growing desire for him to keep kissing me and never stop.

He grazes his hands along my chin, peppering my jaw with kisses. "I've waited so long to do that, Gigi."

"I told you to find me when you were older. Didn't expect you to make good on the threat."

His blue eyes blaze with intensity as his grip tightens. "Would you like me to stop?"

"Never. You'd better not make me wait that long again."

Ryder smiles against my mouth before laying his claim. With every passing second, I fall deeper under his spell.

A peal of laughter carries over the air as a young couple strolls over, settling onto an adjoining couch.

"So much for private time," I murmur, twirling a lock of his dark hair around my finger. "What to do now? I know, tell me all about your fabulous life. Start talking, Ryder."

So, he does. It's funny. Most people love to talk about themselves, but Ryder is different. Perhaps it's the giddiness lining his face as he discusses his racing career or the fact I actually want to know everything about him. The man possesses a self-assured air. He's confident but not arrogant, and confidence is sexy as hell.

HOOK UP

Ryder is sexy as hell. So are his hands, which are intent on touching me at all times.

Not that I'm complaining.

When he talks about the upcoming year, I realize with his talent, he's going places. Fast. "You're going to be a star."

It's not even a question. He will be the biggest name in racing soon, an idea that is both exciting and terrifying. Exciting for him. Terrifying for me. Even though I spent countless weekends at the track, watching Ryder and Greg fly around the turns, I always worried something would happen. A split-second decision could end it all.

Could end him.

Reaching up, I slip a pendant from my neck, placing it around his.

"What's this?" Ryder asks, trying to read the inscription.

"St. Christopher, the patron saint of travelers. Since you travel all over the world and practically at the speed of light around the track, I want you to wear this." Running my fingers over the pendant, I rest my hand on his heart. "It will keep you safe."

Ryder pulls me close, tucking my head under his chin. "I'd rather keep you. You can be my good luck charm."

"Going to pack me in your luggage and take me everywhere?" I tease, pressing a soft kiss to his neck. When I glide my tongue along his skin, his grip tightens, a huff escaping his lips.

Glad to know I affect him, too.

"That's the most tempting offer I've ever heard." Tipping my chin up, I find myself transfixed by his heady blue stare. "Pack your bags and you can travel the world by my side."

"My job would be so thrilled."

"Who cares? Quit. Spend all your time with me."

They might be lines, practiced in front of a mirror until

he perfected their delivery. But for some odd reason, my skeptical brain believes every word from his lips as they flow through my heart to set up residence.

"Now that's the most tempting offer *I've* ever heard." My tongue swirls around his fingertips as they glide across my lower lip, my grip on reality loosening with every second.

"Then say yes, Gigi."

Before I can answer, the voices of millions of New Yorkers fill the air, crowing out the countdown to the new year.

Snuggling closer on his lap, I wind my hands in his hair, unable to look anywhere but at him. "Seems I got my New Year's kiss early. Whatever will I do when the clock strikes midnight?"

"I've got millions of kisses for you. I've been waiting for you to come to claim them."

As raucous cheers erupt across Manhattan, Ryder's lips claim mine. I try to hold on to any thought as the moment deepens, but my emotions win the battle. The din, the fears, and the noise fall away as I fall into Ryder, my hands fisting in his shirt.

"The perfect start to a new year. Kissing the woman I've dreamt about for over a decade."

Any witty retort dies in my throat as I'm captivated, once again, by Ryder's intense energy. It's the way he looks at me, as if I'm the only woman in the world.

No one has ever looked at me that way before.

An icy breeze blows across the rooftop, and I huddle closer to his lanky frame.

"It's downright frigid out here, isn't it?"

"Yes, but you did an excellent job keeping me warm against the elements."

Pulling me tighter, he teases my mouth with featherlight kisses. "Do you want to get out of here?"

"I do." There's no question. My reunion with Ryder is unexpected and moving at warp speed, but I'm certain of one thing.

I don't want it to end.

"Would it be totally presumptuous to invite you back to my hotel? It's only a few blocks away."

"Think you're going to get lucky?" I tease, biting back a grin.

"I already got lucky, Gigi. I'm with you."

The grin slides from my face as a wave of emotions surges through me. Grasping Ryder's shirt, I crush his mouth to mine, claiming, without words, every inch of this man as my own.

Before the sun rises, he will be mine.

"Ryder, there you are. Dude, your date is pissed."

Tearing my lips from Ryder's, I turn my attention to the stranger standing to our left. "His what?"

"Shit," Ryder breathes, and I waste no time scrambling to my feet. "I'll be down in a minute, Sam."

I wait until Sam disappears inside before unleashing my famous Hammond temper. "Your date?"

Ryder huffs out a sigh, burying his head in his hands. "It's complicated."

He is *not* using that expression. "Don't use my line on me, Ryder. You're here with someone? That's fucking perfect," I mutter, grabbing my purse as I prep for a hasty exit.

Ryder grabs my arm, and I see the panic lining his face. "Please sit down."

I shake my head, feeling like an idiot that I fell for his lines. "You're good, Ryder. I actually believed you, but I guess that's the point, right? Your delivery was perfect. No doubt you've done this hundreds of times before."

He flies to his feet, but he's a bigger fool than me if he

thinks I'll believe one word from his gorgeous mouth at this point. "You think this was some ploy to get you into bed? I've been hoping to run into you for years and then boom, here you are. No way in hell was I going to let this moment slip by, and I'm not letting it go now. I'm not letting you go."

"Such a sweet sentiment, except for the fact you have a date downstairs," I seethe, tempted to impale my heel in Ryder's handsome head. "Thanks for making me the other woman. Appreciate it. I always swore it was the one role I'd never play, but you made certain I did."

With a flip of my hair and a shaky sigh, I slip on my emotional armor. "I should have known better. You're just a kid."

Ryder stiffens at my barb, taking the coat I thrust in his direction. "I think we both know that's not true."

"Just because you can kiss, doesn't make you a man. Goodbye, Ryder. Maybe we'll run into each other in another twelve years."

Twirling on my heel, I storm toward the door, intent on one thing—getting inside before the tears fall and I look like an even bigger fool.

Apparently, my footwear and physics have other ideas, as my heel catches on a cord and I tumble toward the ledge.

With lightning fast reflexes, Ryder snatches me to his chest, pulling me flush against him. My breath catches when I gaze over the side of the building. That's right. *Over* the side of the building.

"Oh, my God," I manage, my heart speeding like a runaway train.

You know the claim that your life flashes before your eyes right before you die? Totally false. All you have time to realize is this was not how you wanted to go out.

At all.

"Christ, Gigi, I know you're angry, but could you let me explain before you hurl yourself off the building?"

I pull my head from his chest, glaring into his smiling face. "Aren't you funny?"

"I have my moments." Ryder smooths my hair back, and I hate how soothing his caress feels. "My situation with Jane is no different from you and Austin. We both know the host and although we split up months ago, we agreed to come to the party together. As friends."

"I don't think Jane sees it quite the same way you do."

"Apparently not, but that was the stipulation. Greer, I planned on having a few drinks and some laughs with friends. I didn't plan on kissing *anyone* tonight, but you're not just anyone."

There he goes with his impeccably timed one-liners again.

Huffing out a sigh, I realize I have two choices—continue to be mad or let it go, chalking it up to another dumb decision because of alcohol.

This is why I rarely drink. Alcohol and common sense are terrible bedfellows.

"I'm still pissed you failed to mention your date for the evening, but I owe you for not letting my ass tumble to the pavement."

"You can make it up to me." Ryder grins, a desperate attempt to lighten the mood.

"I'll have quite a list of IOUs if we hang out any longer, which is why I'm heading downstairs. I'm bound to have a hell of a time hailing a cab on New Year's."

I back away from the warmth of his embrace, stepping gingerly over the mess of hoses and cords tangled on the ground. Time for me to return to reality—a far colder experience than my previous few hours.

I walk back into the party, which is no quieter now than it was before the clock struck midnight.

I'm not three steps inside when Ryder pulls me to his chest, his breath hot at my ear. "If you think I'm letting you walk away from me, you're crazy. I have to go deal with Jane and put her in a cab, but I'm coming back. Then, we are going to my hotel to spend the next few days together and plan for Paris."

"Paris? What the hell are you talking about?"

"You're coming with me. I'm showing you the world, Gigi."

"Stop with the lines, Ryder."

He spins me around, his gaze fierce with intensity. "None of what I said to you is a line. Know that. I've been waiting years for you." Cupping my face, he drifts his mouth against mine. "I know you feel it, too. Don't walk away from this. From us."

Am I stupid to believe him? If so, hand me the crown, because I believe every single word. Hopeless romantic leading with her heart, at your service.

"Paris, huh?"

A beautiful smile lights up his face. "To start. But I plan on loving you in every city around the world." Linking our fingers, he brings my hand to his mouth, dusting gentle kisses across my skin. "Will you let me love you, Gigi?"

Every cell in my body comes alive at his question, my heart kicking any of my head's misgivings to the curb. "Do we have to wait until Paris?"

Now his smile borders on smoldering as his lips claim mine in a fierce kiss. "Definitely not. You wait here. I'll be right back."

As he disappears into the crowd, I scope out a quiet corner to await his return. Hopefully, he gets back before my rational side has the chance to debate my spur-of-the-moment decision.

Paris. He can't be serious. But what if he is? What if he means every word?

What if all he wants is to love me?

Or what if I'm absolutely off my rocker for considering his proposition?

"Does he belong to you?" Turning my head, I groan at the sight of Austin, barely upright, with vomit down his shirt. At his elbow is Patrick, this evening's host.

Judging by the grimace on Patrick's face, he's none too pleased. Can't say I blame the man.

With a sigh, I nod. "For tonight, at least. Let me call a cab."

I search the crowd, but there's no sign of Ryder. Looks like our private soiree will have to wait until I get Austin home. Nothing like babysitting a thirty-three-year-old man.

It is absolutely the last time I'm go anywhere with this lech.

Grabbing a pen and paper from my bag, I jot down my number, pressing it into Patrick's hand. "Will you make sure Ryder Gray gets my number?"

Patrick scoffs at my request. "Sure, because you're the first woman to use that segue."

"I'm not a fan. I'm a friend." At his cocked brow, I add, "I've known him since he was ten."

A curt nod. The man doesn't believe a word I'm saying.

With an exasperated huff, I throw up my hands. "Just give him the number, please. If he doesn't want it, tell him to chuck it."

I figure the last line will drive home my point because I *know* Ryder wants to see me again. Hell, he wants to show me Paris.

Patrick shoves the paper into his pocket, motioning toward Austin. "No problem. Just get this guy out of here. He's already puked on one rug."

Austin, you are such an unbelievable pain in the ass.

I scope the penthouse crowd a final time, desperate to find the man who gave me the greatest kisses in all of my thirty years. A man who awakened feelings in me I didn't know I possessed.

A man I want to know much, much better.

Ryder made me tingle. No one has ever done that before.

But luck isn't on my side. Ryder is nowhere to be seen, and Austin looks like he's ready to hurl again. With a sigh, I lead him to the cab, casting one glance over my shoulder as we pull away into the night.

The ball is in Ryder's court now. I left my number with his friend. It's up to him to use it.

CHAPTER 2
RYDER

EIGHT YEARS LATER...

"Ryder Gray! Ryder Gray!" Fans clamor around me as I exit the restaurant, and I can't help but wonder about the absurdity of it all. They think I'm a big deal, something more than human.

Maybe it's because I'm an F1 driver, or because I win—a lot. My female fans claim it's because of my model good looks and reported prowess in the bedroom.

I'm not denying any of it, but I still don't understand the adulation.

What I do know is to the outside world, I'm the luckiest guy on the planet. I make a living—a damn fine living—doing what I love. Racing consumes me, which is a good thing, because when you strip away the tours, tracks, and endorsements, there isn't much left.

The track has been my home since I was a kid; the bleachers and asphalt kept me company when my dad got sick. After he died, it was the only place I found solace.

I guess the women are a perk, too. Don't get me wrong. It's fun as hell having my choice of beautiful bodies to warm my bed, but it never gets further than that.

How can it? I still carry a torch for the one that got away.

Greer Hammond. Eight years ago, she was in my arms, and those were the happiest moments of my life. I was only gone fifteen minutes, but it was fifteen minutes too long. By the time I returned, she was gone.

Worse than Cinderella at the ball.

I waited a couple of weeks, certain she would get in touch with me, but she never did. Then the racing season started, and it seemed no matter how often I tried to call Greg to finagle his sister's number, we never connected. Let me tell you, time zones are a bitch.

Finally, after months and thousands of miles of travel, I spoke with Greg, my determination at an all-time high. I knew what I wanted and didn't care how much shit he gave me; I was a man on a mission. Greg was thrilled to chat and fill me in on all the family gossip. Namely, that Gigi was dating a med student, and it seemed serious. He figured they'd marry soon.

The woman who claimed she wasn't built for relationships was now firmly entrenched in one. And it wasn't with me.

I didn't care to hear anything about Greer after that.

My mother still jokes with me about my feelings for Greer Hammond, but I claim it was a childhood crush. Nothing more. We both know I'm lying.

I dated a few nice women over the years and although I cared about them, it was never near the intensity of my feelings for Greer. But maybe that's not a bad thing.

Hell, my feelings for Greer were likely more pie in the sky

than based in reality. Who knows? We might have spent a week together and ended up hating each other.

Besides, I haven't seen Greg or Greer in years. That's how it works, right? You don't plan to drift away from each other, but time and distance do their worst to break the bonds that once held you tight.

Greg and I still speak occasionally, but I never ask about his sister. Even when he slides in her name, I steer the conversation to an alternate topic. As I said, I don't want to know about her wonderful life. A life without me.

Instead, we focus on his work as a mechanic, or his latest automotive gadget that's guaranteed to make a car faster, smoother, or more economical. With cars, the man is a genius, even if some of his ideas are borderline ridiculous.

With Greg, I'm his buddy, Ryder. Not Ryder Gray, the international racing superstar that graces the covers of magazines. There's peace in that knowledge. His friendship is genuine, and even though he knows how much money I make, he's never asked for a dime. Not one loan, not one favor.

Okay, maybe one.

He called a few weeks ago, asking me to be the best man at his wedding. True to form, Greg bucked tradition, opting for a wedding in Vegas. To quote him, a weekend of drunken debauchery in Sin City.

I declined, even though I know it hurt Greg. It's not that I don't love my friend, but I can't show up and have Greer walk in, her husband and children in tow.

It's safer to exist in my sphere of denial.

Not that I don't think of my Gigi, wondering how her life turned out.

Wishing for one more chance with her. This time, I'd never let her go. No matter what. Hell, I scoff at the idea of marriage, but I'd march Greer's ass down the aisle so fast her head would spin.

But it doesn't matter.

Some wishes don't come true.

To be fair, my current girlfriend is no slouch. She's literally a former Ms. America. Not too damn shabby. But aside from looking good on my arm, there's nothing there.

Mandi and I have an agreement. Love is secondary when you're a celebrity; a sad but true fact. The world doesn't care if you have a happy life, so long as it *looks* fabulous.

Mandi and I had fun for the first few months, until she started hinting around about a ring, and that is one plank I'm not walking. I often wonder how much longer I can delay the inevitable breakup because the glitter wore off months ago.

A little boy tugs my sleeve, jogging me back to the present. "Can I have your autograph?" He hands me a piece of paper and I sign it with a smile. Kids always make me happy, especially since I remember being that boy with stars in his eyes.

Now, I'm the star.

"It's a trip, isn't it?" Mick questions, busy signing his own share of autographs. The man is a racing legend, even if he hasn't competed in years. He's also my mentor and the big brother I never had. Without his help, I doubt I would have made it this far.

Mick moved from the driver's seat to team ownership a few years ago—a far safer position physically but a hell of a gamble financially. Lucky for him, his racing tenure earned him connections. Connections with bottomless pockets. Those pockets helped him finance an F1 team.

That is a monstrous feat, and although we lack the funding of Mercedes or Ferrari, we have something else. Me.

When I'm behind the wheel, I can't lose, and I've proven it time and again, claiming title after title.

When Mick first approached me about joining him, I was flabbergasted and immediately on board. It was a challenge, but I thrive under pressure.

"Mr. Gray, do you ever get scared?" The little boy's eyes widen as I return the signed piece of paper.

Ruffling his hair, I shake my head. "Not when I'm racing."

It's the truth. It's an exhilarating idea that anything can happen when I slide behind the wheel. One wrong move, and it's all over. I know that, and yet I continue to slide behind the wheel, laughing in the face of danger.

Fear never gets a seat.

Not in my car.

Fear is a four-letter word in the world of racing.

"No fear. No consequences. All flow." It's my motto, one I've repeated countless times. But it's more than that. It's a mantra, reminding me the track is home and the only thing to which I owe any explanations.

After a few more minutes of conversing with fans, Mick and I stroll to the parking lot. I don't mind chatting with them, and I'm lucky Charlotte is a cosmopolitan enough city that I blend into the fray most days. Usually, I go about my business without interruption. But it's almost racing season, and Charlotte is a racing city.

Despite a storied history of racing, Charlotte lacked an F1 team, but Mick changed all that, bringing an entirely new level of speed to the birthplace of NASCAR.

"Does Mandi know you got home early?" Mick tries to maintain a straight face, but I see the grimace crawl across his features. He's not a fan of my girlfriend, and I'm sure his wife, Rachel, has much to do with that opinion.

Rachel is my unofficial big sister, and she desperately

wants me to fall in love and settle down. She knows that won't happen with Mandi.

She's 100% correct there.

Not happening.

Definitely not with Mandi.

I shake my head, pursing my lips. "If I had, she would be up my ass wanting to go to dinner and a club. I'm so not up for that."

"Sounds like you're not up for her, anymore."

I nod, chewing the inside of my lip. He's right. She's hot and a decent lay, but I've been over this relationship for months now. Apparently, so has Mandi. Why else would she have cheated on me earlier this year?

At this point, the relationship is built more on logistics than love. Not that it was ever built on love. Lust? Sure. Love? Not even close.

"You're right, Mick, but it's tricky since we live together."

Mick claps me around the shoulder, a knowing smile on his mouth. "No, it isn't. It's your house. If you don't want her there, tell her to leave. See? Problem solved."

"If only it were that easy." I wave him off before sliding behind the wheel of my ride, a noisy exhalation flowing from my mouth.

Time to go home.

∼

I NOTE the strange sedan parked in my driveway as I pull into my garage. Who the hell drives a beat-up Honda? Knowing Mandi, it's some member of her beauty squad, called in to primp her to perfection.

I get it. Mandi bases her reputation on beauty and glamour. I just wish there was something beyond the stunning facade. Something deeper that would last once the beauty fades.

To be honest, it's all a sham. Mandi still lives in my house, but it's partly for show and partly because I lack the motivation to kick her out. Evicting her will no doubt result in a long and drawn-out argument, complete with tears and whining. I should have forced her to leave when those photos of her with another man surfaced in the tabloids, especially after she admitted to the tryst.

Her excuse for knocking boots with someone else? I'm emotionally distant and won't discuss a future together.

If she thinks fucking another guy is going to force me into a long-term commitment, she's dumber than I thought.

If only I had an irrefutable excuse to get her out of my life, before I lose the last vestiges of my sanity.

What was I thinking, letting this woman I barely knew move into my home? Her reasoning made sense at the time —how do we build a relationship when she's in California and I'm in North Carolina?

The truth was I thought we were having fun together. Casual fun that didn't involve any commitment. But she was insistent, and I figured, what the hell, let's give it a shot.

So, we started playing house, which has now morphed into a macabre version of its former self—pretty coats of paint to cover the crumbling walls of our relationship.

And my digs are far fancier than her Los Angeles apartment. It is a beautiful house, but it never felt like home. A home is filled with more than upscale furnishings and top-of-the-line electronics. It oozes love and laughter and warmth.

My house has none of those things, although I pray one day it will. One day I'll meet a woman who makes me feel like Greer Hammond did that New Year's Eve. I was a fucking king. I was her king.

The shortest reign in history.

Pausing by my gate, I let my gaze linger over the lagoon-style pool. Once again, my thoughts flit to Greer. She loved lounging by her parent's pool and I could spend hours watching her. Her body was beautiful at eighteen. At thirty, she was superb. Her curves had blossomed, and the feel of them under my hands as I kissed her was my definition of perfection.

Greer Hammond will always hold a piece of my heart. But she's gone, slipped through my grasp, and married to some doctor on Long Island... or wherever she's living now.

Greer, I would marry in a heartbeat. Everyone else can sit down and shut up.

It doesn't do me any good to live in the past, even if those hours with her still make my mouth water. The way she kissed, the way she tasted. No one else has ever come close.

With a grunt, I step inside, forcing all thoughts of Greer to the back of my mind. There's an eerie silence inside my house, odd considering Mandi's teacup poodle is usually yapping at my feet by now.

I know she's here. Her car—rather, *my* car, is in the garage, along with that strange vehicle in the driveway. Who knows?

I stroll to the fridge but pause with the door open as I hear an all too familiar sound emanating from upstairs.

The grunting and low moans indicate one thing, and I'm pretty damn sure it isn't a porno party.

I wait for the anger to sweep over me, but all I feel is an immense relief. Mandi has inadvertently handed me my ticket to freedom. Now I can hand her walking papers, ending this facade of a relationship.

I climb the steps toward the guest suite, pushing the door open with my foot. "Nice of you to use the guest room."

There's a feeling of power when you slide behind the wheel of a race car, but it pales compared to the thrill I feel as Mandi and her boy toy leap apart.

Hey, they stacked the wood. I simply lit the match on the tinderbox.

Time to watch it burn.

"Ryder. You're home early." Mandi's face pales with shock, her eyes darting to all corners of the room.

"Why does everyone say that when they're caught cheating? Is that the best you can do? Honestly, I deserve something a bit more original."

Crossing my arms over my chest, I stifle a laugh as they scamper about, grabbing their clothes. The guy can't be a day over twenty and looks like he's seen a ghost as he runs past me, his hands covering his dick.

Seconds later, the front door slams. Easy come and easy go.

Now it's time to deal with the real problem. Pulling out my phone, I dial my travel agent. "I want a one-way ticket to Los Angeles, please. Tonight, if possible."

Mandi's eyes widen, but I ignore her non-verbal cues until I finish purchasing the ticket. With a final click, her fate is sealed.

"What are you doing, Ryder?"

"Putting you on a plane. You're going home tonight. You can thank me later for sending you first class."

"I live here."

"Correction. You lived here. Now, you're homeless. Better call your Mom because that friend of yours doesn't look like he can afford a mailbox, much less an apartment."

Mandi moves toward me, but I hold up my hands, stopping her mid-step. "We need to talk about this. I know how it looks—"

I bark out a laugh. "It looks like you were fucking someone else. Do you know why? Because you *were* fucking someone else."

Tears fill her light blue eyes, but she must be insane if she thinks I'm going to pity her predicament. "Please—"

"Mandi, we've been unhappy for months. Miserable, in fact, as made obvious by your extracurricular activities. I'm tired of pretending we mean anything to one another."

"You mean something to me."

"No, I don't, and that's fine." Glancing at the time, I hold out my phone in Mandi's direction. "Better get packing. Your ride to the airport will be here in an hour. Don't worry, I'll have someone send you the rest of your things."

A single tear slips down her cheek, but I feel nothing.

Okay, that's a lie. I feel like an enormous weight has been lifted, along with the overwhelming urge to party it up for the next few days.

I have the perfect solution.

"One hour," I reiterate, as I turn on my heel, marching to the master suite. A small whine sounds from the bed, and I plop down next to the dog, scratching his ears. "So, that's where she hid you. I know, you would have warned me. Guys have to stick together."

With a sigh, I open the door, letting him scamper back to his mistress. Unlike me, he adores Mandi. No accounting for taste.

Time for me to finalize my new plans for the weekend. My childhood friend is getting married, and the idea of Vegas heat and Vegas strippers sounds like an excellent idea.

Fuck love. In all its forms.

And fuck Greer, too. All the love and unrequited feelings

I've been carrying around for two decades can shove off. So what if she's happily married? By the time she arrives in Vegas with her husband, I'll have a woman under each arm... and a few more waiting in my bed.

That's my story and I'm sticking to it.

Greg lets loose with a loud guffaw when he answers the phone. "Holy shit. Ryder Gray, as I live and breathe. How have you been, buddy?"

"It's been an interesting week. Change of plans. I'm going to make your wedding if I'm still invited."

"Absolutely. I don't know if there are any more rooms available, but you can bunk with Jillian and me. The hotel isn't anything fancy, but it's the company that counts. I'd love for you to be there."

See? This is why I love Greg. "Give me five minutes."

Good to my word, I call him back with the surprise.

"Did you change your mind?"

"No, but you are changing venues. I booked a floor of suites at The Cosmopolitan. You've been my friend forever. It's the least I can do."

"Holy shit, Ryder. You didn't have to do that."

"Consider it a wedding gift. Let me send you out in style."

"Wow." I can tell by Greg's voice he's truly touched by my gift. Since he was ten, his life has been focused on survival. It's time he got a bit of luxury thrown in there. "I don't know what to say."

"Don't say anything. This is what friends do."

"Can you do something else for me?"

Okay, apparently shelling out twenty grand wasn't enough for Greg. "Sure."

"Will you stand up with me? Be my best man? Right now, Jillian's brother is filling in, and to be honest, I hate the douchebag."

I relax onto the mattress with a chuckle. "Come on, now I have to wear a tux? Fine, so long as I have time to find some beautiful women beforehand."

"You never had an issue before. Wait, aren't you dating someone?"

"Was. She's moving out, as we speak."

"I'm sorry."

"Don't be," I snicker. "I'm thrilled. It's been hell for months."

"Hey, I've got an idea."

"What's that?"

"You can be Greer's plus one."

I sit up with a start at his words, gripping the phone like a vise. "What?"

"My sister, Greer."

"I know who your sister is, Greg." Does he seriously think I've forgotten Gigi?

"You used to have the hots for her, remember? I get it, because she's beautiful, even if she's still a pain in the ass."

I damn near choke as I spit out the next question. "What about her husband and kids?"

Greg snorts into the phone. "She's never been married. No kids."

"She was dating that doctor."

"Was. He screwed her over pretty bad, but that was years ago. She's totally over it, now."

My mind reels at Greg's words. Gigi is single. I'm single.

Despite the events of the last thirty minutes, a giant grin crosses my face. "Gigi is single." I don't mean to say the words aloud, but Greg chuckles when he hears them.

"Don't tell me you still have a thing for my sister."

"No," I lie, forcing a laugh. "Not at all."

"Fucking liar. I can't wait to see you."

"You, too. It's been too long. I have something I want to talk to you about in Vegas. A job, if you're interested."

"Always up for hearing about new opportunities. I'll see you soon."

Clicking off the call, I fall back on the mattress, running a hand over my beard. Greer Hammond is single.

Not for long.

The thought pops into my brain, my smile widening at the idea.

This time, I won't let her get away.

This time, Greer Hammond is mine.

A thud reverberates from down the hall. Time to check on Mandi's progress with packing. If the banging outside the door is anything to go on, she's none too happy with the turn of events.

Too damn bad, Mandi. Too damn bad.

CHAPTER 3
GREER

I stare at the half-empty suitcase, seriously questioning my brother's decision to marry in Vegas. How the hell does one even pack for this type of event? Bridesmaid dress, bikini, crotchless panties?

Okay, I don't own any of the latter, but that doesn't make this task any easier. With a groan, I toss in another bathing suit. Who doesn't bring a load of swimwear to the middle of the desert?

"Greg, I could kill you for this," I grumble to my empty apartment.

It's not that I don't love my brother. In fact, I adore the man. But his destination wedding is costing me money I don't have, and I seriously doubt I can work any more hours without falling flat on my face.

Isn't being broke grand? I'll be out of debt eventually... if I live that long.

So, despite this being Greg's wedding weekend, I tried to finagle my way out of attending, claiming the clinic was busy and understaffed. Figures Greg knew someone in the unit to negate my claim.

Damn that man. He's like the mayor of our small town.

If only Greg could rein in his drinking, he likely *could* run for public office. He's more than personable, although he abandoned any lofty career ambitions years ago when he had to give up racing. I still bear a grudge against my father for stripping away my brother's happiness.

Have you ever seen the look on a child's face when you tell them the only thing that matters to them is no longer an option? It's the definition of heartbreak.

But my brother, despite losing his chance at the golden ring, continued to go to the kart track every other week to cheer on his best friend.

Ryder Gray.

It's been eight years since I saw the man. More specifically, since we saw each other. I see him everywhere, and I mean *everywhere*. He's the hottest ticket in racing, with the trophies and trophy girlfriends to prove it. Each beauty is more striking than the last, and if I'm not mistaken, he's even bedded Ms. Universe.

Not that I'm keeping tabs on the man. That's something I won't admit even to myself. I try to gloss over the many magazines or television appearances, assuming an air of indifference toward him.

Lord knows he's indifferent toward me.

Ryder has the world on a string, but I know his smile, and the one he flashes for the cameras isn't the one he flashed at me. This smile is practiced and fake as hell.

I hate it.

Hell, I should hate him—plying me with promises but then never bothering to phone after he swore those moments on the rooftop meant something.

Swore *I* meant something. I believed him, too.

Man must have one hell of a short-term memory problem because it's been radio silence for eight years. No call, no text, nothing.

At least he isn't attending Greg's wedding. Yes, I asked. If Ryder was going to be there, I planned to make myself scarce. I have no desire to watch him make out with whatever beauty queen or supermodel is serving as his latest arm candy.

It's pathetic, how well I remember his kisses all these years later. I've had good kisses since then. Plenty of them, but none ever came close to the fire that man ignited in my soul the moment his lips met mine. It's as though he flipped a switch in my heart, only to stroll away and leave it to burn itself out.

Hopefully one day, it will.

My phone buzzes and I shake my head, biting back a chuckle. It's Greg—again. He's called almost every hour for the last day, ensuring I'm actually getting my ass on a plane.

We give each other crap constantly, but he's my best friend in the world. When our world crashed around us, we clung to each other for support, since Dad was too busy with his mistress and Mom in no shape to help anyone.

Some things never change.

"You realize every time you call me, you're interrupting my flow and delaying my packing? What do you want?"

"Are you sitting down, because I have the best news. Seriously."

Damn, but he sounds giddy. "You won lotto and are moving the wedding to the Caribbean."

"Why would I do that? Vegas is much cooler."

Greg would be happy never being near the water again, after a scare with a manta ray when he was nine. Yep, a manta ray. Those large, peaceful creatures scared the hell out of Greg, and it would take a boatload of cash—literally—to get him back in the ocean. "What's your news?"

"An invited but unexpected guest is making the wedding after all."

My hand grips the phone as an unfamiliar feeling floods my body. We have a ton of mutual friends, but my money is on the fact one superstar racer is primed to make an appearance. "Don't even tell me it's Ryder Gray. If he's in, I'm out."

Silence from the other end of the line. Never a good sign.

"Greg, I'm serious. I have no desire to see that man."

"I get you hate him, even though I don't know why, but this is my wedding. You have to be there. It's a law or something."

I huff out a breath, resigned to my fate. He's right, and I know he's right. I'd be a shit and a half if I missed Greg's wedding because of a guest who ghosted me eight years ago. "I'm sorry. I'm being stupid." Tapping my hand along the table, I force out the next question. "It is Ryder that's coming, isn't it?"

"Yes. He phoned yesterday and told me he had a change of plans. He's also standing up with me—"

Groaning into the receiver, I hang my head. Wonderful. Now I not only have to see Ryder, but I have to interact with him.

"What is your deal with him, anyway? You act like he broke your heart or something. Ryder has always had a thing for you, Gigi."

"Not anymore," I mutter. "That was years ago."

And only for a few brief, wonderful hours, at that.

"He sounded pretty damn excited when I told him you were single. You should take advantage of that fact." Greg chuckles. "I can't believe I just intimated my sister needs to get laid."

I scoff at Greg's statement. Ryder Gray is glad I'm single? That means one thing—he's eager to finish the conquest he started all those years ago. Probably thinks I'm an easy lay, and he won't have to wine and dine me like his Hollywood hotties.

But my brother isn't totally off-base. I could use a good roll in the hay. It's been... longer than I care to recall.

Suddenly, inspiration strikes, and a plan formulates. I'm going to flirt and coo my way right into a handsome hunk's arms while staying in Sin City, earning a well-deserved romp while ensuring Ryder Gray knows he will never have a chance with me.

Is it petty? Absolutely, but the millionaire superstar has it coming.

In spades.

"On second thought, this could be fun." I stroll over to my closet, pulling open the door. Time to rethink my wardrobe choices.

"Uh-oh. One eighty change in disposition. Disaster is imminent. Should I worry?"

"Not at all, sweet brother. I'll see you tonight."

∼

MY BRAVADO IS ONLY PAPER-THIN, but at least it's making an appearance. I strut through the Vegas hotel lobby like I own the place, the clacking of my heels reverberating throughout the marble entrance.

Usually, I aim for comfort when I fly, dressing in yoga pants and sneakers. But this is not one of those times. Today, I'm wearing a black lace dress that hugs my curves in all the right places, complete with a pair of strappy heels that make my legs look a mile long.

I'm a short woman, so heels are a bit of a necessity if I don't want to disappear into the crowd. But I rarely show off my body in so obvious a manner, even though it's tighter now at thirty-eight than it was at twenty.

Hey, there has to be an upside to be dumped for a younger woman. When Richard told me he had fallen in love with his secretary, I laughed. Seriously. I threw my head back and laughed at the irony. Just like my mother, I found a man who would throw away years—and I mean years—of dedication in pursuit of a younger lay.

The apple doesn't fall far from the tree. But unlike my mother, whose nerves and self-confidence never recovered from my father's deceit, I refused to hide away.

Fuck that noise.

Instead, I hit the gym, earning a Pilates certification and discovering muscles they don't teach you about in anatomy class. My other focus? Work, and paying off the mountain of debt that schmuck ex-boyfriend left me with. At the rate I'm going, I'll be debt-free by the twenty-second century.

But those bills and that pathetic excuse for a man are not my focus for this weekend. This weekend is about turning heads. Mostly turning Ryder's head.

Men always want what they can't have. I let Ryder near my body and heart once. This time, I'm a no-fly zone—at least where Ryder is concerned.

My plane was delayed, so it's a bonus all I need is a pat of powder and a spritz of perfume to be ready for the rehearsal dinner. By the time I finally landed in the desert, Greg was in full-blown panic mode, certain I was making good on my threat to blow off his wedding.

He's worse than a woman with the way he worries, but I

quickly assuaged his fears and let him know I'd be there for the limo pickup at seven. Greg informed me the rest of the bridal party had already arrived and their mission was clear—imbibe copious amounts of alcohol and commit sins that won't be spoken about outside the city limits.

It is Vegas, after all.

Strolling out the front entrance, I hear my brother's loud whoop, my head swinging toward the group. There are about eight in total, and judging by the volume, they've been in their cups for a while.

My breath catches when my gaze lands on Ryder. He looks so different from the cocky but sweet kid I fooled around with once. The long hair is gone, replaced by a crew cut and neatly trimmed beard. He's bigger too, the muscles evident under his button-down shirt and fitted pants.

Holy hell, but he's all man now.

Seems the resident celebrity has already been claimed. One of Jillian's friends, a redhead named Rachel, is eyeing Ryder like he's the finest piece of ass she's ever seen.

A whole slew of women will agree with her sentiment. Lucky for me, I'm no longer one of them, and I'll keep telling myself that until I believe it.

Ryder, for his part, is eating up her affections, that ever-present and fully fake smile on display as Rachel bats her eyes and mashes her tits against him.

Subtle, darling.

With a final breath to center me, I toss my long hair over one shoulder and stride toward the group. Let the games begin. "Ryder Gray. Breaking hearts as always, I see."

Ryder's head flies up at the sound of my voice, a grin breaking across his features.

But it's not the practiced smile that decorates magazine

covers. It's the goofy, crooked grin I remember from eight years ago. Ryder's real smile.

Suddenly, I'm not feeling as confident in my quest.

Focus, Greer. Don't let this man get the better of you again.

He meets me halfway across the parking area, wrapping his hand around my nape and pulling me to him. Without permission, he presses his mouth to mine, and my hands fly up to his chest as my heart threatens to beat out of my own.

Pulling back, those baby blues twinkle at me. "Greer Hammond. Can I just say how jealous I am of your dress tonight? It gets to touch every one of your luscious curves."

I bristle at his well-practiced delivery. Typical playboy, figuring I'm going to melt at the feet of racing royalty.

Nice try, Ryder. I remember when you used to wet the bed.

With a chuckle that's as fake as his smirk, I reply, "I figured you'd be jealous of my bra and g-string since they have a front-row seat to the goods."

His eyes widen, momentarily thrown by my comeback. But he recovers quickly. "Those I plan to dispose of directly. Can't have them crowding in on what's mine."

What a pompous ass. What did I ever see in him? "I'll let you duke it out with them. Until then, your date for the evening is waiting."

Ryder's face scrunches in confusion. "Who?"

"Rachel."

"Who?"

His ego is enormous, and my temper flares to match it. Leaning in, I pull his head down to mine, my voice a fierce whisper. "Ryder Gray, have you forgotten her already? I know you're a callous cad, but try to remember the name of the woman you plan on screwing tonight. Or is that too much to ask from someone of your status?"

A final hair flip and I step away from him, saddened

that the lovable guy I knew, and damn near fell head over heels for that New Year's Eve, is no more. He's been replaced by a man who believes himself better than others, likely because most people treat him as if he is.

Ryder grabs my arm, pulling me back to him, and for the first time, his facade cracks. "If anyone has a right to be angry, it's me, Greer. Thanks for ghosting me, by the way."

What the hell? He is *not* blaming me for eight years ago. "That's rich. I love your version of events."

"What would you call it? I went to deal with... whatever her name was, came back, and you were gone."

"You have difficulty remembering your women's names, don't you? Her name is Jane." I'm never this caustic, but fury from the past eight years is blasting its way to the surface. All aimed at one man. "Austin puked everywhere and Patrick kicked him out. I had to take him home. I gave Patrick my number and asked him to give it to you. Not that you ever used it."

Ryder crosses his arms over his chest, gaze focused on me. "Patrick didn't give me a damn thing. Do you honestly think I wouldn't have called you if I had your number?"

"Do you honestly think I would have left without leaving my number?"

Now we're in a standoff, my dark eyes flashing in time with his blue ones, as we attempt to deduce what happened that night so many years ago.

Ryder breaks first, running a hand over his scalp. "Greg says you're single."

"He didn't mention your marital status, although the tabloids love discussing your escapades. A new woman every week. Aren't you ambitious?"

I mean the barbs to bring him down a notch, but instead,

a smile quirks his lips, despite his best attempt to appear angry. "You read the tabloids about me?"

A flush crawls up my cheeks, and I'm thankful for the dim lighting. "No, I just... no."

Wow. That was one hell of a comeback, Greer.

That endearing grin reappears as his thumb traces over my lower lip, and I'm torn between biting it or twirling my tongue along the digit. I have a feeling he'd play along with either choice. "Greer Hammond is keeping tabs on me."

That does it. Bite it is.

"Ouch." He pulls his hand away, chuckling. "Still feisty as ever."

"Some things never change."

Grasping me around the waist, he pulls me close. "You're right. Some things never do. In fact, some things get more potent with time."

I refuse to read into his statement, or the look flashing in his eyes which I know matches my own. The electricity between us is enough to put Vegas to shame, and I wonder how I've lived this many years without his light.

No, I can't go there again. He's not the same man. Not anymore.

Breaking my gaze away, I focus on his chest, the flash of silver just visible through the open button. I reach up, fingering the medallion around his neck. "You still have it."

"It was given to me by a very special lady, who I missed much more than I'm willing to admit. It was all I had left of her, so I never took it off."

With those words, I see the same sweet guy I always knew, and I want to sob with relief. He's still there, hiding behind a practiced mask. A mask he uses to protect himself, particularly his heart.

Just like me.

So much for focus. If I'm not careful, I'll be in love with the infamous racer before the weekend it out. A repeat of eight years ago, when my heart was his for the taking.

When he promised to show me the world, starting with Paris. Funny thing, I would have gone with him and likely never left his side.

But falling for Ryder Gray now would be the dumbest idea I've ever had. He's a star, despite his modest roots. Besides, I spent eight years thinking about him. Missing him.

Time to put some room—emotional and otherwise—between us.

"You're very charming, but I won't fall for you again, Ryder."

His grin widens as his grip on my body tightens.

"I take it you approve of my decision?"

"That's not why I'm smiling. You said you won't fall for me *again*, implying you fell once before." Lifting my hand, he presses a kiss to my palm. "Which means, it's only a matter of time."

"Is that a fact?" I try to sound aggravated, but my words are breathy as his lips dust kisses across my skin.

"It's a promise, Greer Hammond. Mark my words."

"If you two are quite through flirting, can we get a move on? I'm parched." My brother shoots me a grin, a knowing look on his face.

Blowing Greg a kiss and wink, I walk toward the stretch limo, acutely aware of how Ryder has fallen into step with me—quite a feat, considering his legs are twice as long as mine.

I'm not sure what to make of the man. He's gorgeous, celebrated and coveted by almost every straight woman in the world.

But deep down, he's still Ryder.

Or is he?

"Hey, stop with all the heavy thoughts," Ryder says, breaking into my internal monologue. "We're going to have an amazing time this weekend."

My eyes dart upward, locking with his. Just like times past, he knows my innermost thoughts without me saying a word.

That knowledge, coupled with the way the man is undressing me with his eyes, is a bit unnerving.

In the most delicious fashion.

My phone buzzes and I groan when I glance at the caller ID. Waving Ryder to the limo, I pace the walkway, explaining to my patient for the hundredth time that just because her blood pressure is under control doesn't mean she can stop taking her ACE inhibitor. After arguing my scientific logic for a minute, she relents, agreeing to take her medicine.

No doubt I'll have another call in the morning, debating the same topic. Never a dull moment in healthcare.

As the last one into the limo, I have the added bonus of climbing over everyone, since the only remaining seat is way in the front. Love the logic there.

Rachel has reclaimed the man of the hour, her entire body pressed against Ryder.

Like I said, subtle.

As I crouch to make my way to the available seat, I'm acutely aware of the up-close view I'm giving Ryder of my ass, made more pronounced by the length—of lack thereof—of my skirt.

I jump when a hand wraps around my hip. Glancing over my shoulder, I see Ryder's digits locked onto me, those azure eyes daring me to complain. "I thought you were going to fall," is his only explanation.

"How chivalrous of you." Flashing him a smile, I plop

into my seat, hiking my skirt up an extra inch as I cross my legs, fully aware of his laser stare on my stems.

The limo hasn't even left the parking lot before everyone has a glass in hand, toasting Greg and Jillian.

I remember how nervous Greg was when I first met Jillian. She was different from all the other women, he claimed. She was the one. He just knew it. He was right, and I couldn't ask for a nicer sister-in-law. Jillian is bubbly, cute, and fun as hell.

Plus, she loves Greg something fierce. That love was tested early in their relationship when my brother had a cancer scare. Jillian stood by his side, never wavering in her dedication. Such a difference from when my mother found a lump in her breast, right after I left for college. My father, despite the years between them, couldn't be bothered to support her during such a trying time. He had affairs to handle and secretaries to screw.

Thankfully for Greg and Mom, their lumps were benign. My father's behavior? Not so much.

"As the best man, I want to say a few words before we're all too drunk to remember them." All eyes focus on the divinely handsome racer, a smirk breaking across his features.

"Speak for yourself. There's no such thing as drunk in Vegas," Greg counters, earning an appreciative laugh from Ryder.

"That's the rumor, anyway. You're my oldest friend, and even though we don't talk enough, true friendship never dies. Jillian, we only just met, but I see how happy Greg is, and I know that's because of you. Congratulations, you two. Here's to the world being your oyster."

Everyone toasts to their happiness, and I shoot a smile at

Ryder from across the limo. He's right. My brother deserves every happiness.

At least one of us does.

With a sigh, I focus my gaze out the window. I'm thrilled for Greg and normally I keep the loneliness at bay by maintaining an insane work schedule, interspersed with the occasional night out with friends. I haven't dated anyone seriously in over a year, but honestly, I don't have the energy for a relationship with my endless stacks of bills.

Perhaps one day.

My reverie is broken as Ryder squeezes next to me, wrapping an arm around my shoulders. He's snuggled as close to me as Rachel was to him, and his proximity threatens my heart's equilibrium.

"I have one last toast. A private one for the most beautiful woman in the world. To you, Gigi."

My jaw slackens, not only at his words but at the softness residing in his eyes as he speaks them. "That's quite a compliment from the king of racing."

Ryder shakes his head, but it's obvious my statement upsets him, which was never my intention. "I'm just Ryder. With you, that's always been enough."

Pressing my hand to his chest, I let down the wall that encases my heart. "It still is."

That crooked grin decorates his face as he tucks my head under his chin, his grip tightening around me. Once again, I feel safe.

Just like eight years ago, Ryder has snuck back into my heart through a window which I no doubt left open for his return.

CHAPTER 4
GREER

I'll be full for a week. The rehearsal dinner is a Greek-style feast with so many platters of food I'm shocked the table doesn't crack from the weight. No surprise to learn the entire weekend is compliments of Ryder, who is also on a first-name basis with the restaurant's owner. There's no way we normal everyday folks could ever score a table in such a place.

Normally, I hate how the ultra-rich flaunt their money, but Ryder isn't doing it for recognition. The man is generous to a fault and I know it's making my brother's wedding special. Judging by the smile decorating Greg's face, he's over the moon to be reunited with his childhood friend.

I'm thrilled to see Greg smile.

I'm also thrilled to see Ryder, even if I'm having a hard time controlling my lustful urges in his vicinity.

Who can blame me? The man is superbly sexy. His hands are strong but lean, with long fingers I've no doubt know their way around a woman's body. Too bad I didn't get the full breadth of that experience eight years ago. Then there's his mouth—full lips surrounded by a neatly trimmed dark beard. When he runs his hand over his beard, connecting my two favorite body parts, I don't stand a chance.

Despite Ryder's nonchalant attitude toward her, Rachel is still gunning for his attention. She snagged the seat next to him at the table—no surprise there—and she's finding every reason in the world to lean against him, her breasts threatening to spill out of her skimpy top.

No doubt Ryder is used to the blatant affection, but he appears to be a consummate gentleman, which I'm sure is terribly upsetting for Rachel.

As for me, I'm seated a few seats down and across the table from him, but I'm happy with my spot. It allows me to sneak glances in his direction without being too obvious. Of course, every time I look his way, he's already looking at me.

But it's the way he looks at me—such intensity and longing—that has every cell firing at the same time. I've had my share of men, but none has ever managed a reaction quite like the one Ryder is bringing out in me, and he's a few feet away.

I can't imagine what it would feel like to remove that space, along with any clothing that might get in the way.

I giggle at my tempestuous thoughts, earning a quizzical glance from Ryder. "Nothing," I mouth, waving it off.

With a sigh and a wink in Ryder's direction, I head for the bathroom, releasing a squeal of excitement when the band plays one of my favorite Bowie songs.

Walking to the small dance area, I spy Ryder and Rachel, her body pressed close as she whispers in his ear, and a twinge of jealousy sparks inside me.

I know he's not mine, but I can still want to break her fingers. It's not like I'm going to act on the notion.

"Would you like to dance?"

Gazing up, I smile into the stranger's handsome face as he offers me his hand.

"She's dancing with me. Only me," Ryder cuts in, a muscle jumping in his jaw. He grabs my hand, leading me to the floor and pulling me flush against him.

"What was that about? You had a dance partner."

"Not by choice," he retorts, his hand resting against my lower back. "She's like an octopus—arms everywhere. Thanks for saving me, by the way."

I tap his chest, offering him a smirk. "So hard being adored. Poor little Ryder."

Cupping my ass, he pulls me hard against his erection. "Gigi, there's nothing little about me."

"Certainly not your ego."

Am I getting flustered, feeling his length pressed against me?

Hell yes.

Will I let Ryder in on this fact?

Hell no.

"Did you really want to dance with that guy?"

"Not particularly," I remark, glancing at the handsome gentleman across the floor.

"Do you want to dance with me?"

Moving my gaze to meet his, I capture my lower lip between my teeth, fully aware Ryder is watching my every move. "If I say yes, that makes it too easy. Women always come easy for you."

Ryder chuckles, his lips moving against my ear. "Greer, I've waited twenty years for this moment. Nothing about you has been easy."

"You weren't waiting for me."

He stops moving, his gaze focused on me with such intensity I fear I might melt into a puddle. "My heart was."

And now my heart pounds like a runaway freight train, my entire body trembling under the weight of his words. "That was really good. Next level good."

Dipping his head, his mouth grazes against mine. "Good enough for a thank you kiss?"

"Definitely." I press a chaste but soft kiss on his lips, pulling back before I totally lose myself to the moment.

Ryder skews his mouth, shooting me a mock glare. "I'm not sure how grateful you are with a kiss like that, and I know you have the most amazing mouth in the world."

"Shall I show you again?"

"A million more times."

I can't fight the high I feel being in his arms, or the sparks flooding my body as his hands press me ever closer. Then I hear the familiar strains of my favorite Elvis song. "Two for two. Lucky guess?"

"Not a guess, a photographic memory. I told you on New Year's Eve that I remember everything about you. It still holds true today, but for the last eight years I've also carried the knowledge of how you kiss." His mouth nuzzles my neck, and I tilt my head to give him better access. "How you taste. Your body has always been gorgeous, but now you're absolutely incredible."

Ryder runs his tongue along his lip, the hunger raging in his face.

Rising on tiptoe, I press a kiss to his ear. "You should see me naked."

His breath hitches, but his grip never falters. Instead, his hands slide down my spine to wrap around my hips. "I plan on it, Gigi. And one more sexy as fuck statement from your delectable mouth and I'll be forced to strip you down right here."

Damn, doesn't that sound tempting? "Is that a fact? What then?"

He grips my chin, his lips hovering against mine. "Then everything. Everything I've waited years to do. I'm not leaving here without making you mine. In every possible way."

Ryder claims my mouth, his kiss hot and demanding as he splays his hands across my ass.

But unlike the slow, sensual kisses from that long-ago New Year's Eve, this kiss borders on possessive, and with every second that passes, my body nears implosion. Ryder isn't holding back as he hauls my body flush against him, his hands firmly against my skin.

A whoop sounds from my right and I glare at my brother, who shoots us a thumbs up. "I knew it."

"What an ass," Ryder chuckles, his mouth dancing against mine.

"He's *your* friend."

"He's *your* brother."

"Exactly. I had no choice in the matter. You went willingly."

"I'd go anywhere to be near you," Ryder replies, and I know my heart doesn't stand a chance against his romantic inclinations. Or his grace on the dance floor.

"Who taught you to dance?" Yes, I'm changing the subject. I need to maintain some level of space between me and the world-famous playboy.

Ryder smiles, inching me closer. "When my dad was in the hospital, my mom wanted to keep my mind off things. To be honest, she wanted to keep her mind off things. So, she taught me to dance in the waiting rooms, swaying to the ridiculous elevator music that all hospitals play."

"I always loved your mom. How is she doing?"

"She's good. I built a house for her up on Lake George. She and Dad always wanted to move there. I wanted to ensure she didn't miss that chance."

I slide my hand along his arm, feeling the muscle flex. "I love how you take such good care of your Mom. You're doing very well for yourself."

"I do all right."

"Bullshit. I've seen pictures of your house. I mean, castle."

"It's just a house." He leans in, his mouth tickling my ear. "You have to come to visit. I'll give you the grand tour."

"Any room, in particular, you'd like to show me?"

The air crackles between us, but I can't look away. His eyes darken, his hands drifting across my skin.

"I'll make love to you in every room, Gigi. One time for each day I've gone without you."

"We'll be busy for a while, then."

"That's the idea, but I'm not waiting until we get back to my house."

"No?" My heart races like a locomotive, pounding against my rib cage.

"We've waited long enough." Stealing a kiss, he rests his forehead against mine, softly singing 'Can't Help Falling in Love' as we sway to the rhythm.

"You really remember." I can't believe he's committed so much of me to his memory.

"It was your favorite song."

"It's still my favorite."

"And you're still mine."

Just like that, I fall in love with Ryder Gray again.

I'm barely able to breathe over the pounding in my heart. Cupping his face, I run my fingers along his soft beard. "I missed you, Ryder."

Once again, it's as though he sees past the simple statement, to the true meaning underneath. "Not nearly as much as I missed you."

When our mouths meet this time, I feel everything—all the passion, the deep ache emanating from us both. His kisses reawaken a part of my core that's laid dormant for years, each slide of his tongue against mine reassuring me that every promise he's made he intends to keep.

Ryder nibbles a path along my jaw, his grip on my hips tightening, and I wonder how much longer I can hold out against this level of electricity. "Let's get out of here, Gigi. I need time alone with you."

I should play hard to get, because I know a man like Ryder Gray doesn't hear the word no, particularly not from women. But I've also been waiting far longer than any of those women. Besides, I know what I want. I've known for eight years.

And yet...

"Hey." Ryder tips my chin up, pressing a soft kiss to my lips. "I just want to be with you. We don't have to do anything beyond that. Please."

"What about the bachelor party?"

"I've hired the best strippers in Vegas for your brother and his buddies. I have a much more private party in mind for us—bubble bath, champagne, and holding you all night. We've waited forever already."

With a smile, I release my doubts, determined to live in the moment. I'll deal with the heartache tomorrow. "Meet you out front?"

Ryder presses another kiss to my lips, his hands tangling in my hair as he holds me close. "Don't take too long."

With a smile tattooed on my face, I strut into the bathroom, ensuring some extra hip shake for Ryder's benefit. Hey, I work my ass out three times a week for a reason.

If you've got it, flaunt it. If you work it, shake it.

Not my motto, but it sure as hell should be.

I'm fixing my lipstick in the bathroom mirror when a woman sidles next to me, casting me a side-eye glance. "You're with Ryder Gray."

And just like that, my back goes up. "Is that a question?"

"An observation, judging by your make-out session on the dance floor."

Closing my purse, I turn to my accuser, verbal barbs at the ready. "What's it to you?"

"Me? Nothing. But I'm fairly certain it will bother his girlfriend, Mandi."

The name Mandi isn't totally unfamiliar, and I seem to recall reading about her and Ryder's romance, but that was months ago. Besides, he would tell me if he had a girlfriend. I refuse to let this stranger get under my skin. "Sorry to break it to you, but he's single."

"When did they break up? Yesterday?" With a final once over, she sends me a smirk. "Honey, do your homework. Men like Ryder Gray are never single. They only pretend to be, in order to get what they want. Best not learn that the hard way."

Thrilled she's put a kink in my step, she saunters out of the bathroom, leaving me to weigh my options.

She's a lunatic, jealous that I have Ryder's attention, and she doesn't.

But what if she's right? He never mentioned not having a girlfriend.

Ryder is a good guy, especially where I'm concerned. He wouldn't do that.

He's also the same man who kissed me and then never called. Do I really want to test that theory with sex?

This is the mental argument doing battle in my brain, and I'm not sure which side has the advantage.

Screw it. The only way to learn the truth is to ask for it, and the man with the knowledge I seek is right outside.

With a final sigh, I stroll out to the limo, watching Ryder's face light up when he sees me. "Ready to go?"

Here goes nothing.

"Can I ask you something?"

"Anything."

"Are you dating a woman named Mandi?"

"Fuck." Ryder runs his hand over his scalp, avoiding my gaze. "Did someone say something?"

My heart sinks at his statement. "That's not an answer."

"I was, but we aren't dating anymore."

Okay, that's a start. I knew that woman was a jealous maniac.

"When did you two break up?"

"Gigi, what's going on? Don't let people get into your head."

And here is where the conversation takes a turn into dangerous territory. After my father's indiscretions, I learned how to read people, particularly when they're not forthcoming. Ryder is the epitome of evasive with this line of questioning.

"Answer the question."

"Two days ago," he mutters, and my stomach flips.

"That's just wonderful."

"What does it matter? I caught Mandi screwing another man in my house. Trust me, she doesn't deserve your sympathy."

"Right now, I feel sorry for me." I shake my head as the

full breadth of his words hit home. "Wait, she *lived* with you, too? God, that's so much worse."

"Mandi was more than happy to end things. Trust me, the relationship has been over for months."

Holding up two fingers, I prepare to stand my ground. "No, it's been over for two days. Here I thought... doesn't matter. Turns out I'm a rebound. At least it's a step up from being the other woman."

He grabs my arms, forcing me to look at him. "That is not the case, Gigi. You know how special you are to me."

"Eight years ago, you kissed me with your date downstairs. Today, after our little dance floor make-out session, I discover you had a live-in girlfriend two days ago. Do you have any idea how bad this looks?"

"How long do I need to be single for it to be acceptable to you?" Oh, good, now he's aggravated.

Two can play that game.

"More than two days would be preferable. Hell, is asking for a week between women too much?" I rub my brow as a headache brews. "I feel like an idiot. Again."

"Gigi, that's the last thing I ever want to do."

He rubs my arms, but I shrug him off. My emotions become too muddled when he touches me, and I must maintain a clear head. "If it's a quick lay you're after, there's a ton of women here who will do whatever you want. No questions asked."

His eyes darken, a storm brewing in their depths. "Is that what you think? Gigi, if I wanted a quick lay, I'd have had one by now." No sooner has the words left his mouth than he realizes what a terrible idea it was to give them a voice. A frown mars his brow as he takes a step toward me. "I shouldn't have said that."

He's right, but contrite or not, the damage is done.

Stepping back, I shake my head, disgusted I ever considered sleeping with this man. Disgusted I believed I wasn't another in a long line of women. "Have at it, Ryder. Don't let me stop you." I turn on my heel, but he grasps me about the waist, his large frame pinning me against the side of the limo.

His fingers encircle my wrists, holding them hostage as his mouth claims me. After a moment's struggle, I relent, allowing my emotions to flow unbidden. With gentle strokes, his tongue slides against mine, coaxing me off my emotional ledge.

Let's face facts—where Ryder Gray is concerned, I have no willpower.

The moment he releases my hands, I slide them around his neck, a heated moan rising from his throat as he presses closer.

When his hands slide under the hem of my skirt, the rest of the world falls away. All I see is him. All I feel is him.

"You're all I've ever wanted, Gigi."

Pulling back, I hold his azure gaze, searching for deception. I find none. Instead, I see years of long-shelved passion aimed at me and desperate for release.

It mirrors my own.

"Let me make you mine."

"Ryder Gray," a voice shouts from behind us, and I groan when I spy the group of reporters gathered on the sidewalk, cameras clicking.

"Oh, no," I murmur, burying my head in his chest.

I can see the tabloid headlines now: *Not a week between women. Way to go, Ryder Gray.*

"Fucking vultures," Ryder mutters. "The restaurant won't allow them on their property, so they hover on the sidewalk, hoping for some action."

"Which we just gave them. What do we do now?"

"I'm going to speak to them. Better they hear from me directly instead of inventing a story of their own. Do you want to come with me? Meet the press?"

"Hard pass. What are my other options?"

Ryder presses a kiss to my forehead, a low chuckle reverberating from his throat. Glad he's so amused. "You can wait in the limo."

I'm halfway in the limo before he finishes his statement. Some people crave the limelight. I am not one of them.

Instead, I spend the next few minutes wondering what the hell I should do now. What are even my options at this point?

See? I knew Vegas was a bad idea.

Ryder slips into the limo, that artificial smile plastered on his face.

"I hate that smile."

He chuckles, the goofy grin I know and love taking center stage. "I love that you know the difference."

"That smile," I reply, motioning to his delicious mouth, "is a recent addition. Nonexistent when you were a kid."

"It's all part of the facade. Total bullshit." Turning in the seat, he slides his fingers down the length of my hair. "Are you done being mad at me?"

Huffing out a breath, I open the bottle of wine, helping myself to half a glass. "I suppose I don't have any right, but I hate the idea of being your rebound. It never ends well for the rebound."

"Gigi, I've waited years for a chance with you. That's hardly a rebound."

I want to believe him. He seems so earnest in his appeal, but I've been burned before—by Ryder, no less. No way in hell I'm racing back into the fire.

Time to change the subject.

"How do you deal with the constant media attention? It would drive me crazy."

"It's not all the time. Honestly, my life is pretty normal."

A snort flies from my mouth at his remark, because it's total bullshit. Nothing about Ryder Gray's life is normal.

He laughs, stealing a sip from my glass. "Somewhat normal? Most of the time, it's photos of me going to dinner or grocery shopping. Normal stuff."

Rolling my eyes, I snatch back my glass. "Does this qualify as normal?"

"Not at all. They love capturing moments like this. It's what they live for."

With a groan, I flop back against the seat. "That settles it. I'm never kissing you again."

He pulls me against him, grasping my chin and forcing me to meet his gaze. "Like hell you aren't. You're going to kiss me a million more times."

"I'm serious. You said the media is going to eat this up. I don't want any part of it, particularly since I now know you're only *newly* single."

I try to jerk my chin away, but he holds me fast. "Well, that's not exactly true."

The hairs on the back of my neck stand up at his blasé statement. "What's not exactly true?"

"I'm not technically single, but don't worry, I explained everything to the reporters."

Suddenly there's no air in the limo, as my respirations increase in a desperate bid to calm my mind. He told me he was single. Now he's reneging on that claim? After the media caught us making out in broad daylight?

It's an introvert's worst nightmare. Hell, it's a woman's worst nightmare.

Ryder picks up on the change in my mood, wrapping an arm around my stiff shoulders. "Gigi, it's all good. I promise."

"What's good about it? What did you tell them to clear everything up? Did you claim I was having a seizure, and you had to keep me from swallowing my tongue?"

I'm freaking out. Ryder, for his part, is totally calm and judging by the upturned corners of his mouth, slightly amused by the entire debacle.

How nice for him.

"Not exactly. I told them our situation."

My headache? It's back with reinforcements. "Which is what, exactly?"

"I told them you're my girlfriend."

CHAPTER 5
RYDER

Greer's eyes darken as a stunned sputter flies from her mouth. "Your what?"

"Girlfriend."

"Why would you tell them that?"

Okay, not the reaction I was hoping for. "They have photos of us making out. I wanted to protect you. What would you have preferred I say?" A muscle jumps in my jaw as I cross my arms over my chest. She acts like dating me is on par with contracting the flu. "Being my girlfriend isn't the worst thing in the world."

"Do you realize how this makes me look? Forty-eight hours ago, you were living with another woman. Now, you're in Vegas with someone new, and *I'm* that someone?" She buries her face in her hands, releasing a loud groan. "I look like a homewrecker. Hell, I suppose I *am* a homewrecker."

I grasp her knee, desperate to calm her emotions. It would thrill most women to have the paparazzi capture an intimate moment with me. Not my Greer—a fact that both entices and infuriates me. Hey, my ego is coming into play and it's getting a bit of an ass-kicking at the moment. A woman *not* wanting to date me is not something I normally encounter, particularly when that woman is the only woman I want. "It's not that bad. We can get pistachio ice cream. Does that help ease the pain of being my girlfriend?"

She snorts, shaking her head. She's trying to appear aggravated, but I see the grin pulling at the corners of her mouth. "Ice cream doesn't come close to cutting it. Does the whole what happens in Vegas stays in Vegas apply to your life?"

"I highly doubt it." At least she's smiling. I know this woman, she likes to appear tough as nails, but she's a marshmallow. She also has a soft spot for me, or, so I thought before she melted down about our relationship status.

Greer drums her nails along the door handle and I see the gears turning in her mind, wondering what my ulterior motive is in this situation.

The truth? The media asked about Greer; I opened my mouth, and without thinking, I announced she was my girlfriend. It was an accident, of sorts. It just came out.

Not that I don't want to date her. Hell, I want far more than that with Greer Hammond. But I hoped to wine and dine her, romance her slowly and steal her heart when she wasn't looking.

Turns out I have far more finesse on the track than I do with love. Don't get me wrong, I have no issues dating women, but I don't love them. I wasn't even certain I still loved Greer until she walked through the hotel entrance. When she called my name and our gazes locked, I knew I was a goner.

Who am I kidding? I never got back from loving her, and by the time this weekend is over, she'll be equally crazy about me.

I suspect she already is if those luscious kisses are anything to go on. Damn that woman and her talented mouth. Shifting in my seat, I adjust myself, realizing I've had a hard-on since Greer walked back into my life.

Time to remedy that situation.

I grab the bottle of whiskey, pouring a finger into my glass. Best bet with Greer? Make her laugh. "I always told you that one day I'd date you."

That did it. Greer's face splits into a grin as she delivers a light smack to my arm. "You could have asked me first. Brought me flowers."

"I can stop for flowers. Hey, Mike," I call to the driver through the window, earning another smack from Greer, "can we stop by a florist?"

"You're ridiculous," Greer laughs.

"You want flowers, you'll get flowers. I'll buy the whole damn shop." I run my fingers along her jaw, trailing them down her neck to dance between her cleavage. This woman has skin like silk, and I can't wait to taste every inch of her. Leaning in, I capture that beautiful mouth, tracing my tongue along the seam in her lips until she grants me entrance.

But Greer has never been one to go down easily. Staying my hands, she fixes me with her dark stare. "That isn't how it works, Ryder."

"How would you know?" I ask between kisses, her mouth hot against mine. "You've only dated me for five minutes."

As luck would have it, the florist is around the block. Literally. I haven't even had time to sink into our kiss when Mike announces our arrival. Damn punctuality and green lights.

Greer shakes her head in amusement when the limo slows to a stop. "You're not really going in, are you?"

"What's the point of stopping, otherwise?" Stealing another kiss, I jump out of the limo, determined to buy the biggest bouquet in the place and get this woman the hell back to my suite.

I have a bevy of romantic plans for the two of us, but at the moment, pent-up sexual energy wins.

Five minutes later, I stroll back to the limo, carrying a tremendous bouquet of lilies and irises. The florist mentioned roses as an option, but I get the distinct impression Greer isn't one for typical sentiments.

Judging by the smile crossing her face when I hand over the flowers, I guessed correctly.

"Ryder, they're beautiful. This is the biggest bouquet I've ever seen in my life." She struggles to hold it against her petite form, and I chuckle, realizing it only took me twenty years to buy her flowers. Better late than never, I suppose.

"Told you dating me wasn't all bad."

I expect a flashy grin as she settles onto my lap to thank me properly. Instead, a frown mars her brow. Uh oh, the gears are turning again.

"What's on your mind, Gigi?"

"Is this some ploy to get me into bed? Checkbox on your to-do list? Sleep with Greer—check. Move on to the next woman?" The frown deepens as she sets the flowers aside. "I'm sure it works with every woman you meet, but—"

Okay, enough of that noise. Seizing her mouth, I silence any further arguments. I'm not dismissing her fears. They're legitimate. But what she can't seem to wrap her head around is that she's not just any woman.

She's the one I've waited for my entire life.

I'm not entirely certain how to prove that fact to her, although I have reached a decision about this evening.

Even if my dick goes on strike.

I'm not sleeping with Greer. Not tonight. She thinks she's another conquest in a long line of women, and although I know I can lure her into the mood, I'd rather she was secure in her place in my life.

Of all the women I've known, she deserves that level of adoration.

Pulling back, she runs her tongue along that pouty lower lip, gazing at me through lowered lashes. "That's hardly an answer, Ryder."

My fingers drift along her cheek, drinking in the beauty that I've admired for years. It's uncanny, but she's more beautiful with every year that passes. She's also more jaded and emotionally distant.

I've got my work cut out for me.

"How about I make a call and get us some tickets for a show? It is Vegas, after all. Or I can rent a boat on Lake Mead and get us away from the Strip. Better yet, I can set up desert camping, and we can really take in nature."

Her eyes widen with each idea, a small smile crossing her lips. "You still haven't answered my question."

Cupping her face with both hands, I force her to hold my gaze, praying she sees the truth in their depths. "Do I want you? Absolutely. I've wanted you for as long as I can remember. But you only get one first time with the woman you've always dreamt about, so I'm not screwing it up."

"You're not trying to sleep with me?"

"Haven't you figured it out? I'm trying to make you fall madly in love with me." There it is, right out in the open.

Sitting up, she presses a hard kiss to my mouth, but she can't hold back the smile. This time, I know her happiness is genuine. "Keep saying things like that and it won't be difficult."

My heart jumps at her words, but I force levity. "See? I told you dating me wouldn't be such a bad thing."

When the limo pulls up to the entrance of the hotel, I beat Mike to the punch, helping Greer from the car and pressing a kiss to her palm. Then I send Mike back to the restaurant to fetch the rest of the crew.

Me? I've got my own plans—ensuring Greer *does* fall in love with me.

Greer's gaze flits around, taking in the luxurious surroundings. "This is quite a step up from the original location. Greg told me you footed the bill."

"He's been a loyal friend for years. He deserves it and you only get married... well, I'm not going there." We exchange a grin as we stroll through the lobby, Greer barely able to hang onto her flowers.

"Mr. Gray," the concierge calls out, waving in my direction. "I have several messages for you. I apologize, but she insisted I hand-deliver them. She was *remarkably* insistent." His lips purse in a frown and I know immediately who's been calling.

Rubbing my hand over my brow, I flip through the pile—and I mean *pile*—of messages from Mandi, ranging from apologetic to apoplectic. Apparently, news of my exploits in Vegas has made its way to her door. "Insistent is an understatement."

"She also wanted me to mention that she's at home in Charlotte and isn't leaving until she gets some answers." He shrugs, a rueful expression coloring his features. "Should I hold all calls from her, sir?"

What I want is to superglue her mouth shut, but since that isn't a viable option, I know I'll have to speak with her. Fucking wonderful. "Mandi and I need to talk, even if it's the last thing I want to do right now."

My statement, although true, should have remained in my head for two reasons. One is that discretion is of utmost importance in the world of celebrity and I don't know the concierge from Adam. The second and more important reason? Greer heard every word of our brief exchange, and judging by the dismay on her face, she's none too pleased.

Talk about damage control. Releasing a slow exhale, I offer Greer a shrug and hope for the best. "I'm sorry." What else can I say at this point? Despite my every attempt to not make it look like a booty call, this latest turn of events is not helping matters. "I'm not even sure how she knew where I was."

"The world knows every move you make, Ryder Gray." Her gaze shifts to the ground as she chews her lower lip. "She's *still* living with you? This keeps getting better and better. What's next? She'll show up for the wedding?"

"She's still at the house, but only because she hasn't found a place, or so that's her claim. I'm dealing with it."

Wrong answer, Ryder.

Houston, we have a major incident—a head-on collision, and the brake lines are cut. Greer shakes her head, her gaze flitting from the enormous bouquet in her arms to my face. "Take your flowers, Ryder."

"They're your flowers."

The head shaking is more insistent now, her lips pursed. "I don't want any part of this situation." She holds out the bouquet, but I make no move to take them. After standing at an impasse for several seconds, she darts across the floor, gifting them to a woman in a wheelchair.

Then, without a second glance, she turns on her heel and heads for the elevator.

I have two choices: let her walk away or chase her down.

I let her walk away once. There's no way in hell I'm letting that happen a second time.

My long legs have no issue overtaking her, and I grip her arm, forcing her to slow. "Easy, Gigi. Can we talk about this without you running away?"

"Running away is the safest option at this point." She motions between the two of us, and it's then I catch the glassiness in her gaze. "What are we doing? We need to stop, or we'll wind up doing something we regret. I've known you your entire life. I don't want to taint that memory."

"I will never regret spending time with you. But I'm ready to leave those memories in the past and start making new ones together."

"You're living with another woman," Greer argues, punching the elevator button.

"Only technically. Hell, I put her on a plane two days ago. I don't know why she's back in Charlotte, but I swear, Mandi and I are done."

"That appears to be a one-sided sentiment. Come on," she mutters, her eyes focused on the floor numbers above the bank of elevators. "Go and speak with her, Ryder. It's obvious she isn't taking silence for an answer."

"What about us?"

Greer pivots, her eyes large and luminous. "There is no us. There never has been. Any time we came even remotely close, your girlfriend suddenly appears, shooting the notion all to hell, and making me feel like a hussy in the process." She runs her hand over her brow, the tension clear in her face. "I knew this was a terrible idea. I shouldn't have come."

No way will I let her throw up more emotional walls. She has miles of them already that I have to break through. When the elevator doors open, I mouth a silent prayer that it's empty, before crowding Gigi against the back wall, caging her in with my forearms. "Do you know why *I* wasn't going to come?"

"Greg said you were too busy."

"Not even close. Yes, I'm busy, but never too busy for my friends, and trust me, I don't have that many of them. Not real ones, anyway." Inching closer, I nuzzle my nose along her jawline, basking in her magical scent. "I waited four months for you to call, using every excuse I could think of as to why you didn't—it was too hard to reach me overseas, you were embarrassed to call, time zones—*every* excuse. Finally, I worked up the courage to ask Greg. I knew I'd have to tell him everything, but I didn't care. A chance with you was more important. That's when he told me about you and the doctor. It was serious. He figured you would get married. I'd heard enough at that point and from then on, I didn't ask about you."

Greer fingers the St. Christopher medallion around my neck, but she won't meet my gaze. "I wanted you to call me. I started dating Richard when I realized you wouldn't."

"Did he make you happy?" I'm not sure why I need this information, but I finally have the courage to inquire about the details.

"It was fun for a while, but med school usurped most of his time. I worked constantly to foot the bills, convincing myself it would all be worth it in the end."

"Did you love him?"

She hesitates, chewing her lip—my favorite of her nervous gestures. "I'm not sure I know what love is, Ryder."

Her words settle over me, and I see the pain reflected in her eyes. She means what she says. "You've never been in love?"

"I told you years ago I'm not built for relationships."

"And I told you that was bullshit."

"Have you been in love?"

The elevator doors open before I can answer, but I'm glad for the interruption. Although the answer has always been the same, I'm not quite ready to speak those words aloud to Greer. Mainly because I doubt she'll believe them, all things considered.

"My suite is this way," she states, jerking her thumb over her shoulder. "I hope your chat with Mandi goes well and you two—"

"Stay broken up? That's the only option." I refuse to let any additional fears set up camp in Greer's mind.

But it's obvious by her stilted stance that she is nothing if not unsure—what to say, how to act, what to feel. "Have fun at the bachelor party. Take good care of my brother. I really appreciate you doing all this for Greg. It means the world to him. *You* mean the world to him."

Grasping her about the waist, I pull her close, desperate to know where her heart lies and if there's still room in it for me. "What about you, Greer? What do I mean to you?"

I expect a sarcastic retort in the classic Greer Hammond style, but she surprises me by standing on her tiptoes and delivering a soft kiss to my mouth. "You're the closest thing to love I've ever known, even if we're destined for nothing to ever come of it." Taking a step back, she shakes her head, a smirk playing about her mouth. "I'm far safer offering up my body and leaving my heart under wraps. What happens in Vegas, right?"

She's halfway to her suite when I find the courage to speak my next line. "I want more than your body, Gigi. I'm aiming for your heart. This time, I'm not stopping until it's mine." My phone rings and even though I silence it, her expression shutters.

"You'd better get that. I'll talk to you later, Ryder."

"You don't have to believe me. I'll prove it to you." Desperate to keep the conversation going, I aim for levity. "By the way, thanks for giving away the diamond bracelet I hid in the bouquet. I hope that woman enjoys it."

Yes, I'm messing with her, but the energy is too heavy. We need to lighten the mood. Have some fun. Hell, haven't we earned it?

Greer's jaw slackens at my words. "Please tell me you're joking."

I struggle to maintain a stern expression, but the look of horror stamping across her features is too much. "I'm joking."

"Thank God."

As she buzzes herself into the room, I can't resist one last zinger. "It was a necklace."

This time, instead of a horrified expression, she flips me the bird with a smile before closing the door to her suite.

At least we're moving in the right direction.

I know Greer is terrified—of my lifestyle, my storied sexual history, my celebrity status—but what she doesn't understand is I'm still Ryder, and she's one of the few people who can see that. One of the only people who wants to see me as I really am.

Besides, her admission opens the door for a future together. Now, I only have to convince her to fall in love with me, all while keeping my hands to myself.

Holy shit, I have my work cut out for me.

∼

It's been an hour. That's about the only way to sum up the last sixty minutes. I spent the first twenty going round and round with Mandi, who heard from a friend of a friend of a friend—or something to that effect—that I was in Vegas with another woman.

After I verified I was indeed in Vegas with Greer, Mandi spent the next twenty minutes ranting and raving. Thankfully for my eardrums, I kept the phone at a safe distance.

I'll give it to the media. When they latch onto a juicy tidbit, they're faster than any F1 race car. The news of my Vegas weekend is already bicoastal, although they haven't been able to identify the mystery brunette.

Only a matter of time.

The final twenty minutes were a mad dash of showering and throwing on fresh duds before heading to Greer's room and sweeping her off her feet. I wasn't able to snag front-row seats for a show, but I got us a table at the hottest French restaurant on the Strip.

Less than five minutes, and she'll be back in my arms. Even that seems too long.

I swing open the door of my suite, stopping dead in my tracks at the harem of half-dressed women trailing behind Greg and the groomsmen.

What in the hell?

Did I pay for these strippers? Absolutely, along with the suites and booze and various amenities. However, I never intended for them to land on my doorstep.

Literally.

"What's up, man?" I ask, forcing a smile.

"Bachelor party," is Greg's only answer as they waltz past me into the suite, a bevy of beauties and liquor bottles in tow.

"Why did you bring them here?" I question, my face scrunched in disgust. "I have plans tonight."

"I know you have plans—with me. It's my bachelor party, and it's set to go down in history as the greatest one known to man, thanks to you. These women are gorgeous." Greg shoots me a smirk, downing a shot as a slight blonde grinds against him.

"I'm glad. Enjoy them. But, can you move the festivities to your suite?"

His grin widens as he wags a finger under my nose. "These must be important plans. Wouldn't happen to be with my sister?"

Christ, don't let Greg start with me now, especially since he's been in his cups. "If I say it's none of your business, will you let it lie?"

"So, it *is* my sister. Dude, you can't abandon me at my bachelor party. That's breaking bro code or something."

Greg has a point, and I do feel bad jumping ship, but here's the thing. I hate strip clubs and strippers. Nothing personal, but they don't do it for me. Still, under normal circumstances, I would suck it up and play along since it is Greg's night.

But these aren't normal circumstances. The woman I've been in love with for decades is literally down the hall from me, and I'll be damned if some body shots get in the way of that. "I get that, but all your buddies are here. Look at them, having a great time. Wrecking my suite."

Greg rolls his eyes, but he's biting back a grin. Just like his sister—a total marshmallow. That's one of the many things I love about the Hammond clan, with the exception of their father. I'd like to punch him in the mouth for abandoning his family. "Man, you've got it bad. I thought it was just some Vegas fling, but you still have a thing for my sister."

"That's an understatement," I mutter, wincing as a groomsman knocks a lamp off the side table. "Look, finish up and then head for the club. I rented out the entire VIP area for you guys."

"You'll meet us there later, right?"

"Sure." I'm lying, and Greg can see through my falsehood. No matter, though. Within an hour, he will have forgotten I ever existed. Hey, endless lap dances can do that to a man.

Closing the door to my suite and offering a silent prayer that the men don't cause *too* much damage, I phone Mike to ensure he's ready with the limo. The last thing I need is those guys driving anywhere.

But a smile replaces any frustration when Greer's door comes into view.

Showtime.

My smile fades when Rachel swings open the door to Greer's suite, a wide smile coloring her features. "Hello, handsome."

"Hi. Greer here?"

"She's in the bathroom getting ready. We convinced her to come out with us tonight." She drags one manicured nail down the front of my shirt. "I'd love to convince you to tag along, too."

I force a laugh as I squeeze past her. I have one destination and it sure as hell isn't a strip club. The bathroom door is ajar, and I catch sight of Greer in the mirror.

Keeping my hands to myself is *so* not happening.

Her long dark hair is swept up, and her dress is cut low in the back, dipping down to highlight those fantastic hips. I shift, adjusting myself and wondering how long we have to stay clothed.

"Holy hell, but you're gorgeous."

Greer smiles at me in the mirror. "I can say the same for you. How did your conversation go?"

"Mandi is furious, but I couldn't care less. My buddy is going to babysit my house and ensure she's out by Sunday." With a shrug, I shoot off my goofy grin. "See? All settled."

"How's the bachelor party?"

"Strippers have taken over my suite."

"And you're here because?"

"I want to be with you." I hold her gaze in the mirror as I close the distance between us, dropping to my knees and gliding my tongue along the line of her hips, dancing in the crack of her ass just visible above the material.

A surprised gasp flies from her mouth, so I wrap my hands around her hips, teasing her further. Fuck, but she tastes good, and I don't want to stop until I've mapped every inch of her with my mouth.

I trace a path up along her spine, nipping the nape of her neck and earning a soft squeal. "You need to behave."

"I think you'd far rather I don't behave. You'll enjoy it more." Wrapping my arms around her waist, I nuzzle her neck, basking in the sexy and exotic scent I'll always associate with Greer. "I made reservations for us at a French restaurant. They have a top-of-the-line late-night menu."

She turns in my arms, a confused expression on her face. "That's an odd location for a bachelor party."

"I left the bachelor party. I'm not interested in strippers."

"Sure," she cajoles, sending me a knowing wink.

"I'm not, although I wouldn't turn down a private dance from you." My hands slide along the hem of her dress, gliding along her inner thighs.

"Greer, are you almost ready?" a voice sounds from the other side of the door, and I drop my head to her shoulder with a resigned grunt.

"Do we really have to endure strippers for the rest of the night?"

"I'm afraid so, along with an assortment of lap dances and body shots," she teases, running her hands along my biceps. "I know, it's asking a lot of you, but you're going to have to admire a bevy of tits and ass tonight."

"I just want to admire you. Over and over again." Resting my forehead against hers, I smile when her slight fingers play along my beard. "How about I rent a private jet and fly us somewhere? Let's ditch Vegas."

"Great idea. You tell Greg that his sister and best friend won't be at his wedding."

"We'll be back in time for the ceremony."

Greer laughs, that gorgeous smile crossing her face. "While that sounds spectacular, I'm afraid we'll have to suck it up tonight. It's a tragedy, I know."

"The tragedy is not spending tonight with you. Naked."

I mean for the words to entice her, but a shadow passes over her features. "In a hurry to fuck me, Ryder?"

I cringe at her crude statement. Any other woman uttering those words would be an invitation for me to bend her over the vanity and sink balls deep.

But this is Greer Hammond, and I'll be damned if our first time is a quick screw in the bathroom while her friends wait outside.

Even if my dick is threatening to find a new employer.

Sliding my hands along her jaw, I frame her face, pressing a soft kiss to her lips. "Fucking implies hurried. I plan on taking my time exploring every inch of you. It will take hours. Days, even."

Her pupils dilate, her lower lip catching between her teeth. "What happens when you've finished your exploration? On to the next conquest?"

There it is—the fear brimming just beneath the surface

of her calm facade. The belief that she's just another notch on my bedpost.

"Are you kidding? This journey will last a lifetime." I capture her mouth then, sliding my tongue along hers. Taking it slow. Easy. Coaxing her out to play.

With a sigh, she twines her hands around my neck, her body flush against me, her mouth getting in on the action.

This woman. She's my everything, even if she doesn't realize it yet.

"Holy shit. You guys are trending!"

We break apart, a curious expression on her face as she opens the bathroom door. Jillian shoves a phone under Greer's nose, her eyes wild. "The internet claims you two are dating. Is that true? What did I miss between the restaurant and here?"

Greer opens her mouth to respond, but I beat her to the punch. "A whole lot, Jillian. I'm off to catch up with the boys. You ladies have fun tonight, and be sure to take extra special care of *my* lady." I press a last kiss to Greer's shocked mouth, ensuring there is ample tongue action and knowing damn well she'll be subjected to a bevy of questions the moment I leave.

Dick move? Not really. Just a man staking his claim.

∽

AFTER TEN MINUTES in the VIP area, I remember why I loathe strip clubs. The booming bass reverberates through my brain as a woman wearing only pasties and a thong grinds against me.

Is she hot? Sure, in a silicone-filled way.

Is she Greer? Not even close.

Shoving a fifty in her g-string, I huff out a sigh of relief when she moves on to her next victim. Judging by the shit-eating grin on his face, he's more than happy to oblige.

"Step outside with me for a second," Greg says, and I follow him to the back patio. It's cooler than earlier in the day, not that anyone considers 100 degrees cool. Unless you're a sidewinder.

"Are you having fun?"

"Ryder, it's a great party. Thank you."

"No need to thank me. I'm happy to be here."

Greg scrubs his face, releasing a huffed sigh. Uh-oh. I know where this conversation is headed. "Jillian texted me earlier. Apparently, you and my sister are dating? Care to fill me in?"

"The media are relentless," I mumble, unsure how to broach the topic without having to spill all the facts. One of those facts being that Mandi is still in residence at my house. "They snapped some photos of us together."

"So, it's bullshit."

"I don't want it to be." With a sigh, I face my friend. "You know how I had a thing for Greer when I was a kid? I still do. I always have. We fooled around once, several years back, but lines got crossed and—"

"New Year's, right? Greer told me."

"What did she say?"

"That you two hung out, and you wanted to take her to Paris, but then you never called. I was pretty pissed at the time, but she told me to leave it alone. So I did."

"I never got her number."

"Why didn't you ask me for it?"

"I was a twenty-two-year-old chicken shit. I figured you'd hate the idea of me and Greer dating, not that it would have stopped me. I also thought Greer would call me when she disappeared from the party, and I didn't want to look desperate. But, I finally caved and called you. That's when you told me about the doctor she was dating and how serious it was. I knew then I had lost my chance."

"Except you didn't, because here you are." He folds his arms across his barrel chest, his expression solemn. "What are your intentions with her? She's been on the receiving end of a long line of assholes, Ryder. She doesn't need another man fucking with her head, or her bank account."

"Come again? Her bank account?"

"That piece of shit, Richard, left her with a mountain of debt. He went through med school, and she footed all the bills, including several loans she took out, in her name, to help him. Then he left her for a younger woman, right after he finished his residency."

"Fucking asshole. You should have told me about her financial situation. I can help her."

Greg chokes back a laugh. "Are we talking about the same woman? Greer would never allow that. She doesn't accept charity, as she terms it."

"It's not charity. I've adored her for decades. She needs help. I want to help her. Show her that not all men will cut and run."

Greg nods, a thoughtful expression on his face. "Yeah, Dad leaving really messed with her ideas surrounding love. She was a diehard romantic as a kid."

"I remember. That summer I spent with you guys, she told me she wanted to get married on a beach at sunset, the light casting off the ocean."

"What are you, planning to marry her now?"

I smirk in my friend's direction, but the idea isn't unwelcome. I always said I would marry Greer in a heartbeat. "Don't you want me as your brother-in-law?" I jest, giving him a jab in the arm.

"Just don't upstage my wedding, okay? Wait a week." Greg downs the rest of his drink and I can't help but wonder how many more he plans to imbibe before midnight. I love the man, but he drinks like a fish. "You really want to help her?"

"Yes. I also really want to be with her, which should show you how much I love *you* that I'm here and not with Greer."

"Fair enough. Too bad you can't set up some sort of trade with my sister."

"What the hell does that mean?"

"You want to help her. She doesn't accept charity. Find something to bargain with, something that helps you both. Even if it's bullshit, it would likely be the only way to get her on board." Greg snorts, waving his empty glass. "Ignore me, I'm drunk."

Drunk or not, the man is right, and the noises around me fade as Greg's words sink in. I need a plan. Then it hits me.

For the first time since fame came calling, I'm thrilled to have the media hounding me. It's a perfect segue.

I know exactly how I can keep Greer by my side and help her, all at the same time.

CHAPTER 6
GREER

"We have an issue." One of the bridesmaids, Marie, pokes her head out of the bathroom door, her expression grim. "Rachel can't stop vomiting. We need a maid of honor replacement."

I roll my eyes, trying to rein in my frustration. These women are not twenty-two. They're in their thirties, but they behaved like college kids last night. Hey, I get it. Cut loose and have fun, but keep it together enough to stand upright at your best friend's wedding.

"Gigi, will you take her place?" Jillian's voice is sad and small beside me.

How am I supposed to say no to that puppy dog expression? Besides, it's the woman's wedding day. She doesn't need any extra stress.

Wrapping my arm about her, I press a kiss to her cheek. "I'd be honored to be your personal fluffer for the day."

We hold each other's gaze in the mirror, smiles warming our faces. Greg did good. Jillian, despite her party girl tendencies, adores my brother, and I know the feeling is mutual.

For the first time in years, I find myself longing for that level of love and commitment. The strains of the Otis Redding song filters through my memory, reminding me I wasn't always this jaded. Once upon a time, I believed in happily ever afters.

Likely, Ryder's reappearance has something to do with my change of heart in the heart department. Okay, he has everything to do with it, but falling in love with Ryder Gray is a dumb idea.

A surefire way to get my heart broken.

Still, a woman can dream.

"It's not fair," Jillian whines, her hands motioning along my body. "You look better than I do."

"Not a chance, Jillian. I just look more sober. Come on, let's get you married."

~

I ADORE MY BABY BROTHER, but I have no idea why he insisted on getting married in Vegas. To hear him tell it, it's the best of both worlds. Plus, since Ryder joined the festivities, it's been luxury level all the way.

I have to hand it to Ryder. He spared no expense for his friend. So often, nouveau rich throw their money around as a way of showing off, but I don't get that impression from Ryder. He doesn't make a big deal of the cash he's dropped, only stating that Greg deserves it for being a true friend.

Turns out, Ryder is a true friend, too.

I don't dare ask what kind of trouble the men got into last night, although they all look less green about the gills than the women. Hell, I was the only sober one last night, but I'm ever so grateful for it today.

Still, I'm no fool. Ryder is a gorgeous, eligible man. At least, I think he's eligible. Not sure what his situation is with the infamous Mandi, a woman I admittedly performed an internet search on last night.

All I can say is damn, she's a looker and a half.

The further I keep my heart from Ryder, the better. Hell, at this point, I need to keep my body from him, too.

Both are becoming increasingly tricky to do.

I take my place next to Jillian, struggling to maintain a neutral gaze as Ryder's baby blues drill into me. It's impossible not to notice, he's hardly subtle. Swinging my gaze in his direction, I widen my eyes and offer a shrug.

"Wow," Ryder mouths, motioning up and down my body.

Fighting the blush that I know is inevitable, I look away, but I can't keep the smile from my face. Wow, is right. Ryder is impeccable in his tuxedo, outshining any of the other men. Even Greg, a good-looking guy in his own right, doesn't stand a chance next to Ryder's chiseled perfection. If he looks that good *in* clothes, I can only imagine what he'd look like with them in a heap on the floor. I've seen a few photos, his muscular chest on display, a couple of artfully placed tattoos decorating his olive skin as he played in the waters of Hawaii, or Malta, or whatever tropical paradise he was visiting.

Always in these photos, there were women. So many women, each one more beautiful than the last. But despite their outer appeal, I know intrinsically that he never loved any of them. None of the photos ever captured his real smile. The smile he wears around me.

I can't explain the connection I feel to Ryder. We don't know each other anymore. But it's there, as palpable as a heartbeat—this bond that can't be broken, no matter the time and distance.

That, and I'm oddly protective of the man, despite him having a foot on me height-wise and scads more impressive people to act as bodyguards.

Stealing another glance in Ryder's direction, we lock gazes.

"You're so beautiful," he mouths, and even though the volume is turned down on his voice, the meaning is clear. Suddenly it's a million degrees, as I flush from his statement.

Such simple words, with such a profound effect.

Even scarier, I believe him.

My heart doesn't stand a chance.

⁓

My brother is a married man. A married man who is currently imbibing the hair of the dog, right next to his wife.

I know this much—I'm not nursing any of them tomorrow morning. They're on their own.

"You know it's the obligation of the maid of honor to dance with the best man." Ryder stands by my chair, hand extended.

I consider declining his request, especially since I overheard him in a heated phone conversation earlier as I made my way to the bathroom. No need to inquire with whom he was conversing; the frown lines made the answer clear.

Another round with Mandi.

At that moment, I made a decision. While I'm wildly attracted to Ryder Gray, and likely always will be, he's unavailable. He has a live-in girlfriend and despite some damning photos snapped by the media, she's obviously still a part of his world.

That's a path I'm not even willing to consider, no matter what my heart says. Besides, we all know my heart is a blooming idiot where the *L* word is concerned. Especially when you combine the *L* word with the infamous Ryder Gray.

His grin broadens at my hesitation, clasping my fingers with his own. "Come on, you know I can dance and that is a rarity among men."

With a chuckle, I steal a sip of champagne for courage before walking with him to the dance floor.

Ryder pulls me flush against him, his hands wrapping around my hips in an extremely possessive and hot as hell manner. "You are a vision, Greer. Absolutely stunning. I damn near missed handing off the rings because I was so busy staring at you."

"You look pretty damn good yourself. I've never seen you in a tux before. You clean up well."

"That settles it. You haven't seen me enough. We're going to change that."

"Is that a fact? Tell me more about this plan." Yes, I'm playing coy, but what's a bit of banter between old friends?

Ryder has flirting on lockdown, along with charm, wit, looks, and deep pockets. He plays his role to perfection, but I refuse to fall at his feet, no matter how tempting the trip.

"The real fun starts tomorrow, so I need you packed by noon."

My brow wrinkles, confused by his statement. "What are you talking about?"

"It's a surprise. Just be ready to leave by noon."

Great. Now I have to address the one subject I didn't want to discuss—the sad state of my finances. Nothing like admitting to a multi-millionaire that you're beyond poor.

Is there anything less sexy than being broke as hell? I think not.

"I can't afford surprises, Ryder. But thank you for thinking of me."

I expect to see a look of confusion cross his face, but instead, he nods, his lips set in a thin line. "Greg mentioned you have a lot of debt."

My cheeks flame at his direct statement. "Why would he say that? My financial situation isn't his business. It isn't *your* business."

Ryder pulls me closer, his eyes darkening with intensity. "I'm making it my business. I want to help you. Will you let me help you?"

"No."

Now he's biting back a laugh, that endearing grin on full display. "I figured that would be your answer, but I need something from you, too."

My mind reels at his words. "What can I possibly offer you, that you can't afford on your own?"

Those eyes, the bluest eyes I've ever seen, lock with mine. "I want you."

I didn't hear him correctly. "I'm sorry. What?"

"I want you, Greer."

"I'm not for sale."

"That's not what I mean."

I step back from the circle of his arms, my gaze narrowing. "You want to fuck me, is that it?"

Grasping my hand, Ryder leads me to a quiet alcove, leaning his large frame against mine. "I need you to stop referring to it as fucking. I told you I had no plans on fucking you, and I still don't."

"Ever?" Wow, that half glass of champagne went to my head. Filter, right out the damn door.

His fingers glide along my chin, a sexy smirk playing upon his lips. "Would you still need me to fuck you if I tortured this gorgeous body every day?" His lips travel along the column of my neck, pressing against my pulse point. "If I make you come several times a day, each time harder than the last, would you still require that I fuck you?"

"I don't understand. You want me but you don't *want* me."

"Gigi, I plan on possessing every inch of you. I can't wait to perform the act several times daily with you, but I'm averse to the term. In regard to you, anyway."

"What don't you like about the term?"

"It's not special enough for you."

God help my heart.

Shaking my head, I force the conversation back on track. "What is this deal, Ryder? Seriously."

He offers an embarrassed laugh, his gaze downward. "I need your help. See, my ex is being difficult."

"I heard your conversation earlier. I wasn't eavesdropping, but it got a bit... loud."

Ryder winces, running a hand over his beard. "I hate you heard that argument. Anyway, with race season coming up, I need to lie low and focus. The last thing I need is a media storm."

Ah, message received, Ryder.

"I fly home tomorrow. You won't see me again. Problem solved."

He moves in closer, every inch of his body pressing

against mine. "Never say that again, Gigi. I don't need you further from me. Quite the opposite, in fact. Besides, the media already knows about you and they're loving the angle of reunited childhood friends."

Pushing my hands against his rock-hard chest, I force a few inches between us. "What are you saying?"

"We need to keep dating."

"But we're not dating, Ryder. I mean, according to the media we are—"

"And it needs to stay that way," Ryder interjects, his tone firm and unrelenting.

I choke on my breath, stunned by his request. "To appease the media?"

"For many reasons, the media among them."

"You're joking."

Please tell me you're joking, Ryder.

"I'm serious, but this isn't some one-sided deal. I'll make it worth your while. All the debts that bastard left you with? I'll pay them off, in full."

To my dismay, I feel tears backing up in my eyes as the truth settles over me. I'm so stupid and naïve. Here I thought Ryder was falling for me, as he spouted such sweet and sexy lines. In truth, I'm his way out of a sticky marital situation.

"I need a drink." It's all I can manage before I slip from his grasp and make a beeline for the bar. I rarely imbibe, but this kick to the heart is enough to push me over the edge. Ryder doesn't want to date me, but he's willing to pay me to play the part.

I'm not sure whether to be flattered or mortified, but my heart is definitely leaning toward the latter.

Ryder slips into the seat next to me, ordering his own drink. "The last thing I want to do is upset you. I'm trying to help."

A curt nod. It's the best I can do as I swallow back some whiskey, feeling the burn wash down my throat. "It wouldn't work."

"Why?"

So many reasons, Ryder, but I'll leave emotion out of it since that's certainly a one-sided deal.

"We live several hundred miles apart, so it's not like we'd see each other, anyway. You should find someone local to fill this position. I can't even imagine why you'd want me... for the job." The last words are strangled, but I manage a harsh laugh.

His hand skates along my spine, but I shrug off his touch. Let's not mix business and pleasure. "First, you'd live with me in Charlotte. I need you close. Second, there are a million reasons why I want you. I've always wanted you. I trust you, Greer, and I don't trust women. You knew me before all of this celebrity bullshit. You know me, the real me. I need your help, and I know you need mine."

"What about my job?"

"According to Greg, you hate your job. You're overworked and underpaid."

I pivot toward him, the whiskey already working as my snarky side comes into play. "Strippers surrounded you men last night, yet somehow you spent the evening discussing *my* inadequacies. Glad to know I provide such interesting fodder for you two."

Ryder grabs my hand, pressing a kiss to my palm. "There is nothing inadequate about you. You're my definition of the perfect woman."

He rocked my world with this cockamamie plan, now it's time to return the favor. "Richard left me with twenty thousand dollars of debt. Bet you didn't know it was that much, right? Care to change your tune? Find someone else now?"

"I'll gladly pay every dime."

I can't think or breathe. I need space. Somewhere to clear my head. "Will you excuse me, please? I need a few minutes."

"Gigi—"

I cut him off, holding up my hand and turning on my heel, searching for the closest exit.

Once outside, I suck in lungfuls of desert air. Nothing like 105-degree heat to settle the nerves. Said no one, ever. My brain is racing like a horse on speed, circling the offer Ryder laid out in front of me.

Date him for the next two to three months, all while living in his luxurious digs in Charlotte. I'm not sure what his angle is in this situation. What does he stand to gain? Avoid a media storm? What does that even mean? He's been plastered across numerous tabloids for years, what's the big deal now?

My heart and mind wage a war over the offer, but any peace is interrupted as the door swings open.

"Hey, Sis. You okay?"

I pull Greg into a tight squeeze, the tears finally breaking free of their chains.

"Why are you crying?"

No way will I involve Greg in this debacle. "I can't believe you're married. It seems like yesterday I was making you ice cream sundaes."

"No need to stop that," Greg jokes, wrapping an arm around my shoulder. "Thank you for always looking out for me."

"Eh, you're worth it."

"I have some news, Gigi."

"Is Jillian pregnant?"

Greg's eyes widen as he sputters his beer. "She'd better

not be. I'd like a few months of newlywed bliss. No, I'm moving to Charlotte."

"What?" That's it. I've definitely fallen into an alternate universe.

"Ryder has an opening on his pit crew. He offered me the job last night."

Now how am I supposed to hate the man?

I give my brother a soft jab in the ribs before hugging him about the waist. "That's amazing, Greg. What an opportunity."

"For us both. You and Ryder, I like you together. You two make sense."

Well, Greg cracked open the door. Might as well let him in on my quandary.

"Ryder asked me to move to Charlotte, too, albeit temporarily. He needs my help with the brewing media fallout from his ex-lover. Whatever that means."

I expect Greg to huff in anger, like a bull in front of a red flag. Instead, he smirks, biting back a laugh. "Did he now?"

"He most certainly did. I don't plan on accepting his offer, obviously."

Greg's brow shoots upward. "Why not?"

Is my brother serious? "For so many reasons."

"Such as?"

I stand there for a few seconds, my brain rattling off all the talking points that ten minutes ago sounded valid but now sound ridiculous. "It's dishonest."

"Please tell me you're not worried about hurting the integrity of the media. Seriously, what has he asked you to do?"

"Move in with him and pretend to be his girlfriend for the next two to three months."

Another smirk. If he keeps it up, I'm smacking it off his face, wedding day or no.

"What is so funny?"

"If a rich, beautiful woman that I was crazy about asked me to move in with her and pose as her boyfriend, I sure wouldn't be out here pouting about it."

"You think I should do it?"

"Absolutely. What do you have to lose?"

"Twenty thousand dollars in debt?"

That got Greg's attention. "Come again?"

"In exchange for being his girlfriend, he's offered to pay off the debt that Richard gifted me." Holy hell, when I say it aloud, I realize how spectacular this deal is, even if my heart gets mangled in the process.

Now his smile is full-blown. "If you don't take this deal, I will. Holy hell, *I'll* pose as his girlfriend for the next couple of months for way less than twenty grand. Gigi, don't look a gift horse in the mouth. Unless you don't think you can stand Ryder for the next couple of months."

"I think the idea of you in a dress is going to give me nightmares." I squeeze his neck, smacking a kiss on his cheek. "Thank you."

"Remember, if you pass on the deal, let him know I'm interested." A final smirk after I flip him the bird. "Get out of here. Go find your man."

"Exactly where I'm headed." I open the door, colliding with Ryder's firm chest. He looks even better than before, infinitely hotter. He's ditched the jacket and tie, his sleeves rolled up to reveal his muscular forearms. And his hands. Good lord, I can only imagine what those hands could do if given free rein. "Fancy meeting you here, Ryder. Getting fresh air, or did you miss me?"

"I've missed you for twenty years."

Gazing into his eyes, I see the passion burning in their depths. Granted, I'm likely part of a sexual bucket list, but two months of mind-blowing sex with Ryder sounds pretty damn tempting.

I need to stay focused. Idle flirtation works. "You have very sexy forearms."

A random statement, but I stand by it.

His eyes widen, a smile splitting his face. "Glad to see you're turned on by at least one part of me."

"Oh, it's more than one."

Desire blazes in Ryder's eyes as he leads me to a quiet seating area, pulling me down on his lap and laying claim to my mouth. His hands slide along my body, cupping my breasts and gripping my ass. "I want you so much, Gigi."

"For real or for this deal of yours?"

"You know the answer to that. Have you decided about dating me?"

"You mean, the *deal*?" I suck in a deep breath, forcing back a smile. "I just don't know. Maybe?"

"Greg is moving down there."

Damn him for hitting me in the sweet spot. "He told me about his new job. Greg has tried for years to get on a crew. He'll be perfect."

"I know. It's why I hired him."

"But that has nothing to do with me. You want me to move in with you, but there are a few issues. North Carolina has snakes, and I hate snakes."

"Long Island has snakes, too." His fingers drift down my arm, setting my body awash in tingles. "I have a pool. I recall one summer where a certain girl spent every day by the pool."

"I like pools. Do you have a jacuzzi?"

"I do, and a sauna."

"Hmm. All things to consider."

"Greer, you're giving me a serious complex here."

"Ditto for you, Ryder."

He pulls me close, burying his head against my neck. "Final offer, just to let you know how much I want you to do this. Move to North Carolina with me—"

"For sixty to ninety days and pose as your girlfriend. Yeah, I understand the arrangement."

"Be quiet, Ms. Mouthy. If you do that, I'll pay off *all* your debts. Student loans included."

My mouth drops open. "Are you insane?"

"I race cars for a living, so my money is on yes, but I'm serious. Do we have a deal?"

"Do you have any idea how much my loans are?"

"Do you have any idea how much money I make?"

"Conceited ass," I giggle, my brain fumbling to make heads or tails of this scenario.

He wants me to leave my life and job—my miserable job and passionless life—to move into his mansion and pose as his girlfriend. Sexual favors from this hunk of love a distinct option. In return, he'll pay off every debt I have. Damn near one hundred and twenty-five thousand dollars.

Even if my heart wasn't involved, I'd be an idiot to turn down this offer.

"It's over a hundred grand." That's it. My final argument.

"Okay." Not a look of surprise, fear, nothing. Ryder is absolutely calm and collected.

I tilt my head back and laugh. "For that sort of money, we might as well up the ante."

Ryder presses a kiss to my neck, his mouth so warm against my skin. "How so?"

Time to turn him on *his* head. "We get married. Show the world you *really* mean business."

I expect him to run screaming in the opposite direction. Or laugh. Or sit there shell-shocked. It would be the ultimate payback.

He does none of the above.

Instead, a slow and sultry grin spreads across his face. "Good idea. In fact, since you mentioned it, it's now a stipulation."

"I'm joking, Ryder."

"I'm not, Greer. We're getting married."

I hold out for several seconds, waiting for him to crack, but he's determined to have the last laugh. Fine. Let him have it. It's not like I ever planned on getting married. Might as well do it as part of a business transaction. "That is the least romantic proposal I've ever heard. Why am I not surprised it's for me?" I hold out my hand. "You have a deal, Ryder Gray. Here's to love and marriage in all of its contractual glory."

His hand envelops mine, but instead of shaking it, he brings it to his lips, dusting kisses across my knuckles. "You haven't given me a chance to be romantic, Gigi. Let's get out of here. Spend some time together."

Even though I just sold my soul to the gods of enterprise, I need a few hours to process the upheaval I've brought upon myself. "I think you need to enjoy your final nights of bachelorhood. I've been up most of the night with the bridal party, so my bed is calling me."

"Can it call me, too?"

"No. Not until the ink is dry on our marriage certificate." It's a bullshit statement, but at least I get the reaction I'm hoping for when his jaw slackens.

No one says no to Ryder Gray, except Greer Hammond.

With a last smile, I press a kiss to his cheek, pay my respects to the bride and groom, and head for my room, with one thought in mind.

What the hell have I gotten myself into?

CHAPTER 7
GREER

"Rise and shine, beautiful." Ryder's lips graze my ear, and I grumble into my pillow, not fully willing to leave this comfy cocoon.

"Five more minutes."

"You said that five minutes ago. No can do." He rips the blanket back, and I scramble to a seated position, my eyes flying open.

"Never mess with a nurse before coffee. Hasn't anyone ever told you that?" I snatch the sheet to cover my naked body, but judging from the smirk gracing Ryder's features, he didn't miss the view.

"I've never dated a nurse before. But, I do recall your caffeine addiction. Breakfast just arrived."

You're not dating a nurse now, I muse, slipping on the robe that Ryder offers and padding out to the dining area. My body is sore, but I'll bet money I'm feeling loads better than the rest of the bridal party, who are currently passed out in my suite.

Likely with all manner of vomit decorating the floors.

Ugh.

"Thanks for letting me crash here," I offer, sighing as I gulp down a mouthful of coffee.

"Gigi, I wanted to spend the night with you, but you refused. Not until the ink is dry," Ryder states, mimicking my previous night's declaration. "You knocking on my door was a welcome surprise."

"Guess I'm lucky I didn't interrupt you." Am I being saucy? Difficult? Yes, to both questions. But this entire deal, no matter how lucrative for my pocketbook, is wreaking havoc on my heart.

Deep down, even though I'd rather die than admit it, I wanted Ryder to fall in love with me. Instead, he offered me a job, albeit the highest paying one of my life.

But what will the cost be to my emotional well-being once these few months are up? Once the media storm dies down, and he no longer needs a stand-in girlfriend?

All these questions rattled around my brain last night as I sat in my suite, until the utterly soused wedding party appeared at my door, interrupting my internal monologue as they insisted they had to stay with me for some inane reason.

I tried arguing with them, but it's absolutely fruitless to battle drunkards.

So, I packed my suitcase and headed down the hall to Ryder's suite, never thinking he might be entertaining someone.

"You thought I had another woman in here?" Ryder questions, crossing his arms over his muscular chest. Damn him for looking so delicious with so few articles of clothing.

"I wasn't sure. It seems I was the only one who didn't get laid last night, not that most of the bridal party will remember their antics."

Ryder strides over to me, setting the mug on the table

and sinking to his knees on the carpet. "You're the only woman. Got it? And all you had to do was ask, and I would have spent the night savoring every inch of you." He leans in, stealing a kiss. "But you chose to be difficult, so neither of us got any loving last night."

"I'm not difficult," I grumble, earning an incredulous look from Ryder. "Fine, but I'm entitled to parameters with this deal, too."

A smile splits his face as he nuzzles my neck, his hands prying apart the panels of my robe. "Denying yourself sexual satisfaction is one of your parameters? Gigi, you need to learn better negotiation skills."

All the while, his fingers slide along my thighs, drifting ever higher, until they hook on the edges of my underwear. But it's the look on his face that gets me, those sapphire eyes lit with an inner fire.

"Tell me what you want, beautiful. I'll give you anything."

My eyes rake over his half-naked form, while my mind lists off a hundred things I'd like for him to do to me. But women have always come easy for Ryder Gray, and I'll be damned if I fall into that category. He may not love me, but he is going to work for a roll in the hay with me.

"I'd like my coffee back." I bite back a laugh as his jaw slackens. "What? You asked."

Ryder quickly regains his composure, a chuckle escaping his lips. "Playing it that way? Okay." He leans in, his tongue circling my nipple before sucking it into his mouth. "You drink your coffee. I'll find other ways to keep myself occupied."

His hands slide along my spine, pulling my body flush against him, his mouth working overtime as he teases first one breast and then the other. I feel him smile against my skin when a low moan slips from my lips and my hands press into his scalp.

Coffee? Who the hell needs coffee?

Ryder pulls back, running his tongue along his full lips. "See? There's more than one way to wake up in the morning." He hands me my mug, pressing a kiss to my mouth before popping up to answer the knock at the door.

At least my libido is going to get a hell of a ride these next couple of months. Something to be said for great sex. Hell, there's a ton to be said for great sex and I know, without a doubt, sex with Ryder will be incredible.

Grabbing my mug, I stroll onto the balcony. It's already hot, but nowhere near as scorching as my body when Ryder is near.

"We have one hour." Ryder interrupts my thoughts as he joins me on the balcony, his eyes riveted to me.

"What are you looking at?"

"You. I'm admiring the view."

It might be a line, but there's something so earnest in his words that they warm my heart and my hormones all in the same breath. Maybe it's the Vegas heat or the surreal nature of this weekend, but I drop all my inhibitions.

"I can offer you a much better view than that." Holding his gaze, I pull open the panels of my robe, letting it slide off my shoulders. Then, I slip off my g-string, shooting him a sultry smirk as I lean against the railing. "Better, right?"

His expression smolders, his eyes raking down my form. "Keep it up and I'm bending you over this railing in full view of everyone."

"Likely story."

It takes Ryder three steps to close the distance between us. With a heated breath, he places one hand on either side of the railing, trapping me in his embrace. "If you think I won't strip you naked right now and kiss every inch of your body while the world watches, you're wrong."

"I think your money is on the fact I'll tell you no."

Inching closer, his mouth hovers against mine. "Try me."

"Do it, then." I'm never this brazen, but the look in his eyes, the blatant desire blazing in their depths, has caused me to throw any last vestiges of common sense out the window.

Tangling his hand in my hair, Ryder's mouth claims me while his free hand pushes the robe from my body.

Holy shit, he's not kidding.

He's also not stopping. His hand slides along my slick skin, and I moan into his mouth as he plunges two fingers inside me.

"So tight and wet. You want me, don't you, Greer?"

I release a purr when he adds a third finger to the mix, grinding against his hand, my naked body on full display. "So much."

Sinking to his knees, Ryder buries his face between my thighs, his tongue teasing me open as I writhe against him. His hands slide up my legs to cup my ass, all the while his mouth eating me like I'm his favorite treat. I whimper and hold his head in place as a low groan rises from his chest.

"Fuck, you're delicious."

The man is relentless as he coaxes me to the edge and holds me there, again and again. He's savoring every second, knowing damn well the effect he has on my body.

My legs shake, threatening to give out, but his grips tightens, holding me in the exquisite pleasure.

With a final flick of his tongue against my clit, every cell in my body blasts apart, and I'm fairly certain the entire city hears my cries.

Ryder presses kisses to my thighs before standing, a satisfied smile on his face. Hey, the man earned it.

"That was spectacular," I breathe, trying to slow my heart. "Where did you learn to do that? You know what? Don't tell me."

He presses his body against mine, and I'm tempted to yank down his shorts and return the favor. Let the world watch how quickly I make Ryder Gray come. He's not the only one with hidden talents.

"You have the most delicious pussy in the world. I want to lick you several times a day."

"Will I get to play, too?" I glide my fingers across his cock, earning a grunt of satisfaction.

Ryder frames my face, claiming my mouth and pulling me into a slow, intoxicating kiss. This man and his kisses. One for every mood.

My fingers loop into the waistband of his shorts, intent on finishing what we started, but Ryder stays my hands. "We'll have plenty of playtime. But first, we have to hurry and get the hell out of here."

My gaze narrows in confusion. "I thought check-out wasn't until noon."

"For us, it's earlier, and that's all I'm telling you. The rest is a surprise." Ryder scoops me into his arms, littering kisses along my jaw, seemingly oblivious to the fact that he's showing off my naked body to all of Vegas. "I promise, I'm all yours the second we land."

"But—"

Ryder holds up a hand, slowing my verbal rebuttal. "I know you're off work the next ten days. You mentioned a few times that you didn't go back until the twentieth. Even claimed how you didn't have plans. Now, you do."

He can't be serious, can he? "Where are we going?"

"That's for me to know and you to find out," Ryder responds with a wink. "Now go get packed."

∼

I'll give it to Ryder. The man is incredible with surprises.

First, a private jet to Barbados.

Then, a ridiculously opulent private villa overlooking the ocean.

Finally, our own personal staff to attend to every whim, with the first order of business being a scrumptious dinner.

I've never experienced this level of grandeur before. Even the suites in Vegas pale compared to this palatial spread.

After the staff clears the dishes, reminding me that I don't *have* to clear the dishes, they excuse themselves for the evening, although they're on call twenty-four hours per day. Who needs a cook at three in the morning? Apparently, the ultra-wealthy and important.

Wandering to the teak wood great room, I breathe deeply of the sea air flowing through the open windows, reminding myself I'm really here.

With Ryder.

Talk about surreal.

"For you." Ryder hands me a cocktail before pulling me close, his mouth slanting over mine. "We're alone, at last."

"So this is how the other half lives." I place my hand on his chest, putting a couple of inches between us. "This is how *you* live."

"Not exactly, but this is a special occasion. It calls for a celebration."

"What are we celebrating?"

"Us. Together. Living the life we're supposed to live. How does that sound?"

Blinking back tears, I raise my glass in a toast. "That sounds incredible."

"You're incredible." Ryder sets our drinks aside as he holds out his hand. "I want an entire dance this time, so I pulled out the big guns."

I wrinkle my brow at his words, but then the strains of my favorite love song since the age of ten floats into the air, and I give up the ghost. My heart doesn't stand a chance. Even if all of this is an elaborate ruse, I'm jumping into the deep end with no lifejacket. I suppose where Ryder is concerned, it's the only option for me.

Even if he smashes my heart to smithereens in a few months.

Ryder wraps his arms around me, a softness in his azure eyes that I know is reserved for me.

"You remembered," I sniffle, a tear rolling down my cheek.

"I don't know how many times you've danced to this song, but I always considered it ours."

"I've never danced to it with anyone before. I never wanted to."

"And now?"

Raising on tiptoe, I steal a kiss, desperate to be closer. "I never want to stop."

So we don't. Instead, our gazes remain locked on each other, our bodies pressed close, until the last note rings out. There's no need for words in those precious moments. Our hearts already know what we're desperate to say, but scared to speak aloud.

After the song ends, Ryder leads me outside to the patio, the full moon playing off the pool and ocean waves just beyond the estate walls. Suddenly, I don't want to wait any longer to make Ryder Gray mine.

We've both waited long enough.

Crooking my finger at him, I offer up a mini striptease, lowering the zipper on my dress and letting it slide to the ground.

Even in the dark, I see the fire blazing in his eyes. There's no mistaking the desire.

"I was thinking," I murmur, edging closer to the pool as I pop open my bra and toss it aside, "it's such a nice night to go swimming. Care to join me?" Sliding off my thong, I stand naked before him, smiling when he adjusts himself, a grunt of approval escaping his mouth.

With a saucy grin, I dive into the warm water, letting the exquisite beauty of the place sink into my bones.

Strong hands grab me as I break the surface, and I wrap my body around Ryder as I claim his kiss. This time, I'm taking the lead.

Scratching my nails along his shoulders, I drag my tongue against the side of his neck, smiling as his hands tighten on my ass, pulling me flush against his erection.

"Gigi," Ryder moans, his fingers sliding inside me and curving to hit the spot that makes me scream. "Tell me what you want. I mean it, I'll give you anything."

Pulling back, I capture his lower lip between my teeth. "That is such a tempting offer. The possibilities are endless. Anything?"

Ryder smirks, walking us over to the side of the pool. "What would you like? A new car? A diamond necklace?"

"Much bigger."

"Bigger than a car?"

Even though his tone is light, I sense the hesitation underneath. The idea that I, like so many other women, are more into his deep pockets than him.

Time to put that one to bed.

"Make love to me." A silence descends on us as I breathe the words to life, his blue eyes glittering in the moonlight. "Please."

"You never have to beg. I've waited forever for you."

"Let's not wait anymore."

Ryder carries me from the pool and lays me on the lounger, his muscled frame settling over me. His mouth captures mine, but it's not frantic or hurried. It's as if he's trying to convey all the emotions he pent up for years.

Stroking along his jaw, I release a soft squeal when he nibbles my palm, his eyes intent on me as his hands drift across my skin.

Still, an undercurrent of hesitation remains.

"What is it, Ryder?"

"I want this to be perfect for you."

A quiver rushes through my body as years of desire course through me. Rising up, I wrap my hand around his nape, dusting kisses across his lips. "It will be perfect. It's with you."

My words release the bonds holding him back, as desire flames in his face. Ryder reclaims my mouth, teasing me to new heights as his fingers dive into my heat.

Arching against him, I let the fears fall away, replacing the emotion with pure fire. A fire that grows with every rasp of his tongue against my skin, my muscles tensing with the rising feeling.

He slides his cock along my slick skin, and I tighten my grip about his waist, desperate for more.

So much more.

Hovering over me, our gazes lock, his breathing heated against my skin.

"Be mine, Ryder," I beg, my voice a soft request.

"I've always been yours." With a heated groan, Ryder

buries himself inside me, and I want to scream from the flood of sensations. Grasping my hips, he slides home, again and again, his movements slow and delicious, drawing out each second into a lifetime of exquisite pleasure.

When his mouth seizes mine, I slide my tongue against his, my fingers digging into his neck and holding him close.

Never close enough.

"You're perfect, Gigi. You feel so perfect," Ryder moans, arching my hips to penetrate even deeper. Filling me more.

Taking all of me and making me his.

"We're perfect," I breathe, my blood pounding in my ears as my body threatens to implode.

That slow, sexy smile crosses his features as he continues to drive me closer and closer to the edge. "I feel you. Let go, Gigi."

With a cry, I dig my nails into his back, scratching along his smooth skin as every cell in my body blasts apart.

Nothing has ever felt this good. Not even close.

But Ryder has no intention of leaving me with only one incredible climax. He works my body over, wringing another one from me within moments of the first, this one even more powerful than the last.

Gripping his shoulders, I pant out my demand. "Come for me, Ryder."

Ryder's body jerks as he collapses onto his forearms, bellowing out his release.

Our breath mingles as I wipe the sweat from his brow, tracing my fingertip over his lips. "You make me feel incredible," I whisper, stealing a kiss.

Nuzzling my nose, Ryder smiles, his eyes soft with affection. "You are incredible. You're the greatest thing that's ever happened to me."

WE'VE BEEN in paradise for the last four days, and every day, I fall more deeply under Ryder's spell. My intention to hold my heart at a safe distance went out the window the night he made love to me.

We made love for hours, until my body fell limp against his chest. Nothing has ever felt so right as his arms wrapped around me, and all my preconceived notions about love and affection were shattered the moment we became one.

Ryder hasn't mentioned our deal since Greg's wedding, and honestly, I don't care to know. Right now, I'm enjoying each and every moment by his side, a place where time and truth can't reach. I'm lost in him and I never want to be found.

My guess is that once the vacation ends, so will our tryst.

Does it break my heart? Absolutely.

Was it worth it? Every second.

We exist in different worlds, but he's given me one hell of a stack of spicy memories for those cold New York nights. As for Ryder, he will continue with his celebrity lifestyle, but I know he'll always look back fondly at the time we spent together.

But I rarely give these thoughts much space. Why bother wasting minutes worrying about what happens next? I'm more interested in what is happening now, especially since my present involves the hottest, sweetest, funniest man I've ever had the pleasure to know.

"Rise and shine, handsome," I whisper into Ryder's ear, a play on his greeting only a few days ago in Vegas.

Ryder rolls over, propping a hand behind his head, a goofy grin on his face. "How long have you been awake?"

"Long enough to cook breakfast. I took advantage of our trip to the market and made us omelets."

"That's what smells so good."

"No, it's me, but the omelets are okay, too," I tease, squealing as he pulls me onto the mattress.

"It's definitely you." Ryder traces a line of kisses down my body, and I know just where he's heading. I also know I'm sure as hell not stopping him. The man has a ramped-up sex drive, but nothing seems to get him as hot as getting me off.

He nuzzles my inner thigh, sucking my clit into his mouth as his hands slide under my ass. I release a groan of contentment, my hands holding his head in place, my hips grinding against that exquisitely talented tongue.

"Don't you want breakfast?" I murmur, a soft gasp flying from my mouth as his fingers plunge inside me.

"That's what I'm eating right now, and I'm starving."

Far be it from me to deny myself such insane levels of pleasure. With a sated sigh, I grip his scalp, my fingers grasping his short strands.

Even though we've only been lovers a short while, he instinctively knows how to touch me, and he's overly generous with his affections. Not that I'm complaining. I never knew a woman could feel this sexually satisfied, and trust me, I love giving as much as receiving.

At least where Ryder is concerned. That man's cock is a thing of beauty. Utterly delicious in every possible way.

Within minutes, I blow apart, my mind blanking and my world turning white as he tongues me over the edge.

Ryder frames my face with his hands, capturing me in a soft kiss. "I get the distinct impression you enjoyed that."

"Did you? What gave it away?"

Rubbing his scalp, he shoots me his trademark smirk.

"I'm going to have to cut my hair shorter. I think you damn near ripped it out of my head."

I glide my fingers along his scalp, offering a giggle. "Totally your fault. You're ridiculously good at that. The best ever, if we're being honest."

"I plan on being the best overall. With everything."

Tracing his lower lip with my thumb, I smile when he gives it a gentle nip. "You already are. By far the best I've ever had."

"You're referring to sex and while I know you are the most incredible woman in the fucking world, that wasn't what I meant." Nuzzling my nose, he offers a final smack to my ass before hopping out of bed.

"What did you mean?" I ask, kneeling on the bed, a curious smile on my face.

But Ryder only offers me a wink as he heads into the kitchen.

A fluttery feeling rushes through me as he disappears down the hallway. No way in hell is he getting away with that cryptic statement. Chasing after him, I capture him by the counter, wrapping my arms about his waist. "No food until you clarify your earlier statement."

"Only trouble there? I'm taller and have longer arms." With that, he takes a huge mouthful of the omelet, earning a fake huff of annoyance from me. "Want some?"

He offers me a forkful, snatching it away at the last moment and shoving it in his mouth.

"Jerk. Forget it, I didn't want to know, anyway." I shoot him a glare, but he sees right through my facade. He calls me a marshmallow and, where he's concerned, he's right.

"Hey Gigi," Ryder calls after me.

"Yes, Mr. Gray?"

"This is the best week of my life."

I pause in the hallway, my breathing shallow as my heart pounds in my chest. Ryder is a man used to worldwide adoration and accolades. That a few days of sex and sun with me can even come close? Talk about thrilling. "I doubt that. You've won countless championships, stood on numerous podiums, and are worshiped by women and men around the globe. This pales in comparison, I'm sure, but it's a lovely sentiment."

"No," Ryder argues, his voice firm as his eyes dare me to look away. "Everything pales in comparison to you."

"You keep saying things like that and I'll fall head over heels in love with you."

He releases a sigh, a frown crossing his features. "I thought you already had."

I'm not sure whether it's the tone of his voice or the slight slump of his shoulders, but suddenly, I don't want to respond with some pithy barb.

I want to respond with the same brutal and beautiful honesty he offered me.

Crossing the kitchen, I grab his hands, reaching up on tiptoe to kiss him. "I have."

It's only two words, but they're the hardest words I've ever uttered. They lay my soul bare. Ryder's for the taking.

The energy between us changes in that moment as he hoists me into his arms and sprawls me across the dining room table.

Within seconds, he sinks inside me, a low moan rising from us both as he fills me.

"I'm addicted to you."

There's such emotion in the words and the intensity with which he speaks them. So much so that I believe him. Some may call me mad or naïve, but I believe him.

I can't hold back the emotions any longer. The dam

around my heart breaks, and the flood of feelings rushes through me. "I love you, Ryder. I'm so in love with you."

There's a split-second where the words hover in the air before the most beautiful smile breaks across his face and his lips claim me. "I've loved you for as long as I can remember. I'm glad you finally caught up to me."

"I caught up eight years ago, but you broke my heart."

"May I have it one last time?"

Does he know what he's asking? How desperately I want to be his and for it to be real? Belong to him and only him? "You won't break it?"

Ryder dusts kisses across my jaw, smiling against my skin. "Be mine, Greer. All mine. I want to build a world with just the two of us, our family, and a lifetime of memories. What do you say?"

Tears prick my eyes, the love for this man flowing through my every pore. "Best idea ever."

CHAPTER 8
RYDER

I've spent the last week in paradise. Literally. I pinch myself several times per day, just to prove I'm actually here with Greer.

My Gigi.

My ten-year-old self was correct—Gigi and I mesh perfectly. Hell, I'm not even talking about the sex, even though the sex... dear God, I've never felt anything like it.

Like her.

The best part is she loves it as much as I do, and in seven short days, we've screwed on every surface that will stand still long enough. Multiple times.

Then there's the blowjob she gave me on the beach, in full view of a ship docked across the cove. I claimed they couldn't see us. She claimed she didn't care.

Our days are filled with laughter and adventure, even if Gigi is terrified of heights and flat out refused to go ziplining. She was my personal cheerleader on the ground, wrapping that delicious body around me the moment my feet hit the dirt.

She's completely unused to the level of luxury here in Barbados, insisting on making the bed and bussing the dishes from the table. That and her wicked sense of humor have made her a hit with the staff at the villa.

Everyone loves Gigi.

But no one loves her as much as I do.

I'm lost in her, and for the first time in my life, I can see a world beyond the circuit.

Don't get me wrong, I love racing. There's nothing like sliding behind the wheel and feeling like a god as I cross the finish line. But before, that was all there was—racing and the inevitable fame associated with it.

Now, there's a whole new level to my life, one where Greer fills every nook and crevice.

There are a ton of women in this world, but only one who makes my heart race the moment she enters the room.

I called my Mom and told her about my spur-of-the-moment vacation. She damn near took my eardrum out with her shout of excitement when she learned I was finally —*finally*—together with Greer.

Her exact words? "Now that you have her, how do you plan on keeping her?"

Let's just say I have a plan, which I'm executing tonight.

∞

GREER SETTLES AGAINST ME, gazing up at the starlit sky. "It's so beautiful here. So peaceful. I can almost forget the chaos that is my normal life."

I stroke her hair, pulling her closer. "Why is your life so chaotic?"

"I work all the time. I have to if I want to keep up with my bills. Vacations and other luxuries are not in the cards for me.

Well, until now." She claims my mouth in a slow, leisurely kiss; one I'm all too keen to get in on.

She straddles my lap, allowing herself greater access to my body. Not that I'm complaining. If I had my druthers, this woman would be naked 24/7, but only I could look at her.

Admire her.

Worship her.

It's true. She's the only woman in this world I've ever truly adored. The one I would give up everything for, just to stay by her side.

"I'm going to miss you," she murmurs, and I pull back, meeting her curious gaze. "What?"

Okay, not exactly the segue I planned, but this can work. "No, you won't."

"I will. I feel whole around you. Safe. Happy. Hard to imagine not seeing you again for months or even years. I think you'll miss me, too. At least a bit. You may be the great and powerful Ryder Gray, but you have a soft spot for me."

A smile cuts across my face. It's now or never, but first, I'm going to mess with my lady a bit. "I definitely have a soft spot for you, but I won't miss you."

Greer stiffens, a scoff flying from her mouth as she pushes herself off my lap. "Thanks for that. You could have lied a bit with that statement."

I love getting her worked up. Not to worry, I'll calm her back down in a few minutes. "Not my style. Come on, let's take a walk."

"Fine." Greer falls into step beside me, her face marred with a frown. "You're still a jerk for saying that."

"Duly noted, but I need you to cheer up, grumpy girl."

We stroll in silence for several minutes, my heart rate increasing with each step. I know what I want. I just pray she wants it, too.

Suddenly, she jumps ahead a few steps, loosening the hook of her bikini top. "I think I may go skinny-dipping again."

"Please do," I murmur, my cock begging for release.

Tracing a finger down my chest, she sends me a scowl. "You're not invited."

"That's just mean."

"Takes one to know one." Greer turns on her heel, but I'm not giving her a chance to walk away.

"Greer Harlow Gray, get back here."

She pauses mid-step, turning back to face me, a look of confusion on her features. "What did you call me?"

"Your name. Or it will be if you say yes."

Am I terrified? Absolutely, but not because of what I'm about to ask. I'm scared shitless of how she's going to respond.

Swallowing back the fear, I smile, sliding my hands along her face and stealing a kiss from her lips.

My lips.

My woman, or she will be before the trip is over.

"You're not going to miss me, Gigi. Do you know why?" I sink to one knee, grasping her hands like lifelines. To be honest, she *is* my lifeline. "I'm not going to give you a chance to miss me. I have a better idea. Marry me. Be my wife. Live every day with me. Have a boatload of kids with me. Just *be* with me. Be mine."

Her dark eyes widen and I feel the trembling beneath her skin, but she's yet to say a word.

"Some might say it's fast, but they don't realize I've loved you my entire life. I've been waiting for you for decades. I don't want to wait anymore." I fish into my pocket, pulling out a velvet pouch and dumping out the contents into her palm—two platinum wedding bands. "One for you and one for me. I even had them inscribed with our initials and the words forever us."

Greer's silence is killing me, but I forge ahead. I have to. My one mission is convincing this woman that she needs to share her life with me. "I'll get you an enormous diamond but I want it to be perfect, and they couldn't finish it in time."

Now her jaw slackens, a single tear drifting down her cheek. I only pray it's a happy tear and not a sign she's about to flee into the water, never to return.

"For a woman who's never without a retort, you're very quiet, Gigi." With a deep breath, I prepare to deliver my final argument. "I know you don't believe in marriage, but you believe in love. Run with that. Believe in us. I'll take care of the rest."

She wipes away the tears, her hands shaking in mine. "You want me to take all my ideas about love, marriage, and children and throw them out the window?"

"Yes."

I barely get the word out as she tackles me into the sand, peppering my face with kisses. "You're crazy."

"We've established this fact already. But am I the kind of crazy you want spend your life with?"

Straddling me, she leans over, that gorgeous smile lighting up her face. "You're the only one I want to spend my life with."

"You'll marry me?"

"Yes, Ryder, I'd love to be your wife."

A euphoria washes over me, far stronger than any finish line or championship. Rolling over on top of her, I claim her lips, my hands hiking up her skirt as I free myself, sinking inside her, a low groan rising from us both.

I normally reserve my affections for behind closed doors.

That concept flew out the window the second Greer crossed the parking lot in Vegas, those long legs moving her ever closer to my side. With Gigi, I can't hold back. I *won't* hold back.

I don't give a crap who sees us, as I thrust inside her, those stems wrapped around my waist, her nails scratching along my shoulders, spurring me on. The water licks our skin with feather-light kisses as I push her over the edge, feeling her body quiver around me.

Nothing in the world feels this good. Nothing.

∽

BARBADOS IS KNOWN for being lenient with marriage laws for visitors to their tiny island. Okay, not Vegas lenient, but far easier than my current state of residence.

Was that a factor in my vacation destination? I'll only admit that it might have crossed my mind. It's an amusing aside that Greer mentioned us getting married as part of our deal, but what she doesn't know is that was the *only* plan all along.

I left for Vegas miserable and jaded. I'll return home with the most beautiful woman in the world by my side. How's that for beating the odds?

Gigi wanted a wedding on the beach, the sky kissing the water as we exchanged vows. There was no way that dream wasn't coming true, despite some uncooperative weather earlier in the day. By the time the sun hit the horizon, the sand was warm and dry, and fluffy clouds danced across the sky.

Perfect. Just like her.

As she walks toward me, wrapped in a flowing blue gown, I pinch myself once more. I'm a diehard romantic, but only for Greer Hammond. She was my first love and now I realize she'll be my only love.

I couldn't ask for more.

We exchange vows in the fading light, but our gaze never falters.

She slides the ring onto my finger, her brown eyes misty with tears. "I told you to find me. And you did. You're the only love I've ever believed in."

Pulling her to me, I claim her lips, tasting the salt of her tears as the deacon pronounces us husband and wife. "I'll show you how much I love you every day, Mrs. Gray."

A giggle explodes from her chest. "Mrs. Gray. I'm married. I'm married to Ryder Gray." Another laugh bubbles up as she shakes her head in disbelief. "I totally didn't see this one coming when I flew to Vegas."

"Not at all?" I inquire, cocking a brow at her.

She bites her lip in that endearing fashion, holding back yet another chuckle. "I may have hoped, but you are beyond my wildest dreams."

"See? Dreams do come true. I knew when I discovered you were single that I was making you mine. End of story. I think I did pretty well." Lifting her into my arms, I carry her back into the villa. Enough of the ceremony and its niceties. I have a private party with only one other guest—my wife. "How would you like to spend the rest of our wedding night?"

"You. Me. Clothing optional. Sound good?"

"Sounds absolutely fantastic."

And she is fantastic. Each and every time.

WE LIE TOGETHER, the sound of the ocean a calming backdrop for our three hours of passion. My wife is insatiable with sex, and I'm taking full advantage. She loves getting off, and I have made it my personal mission in life to get her off multiple times per day.

What a chore, I know.

My hands drift down the length of her body, her skin softer than silk. To say I'm addicted is an understatement.

"What is your daily life like?" Greer asks, propping her chin on my chest. "Perhaps this is a conversation we should have had before we got married."

I chuckle, stealing a kiss. "Fairly normal, in the off-season. During race season, I tour the circuit. But, you grew up around enough racing to know that scenario."

Pressing kisses to my chest, she bites her lip, gazing off in the distance. "I worry about you getting hurt. I know that's not what you want to hear, but I've always worried."

Stroking her hair from her face, I grasp her chin, directing that dark gaze back to me. "I like hearing that, actually. Good to know I've got you in my corner. I want you to travel with me, Gigi. I really want you there."

"Won't I get in the way?"

"Never. Besides, I owe you a trip to Paris."

She nods, but I feel a niggling in the back of my mind. We're running on pure emotion this past week. Hell, we reunited, hooked up, vacationed together, and now we're married.

That's a whirlwind if I've ever seen one. But, as my mother always said, I don't do things slow and I don't do them halfway.

I don't have a single regret. Here's hoping she's not second-guessing our nuptials. "Hey, where's your head at, Gigi?"

"You don't owe me a trip to Paris. You don't owe me anything, Ryder. I guess I feel a bit out of my element, wondering how I'm going to contribute to this relationship. You earn in a day what I earn in... ten years."

"I didn't marry you for your money, Gigi. I married you for this sexy as hell body." Delivering a firm smack to her ass, I earn a squeal of approval.

"I didn't marry you for your money, either." I believe her. If there's one thing I know about Gigi, she's honest to a fault. She's also generous with her heart and her time.

She's my perfect.

"Good to know, even though you are rich now."

Her eyes glaze at my humorous retort. "I don't want your money, Ryder."

Pulling her close, I knit my fingers in her dark hair, forcing her to meet my gaze. "I want you, by my side, every day. Is that okay with you?"

Now the smile returns full force. "That's perfect."

"So, you'll travel the circuit with me?"

"Of course, even if I spend most of the race averting my eyes and praying for your safety."

"Fair enough, so long as you cheer the loudest when I win."

"Deal." Leaning forward, she claims my mouth, her tongue slow and coaxing against mine. "Can I tell you something?"

I nod, winking at her when she straddles my waist. "I like this conversation already."

"I didn't want to go to Vegas and see you. I worried you'd be with another woman. But at the last minute, I decided to go. I planned on bedding some hot guy and making you jealous that you missed out."

Typical Greer. I love that her emotions ran so hot all these years later. Proof they'll stay that spicy for a lifetime.

"Well, you did bed a hot guy. Hell, you married him."

A snort of laughter flies from Greer's mouth as she smacks my chest. "Conceited ass."

"Am I wrong?"

She cocks her brow at me. "You have your moments."

"Take it back."

"Or what?"

Rolling her onto her back, I move over top of her, cupping her head. "I'll spend the rest of the night convincing you of all the ways you're wrong."

"I think I'll enjoy your form of punishment."

∼

REALITY SINKS in the next morning, as we scramble around the villa, packing our things. Despite my repeated pleas, Gigi has to return to New York. She needs to give notice at her job and pack up her apartment.

I have to return to Charlotte to prepare for race season.

I don't want to go anywhere without her.

"I wanted you with me," I groan, falling back on the bed.

"You're going to be so busy these next couple of weeks you won't even miss me."

"Bullshit."

"Okay, maybe you'll miss me a little bit."

"I already miss you."

"Damn, I wish we had time for another quickie," she smirks, sending me a saucy wink. "I'll jump your bones the next time I see you."

"Two weeks, right? That's it. And then you move to Charlotte." Yes, I'm pressing her. I want her near me. For some reason, even though we've only been together a minute, I feel whole with her by my side.

That and the idea of going without her luscious curves for fourteen days sounds like an experiment in torture.

"I'll do my best. Ryder, I have to pack my entire life, while also settling up at work. Not an easy feat in two weeks."

"I'll hire movers to pack your stuff."

"Most of it isn't worth anything, to be honest. I also need to find work in Charlotte."

Grasping her hand, I pull her onto the bed with me. "Let's explore that after race season, okay? I'll take care of you. Hell, you never have to go back to work as far as I'm concerned."

"I enjoy working. Besides, you'd get sick of me, eventually. Always there, bumbling about."

"Not a chance." Sliding my hands along her jaw, I pull her mouth to mine, my tongue tangling with hers and earning a purr of approval. "I need you there. You're my good luck charm."

She fingers the medallion around my neck. "I thought that was your good luck charm."

"Don't need him when I've got you. Talk about one hell of an upgrade."

We dally for the next twenty minutes, until the knock at the door snaps us from our reverie, reminding us that time isn't on our side. The drive to the airport seems to take a minute, and her flight is an hour before mine.

Figures.

I walk her to the gate, pulling her against me and hating that I have to be more than three feet from her side. "My first race is in two weeks. Sunday. Promise me you'll be there. At least promise me you'll try."

Tears roll down her cheeks as they announce first-class boarding. "I don't want to leave you."

"Don't. Screw your job and come home with me. I told you, I'll take care of you." I mean it, too.

"If only I was a total asshole and capable of that. I have to go. You be careful, Ryder. Promise me? I only just found you."

"I've always been here, Gigi. Waiting for you."

I force a bright smile for my wife as she hands her ticket to the attendant, turning back to blow me a kiss before walking onto the plane. I know it's only two weeks, but having to watch Greer walk away from me—again—tears at my heart.

I'll always be a fool for that woman. Glancing down at the ring on my hand, I give it a twirl, feeling the connection between the two of us.

There's another hour before my plane boards. Time for a drink and some catch-up.

In the last ten days, I tossed my phone—and cares—aside, choosing to focus all my attention on Gigi. She's the first time I've ever been able to accomplish that feat, at least since I turned pro. There's a certain level of exhaustion you learn to live with when you're a household name, one I wasn't fully aware of until this vacation in Barbados.

Greer doesn't want me for my money or celebrity status. In fact, I get the distinct impression it turns her off. I know it intimidates the hell out of her, although she's worth more than every F1 team combined. She's priceless.

My only worry? The fear I saw in her eyes when we discussed my racing career. She understands it's what I do and who I am, but the terror was palpable as I discussed some of my near misses.

My reassurances that I've never had an accident did little to assuage her fears. The other women I've dated loved the thrill of the race. Likely, they loved the notoriety that went along with it—the flash of cameras, the reporters, and the guarantee that their picture would grace magazines was fodder for their egos.

Looking back, I realize that not one of them had ever worried for my safety. At least none had mentioned the fact before I sat my ass in a car flying around a track at over 200mph.

But Gigi? She's scared to death I'm going to get hurt. She doesn't believe me when I say she's my good luck charm, but that medallion has brought me plenty of wins and no serious incidents. I used to look at it in the mirror, glistening against my chest, and feel her hands when they slipped it around my neck all those years ago.

Now, we share another piece of jewelry, along with the same last name.

Life is a trip.

I plant my ass at the airport bar, ordering a drink before dialing Greg. My buddy and his new wife moved into my guest house as they search for a home in the Charlotte area. I love that I'm able to provide an avenue for him to reenter the racing world, even though my blood boils when I realize what he lost because of his father's selfishness.

"Hey, Greg, are you settling in okay?"

"Ryder, you don't own a house. You own a castle. This place is enormous, and I haven't even entered the main residence."

I chuckle, swigging back my drink. "It's not that big. How does Jillian like it?"

"She isn't here yet. We figured I should get settled in first. Where are you, anyway?"

"Barbados. I'm flying home today."

"One vacation wasn't enough?" Greg chuckles. "Did you have fun?"

"That's an understatement."

"Wait a damn minute," my buddy bellows into the phone. "You're with my sister, aren't you? I stopped at her apartment to say goodbye before I left Long Island and her neighbor said she hadn't been home in over a week."

"I was with Gigi, but she's on a plane back to Long Island as we speak."

"How did that go?"

Okay, sticky subject. When you have a public image, you want to control big announcements... like impromptu weddings. That's why I'm not saying anything about my recent nuptials until *after* the first race. This ensures my head stays in the game and the media's focus remains on the race and not my new bride.

It also ensures Greer won't have to deal with a barrage of media attention when she's several hundred miles away from me.

My primary goal is to keep her safe. And sane.

"It was amazing. Your sister is amazing."

"Too much information, dude."

"Hey, your mind went to the gutter all on its own." Twirling the ice in my glass, I dread asking the next question. "Has Mandi been around?"

"Twice, yeah. She was none too happy you weren't here, or that I had no clue where you went. She told me to tell you she's moved out her things, *but* she plans on having a serious conversation with you once you get home. I don't envy you."

"At least she's gone. Thanks for watching the place for me. Mick had to return to California, and I didn't trust that she wouldn't camp out there, lying in wait."

"Does Greer know about Mandi?"

"She does, not that there's anything to tell. Mandi and I are over. Done. Kaput."

"And what are you and Greer?"

See? I knew it would come around to this at some point.

Clearing my throat, I swallow the last of my whiskey before offering a safe, but true, response. "I'm crazy about her. Just like I've always been. Gotta run. They're boarding."

I know Greg won't let me slide without a full explanation, but I'd rather give him the details in person. I figure the conversation will go one of two ways—a bear hug welcoming me to the family or a punch to the jaw, followed by the bear hug.

Either way, I'm ready.

CHAPTER 9
RYDER

It's been ten days, and I miss my wife more than I miss breathing. We video chat daily, and I drag out every conversation because I hate ending the call, knowing I'll face my king-sized bed without her gorgeous body next to me.

Greer, on the other hand, looks exhausted, the bags under her eyes visible through her makeup.

She didn't have bags in Barbados. She glowed.

She's less than two weeks into her former life and already she's running on fumes. Her job was less than thrilled with her resignation and dumped all the crap cases on her as a parting gift. I begged her to quit, but she feels an obligation to her patients, despite her employer being a total prick.

Personally, I don't think she owes them a damn thing.

The only upside? Every day we're apart brings us one day closer to being reunited, and I remind her of this as soon as our call connects for the evening.

A smile splits her face, but it fades as she glances at my

hand. "Where's your ring?" she asks, pointing to her own wedding band.

I have a choice. I can make up some excuse she'll no doubt believe and then change the subject. But I never want to lie to Greer. Her father and that piece of shit Richard spent years lying, wrecking her emotional stability in the process.

So, I opt for the truth, praying she understands my logic. "I'm not wearing it." When her face falls, I realize I have seconds to prevent this chat from careening into the wall. "It's not that I don't love it. I do, but we haven't announced anything yet."

"Right," she mumbles, her gaze intent on her hand. "Should I take mine off?"

"The press doesn't know who you are yet. I plan on announcing our marriage after the first race. I want to keep the media's focus on my training until that point."

Please understand, beautiful. Please.

A sad smile colors her face, but she nods in agreement. "Whatever you need to do, Ryder. A few people asked me about the ring, but I never told them who I married. Your secret is safe."

Hell, that's not how I meant it. "I'm telling the world about us as soon as the race is finished. But I want you by my side when I make the announcement." Wincing at my unintentional faux pas, I shoot her a rueful smile. "I should have spoken to you about everything first, ensured you were okay with my decision. I'll put the ring on right now."

Yep, I'm scrambling. I'm terrified she'll slide on her trusty emotional armor again. It was no easy feat getting her to lay it aside the first time.

"It's fine. Honestly. No big deal." But the flat tone of her voice belies her innocent words. I've hurt her, which is the last thing I want to do.

"Gigi, it's not like that."

"How's Greg settling in?" With that question, her armor snaps into place as she switches to a different topic.

"The man is a genius with automobiles." Clearing my throat, I run my hand over my beard, uncertain how to proceed. "Can I ask something without you getting angry?"

Greer releases a short bark of laughter, averting her gaze. "That's always the setup for a terrible question. Fire away."

Yep, I have some serious damage control to handle after the ring fiasco. I see it in the set of her jaw, along with the fact that she's barely meeting my gaze. Now, I've shot out another cryptic question and judging by the apprehension lining her face, she has no clue what I'll hit her with next.

As I said, I have *way* more finesse on the track than with romance, but I'm trying. For Greer, I'll never stop trying.

"Hopefully, it's not a terrible topic. I pray it's something benign and I'm overreacting." It's meant to soothe her nerves, but as soon as her dark gaze flies up to meet mine, I realize I'm only making the situation worse with every second wasted.

"Benign? Are you okay?"

"Bad choice of words. It's about Greg and his drinking."

"Don't scare me like that." Greer rubs her hand over her brow, a small sigh escaping her mouth. "I hoped he would rein in his drinking after the hubbub of the wedding and starting this new job. He's not a mean drunk—"

"I know that, but he's always got a drink in his hand. Except at the track, of course. But the minute we're done, he's in the cooler, popping open a beer. Should I be worried? You know him better than anyone, Gigi."

"Mom and I have worried about his drinking for years. My father had a drinking problem, and we all know there's a hereditary link. I've never known Greg to mix business and pleasure, although their borders lie really close together. Do you want me to talk to him?"

"No, I'll do it. You have enough on your plate." Drumming the table, I stare at her image, the apprehension wafting off her in waves. Time to get to the bottom of whatever is eating at her emotions. "Hey beautiful, what did you think I was going to ask?"

"Nothing." Once again, Greer won't meet my gaze. A sure sign she's lying.

"Don't nothing me. What did you think I was going to say?"

"That you wanted an annulment."

Her off-the-cuff reply knocks me sideways. "Where did that come from?"

She shrugs, her gaze fixed on the floor.

"Gigi, we are never getting divorced. Not happening."

But instead of a smile lighting up her face, she only offers a slight nod. "It just seemed odd that you weren't wearing you ring, so I thought...who knows what I thought? I'm beat from work and I have an early conference call in the morning. Can we talk tomorrow?"

No way will I end this call with her on that note. She needs to understand how much I adore her.

"I love you, Greer Gray. Do you hear me? I'm a total shit for not wearing my ring and I'll tell the world tomorrow, I promise." I send her a smile, trying to coax one in return. "I just wanted you by my side so I could make every man jealous that I had you and no one else ever would. Actually, I'm desperate for you to be here. I've spent so many days without you, and I'm not sure how many more I can stand. When you boarded that plane, you took the color out of my life."

Greer releases an exasperated sigh, those wide eyes

finally meeting my gaze. "Damn you. That was good. How am I supposed to stay mad after such a romantic sentiment?"

I chuckle, letting my fingers trace the lines of her face on the screen. "An annulment? You are way off. In fact, I want to know when we can start prepping for our next phase."

"Phase?"

"You. Me. A ton of sex. Nine months later, you get the picture."

"A secret marriage and I lose my bikini body? I don't know. That might be too much to ask."

"You know I'm knocking you up, right? You'll rock a bikini, even at nine months pregnant."

"I highly doubt that fact." She's trying to maintain a serious expression, but I see the mischievous glint in her eye. "My bed is calling."

"Damn thing never calls me." Even though we're now jovial, I need to drive home how serious I am about our marriage. Our future. The last thing I need is for Greer to distance herself. The woman is a master at shielding her emotions, even if she's never been good at hiding them from me.

Somehow, we always got each other.

"I'll issue a press release in the morning. Just be prepared. The media are going to have a field day with the news."

"It will keep, Ryder. Your only focus should be ensuring that sexy ass is safe during the race. But once I'm back, and the race is over, that ring goes on your finger. Deal?"

"Forever and always." I pull open my shirt, showing the medallion. "I'm ready to retire this guy. I want you as my good luck charm."

"I'll be there soon."

"Not soon enough."

We end the call, but I continue to weigh my options regarding our marriage. Maybe I should announce our betrothal and fuck anyone who doesn't understand.

My doorbell peals, jolting me from my thoughts. Who the hell is stopping by now? My money is on Greg; he's already managed to lock himself out of the pool house once today.

But it isn't Greg standing on my vestibule. It's Mandi.

Isn't this a wonderful way to end an evening?

"What are you doing here?"

Shifting her weight, she sucks in a breath. "Can we talk?"

"About?" Yes, I'm curt, but I have no desire to rehash our sham of a relationship. Mandi has already chewed my ear several times over the last couple of weeks, volleying for a second chance.

She fails to realize she's out of chances. The moment the love of my life walked back into my life, everyone else failed to exist. At least as far as I'm concerned.

What I felt for Mandi, even in the beginning, pales compared to the adoration I feel for Greer. It's not even close. Hell, it's not even the same ballpark. And no matter what Mandi claims, she cheated on me. Twice.

Leaning against the doorframe, I block her forward movement into the house. "I don't think we have anything to say to one another."

"I have a few things to say to you if you can spare the time."

Calling on all my patience, I hold back from rolling my eyes as I wave her into the house. The woman is a born drama queen. She won't go away quietly. Best to let her speak her mind and then show her ass to the door.

Again.

I stop by the bar, pouring myself a glass of wine. Hey, I'm

pretty damn positive I'll need a drink for this conversation. "You want one?"

Mandi accepts my offering and we walk out to the patio. I consider it neutral territory, the proverbial no-man's-land for her forthcoming painful diatribe.

Crossing her long legs, she glances around at the place she used to call home. It's crazy how much can change in thirty days. "How have you been?"

I sputter my drink, glaring in her direction. "Save the pleasantries. Say what you have to say."

"You claim we aren't good together, but I disagree. We had several wonderful months and there was love there, even if we lost our way in the end."

"Why are you involving me in that statement? You cheated, remember? That's what ended this relationship."

"And the first thing you do is fly to Vegas and hook up with another woman. Who is she, anyway? Some high-dollar stripper?"

"How is that your business?" I refuse to divulge any information about my wife to Mandi, especially before the press release. All Greer needs is to be harangued by my ex-girlfriend about how she stole her man, or whatever inane story she creates in her mind. That will definitely send her scrambling for the hills.

"Is she here? I'd like to meet the woman who's taken my place. Have you moved her in yet?"

"Was this your plan? Barrage me with questions about the woman in Vegas?"

"Does she mean anything, or was she just a fling?"

"Again, none of your business." I sit forward, my foot tapping ceaselessly on the ground. "You should go."

"Do you know why I cheated?"

This time the eye roll wins out. I don't give a damn why

she cheated. It's over and done with, and now I need her gone.

Unlucky for me, Mandi is far from finished.

"You were emotionally unavailable, Ryder. All you care about is your stupid car and your stupid races."

A harsh bark of laughter shoots from my lips. "First, that isn't true. Second, that *stupid car* afforded your lifestyle here. But instead of appreciating it, you threw it in my face. Fucked someone else."

"So did you. Don't forget you stepped out on me, too."

It's a low blow, but I should have known it would come around to my indiscretion. Was I unfaithful to Mandi? Depends on how you look at it. After she cheated the first time, I dumped her ass, went to the club, and screwed a woman whose name I don't recall.

It was a real low point, but I own my past—the good and bad parts.

"We also said after our reconciliation that we would focus on making this relationship work. Do you recall that discussion? Apparently not, since you screwed a man in my house while I was away." Another bark of laughter cuts through the night air. "Well, you thought I was away. We both got one hell of a surprise that day."

Mandi grasps my hands, an unexpected and wholly unwelcome move. "I know I messed up, but I'd like you to consider giving us another chance. A real chance."

I open my mouth to object, but she waves her hand, silencing my argument.

"Give it some thought. That's all I ask."

She stands suddenly, pressing a kiss to my mouth before turning toward the door.

If I don't set the record straight now, Mandi will never cease and desist. Chasing her into the house, I grasp her shoulders, spinning her around. "While I appreciate your pseudo apology, I'm not interested in reconciliation. I've moved on. I suggest you do the same."

"I'll give you a few days to think it over."

How dense is this woman? Holding open the door, I force a smile. "My answer isn't going to change. Good luck to you, Mandi."

I sag against the wall the moment she leaves, releasing an aggravated sigh.

I assumed after our last call, where I reiterated—*again*—how I was done with our relationship, that she would take the hint.

I thought wrong. Apparently, Mandi doesn't enjoy being told no.

Too bad for her, because I'm not changing my mind.

∽

"You did what?" Mr. Givens, my lawyer, is less than thrilled with me. To be honest, I worry he might have a coronary at my breakfast bar. "What is wrong with you? You married this woman without a prenup?"

"I did." I'm not sure why he's so bent out of shape. It's my money.

"You realize she could take you for half."

"She wouldn't do that."

"Right. Because I've never heard that line before."

"You don't know Greer."

"Forgive me, Ryder, but neither do you. I notice she's not here. Where is she?"

I bristle at Mr. Givens' tone regarding my wife. "She had to finish up her work on Long Island."

He buries his head in his hands. "I'm going to call her

and see if I can't get some agreement drawn up. Likely won't stand in court, but let's hope it doesn't come to that."

"Don't you dare," I warn.

"I know you think you're in love, but you've worked so hard for all of this. Don't throw it away on a decision made in the heat of the moment."

I understand his point. It's valid. To the outside world, my decision would appear impetuous and rash. But what the outside world doesn't know is my long-standing desire to be with Greer.

They also don't know her.

Although they will now.

Mr. Givens appeared on my doorstep, a stack of tabloids in his hands, demanding to know if there was any truth behind the rumors flooding the gossip mags. Those rumors being my surprise nuptials. Although they haven't clinched any definitive proof, it's only a matter of time. After all, marriages are a public record.

I wonder who leaked the news, although my money is on the maid who cleaned our villa. She was highly attentive to our needs, even claiming to be a huge fan of racing. Now I realize she was really a huge fan of dollar signs.

Mr. Givens expected me to be furious, but I simply shrugged and chuckled before letting him in on the events of the past few weeks. Granted, it's not the way I planned for the news to hit the airwaves, but my hope is the race this weekend will overshadow any gossip, just long enough for my wife to get her sexy ass down here.

Then, I'll let the truth hang out.

"What am I supposed to do here, Ryder? You hired me to protect your investments, then you throw them away on a spur-of-the-moment wedding to some woman I've never heard of. Please tell me she's not a Vegas showgirl. Showgirls are notorious for this type of garbage."

"She's got the body of a showgirl," I reply, smirking at Mr. Given's horrified expression. "I've known her since I was ten and I've loved her that long."

"Then why haven't I heard about her?"

"I thought she was married. Turns out, she wasn't. But I fixed that problem. Next on the agenda is a baby, in case you want to throw another apoplectic fit."

"I'm so glad you find this amusing."

"I got married. I didn't murder anyone. Relax. Have a cocktail. I need to call Gigi because it's only a matter of time before the press gets hold of her name."

Strolling out of the kitchen, I glance over my shoulder, laughing when I see my lawyer grab the bottle of gin. Hey, it's five o'clock somewhere.

Greer picks up on the first ring, her voice hushed. "I swear I didn't say anything. Are you okay? Are you freaking out?"

"I'm fine." Actually, I'm thrilled the truth is out. The look of disappointment on Greer's face when she discovered I wasn't wearing my ring haunted me the entire night.

"Are you lying?" I hate the hesitation in her voice, the uncertainty.

"No. My only concern is your safety and the media bothering you. Has anyone said anything?"

"Not at all, except for one of my coworkers, who claims to be insanely jealous of whoever your wife is because you are, as she puts it, the hottest man in the world of racing."

I chuckle into the phone. "She's not lying."

"Your ego is intact, thank God. Had me worried for a minute. How long until they figure out my name?"

"Depends, but not long. A couple of days at the most."

"What should I tell the media, if someone corners me?"

"Tell them you're married to the hottest man in the world of racing."

"How about no comment?"

"I like the first option better."

"You would," Greer chuckles. "Let me run. I have some paperwork to finish before I squirrel myself away in my apartment."

"I love you, Mrs. Gray. I can't wait for you to be back here. Hey, before you go, what day are you flying in? I'll book your flight. The race is Sunday, but I'd love for you to be here Saturday."

Silence. Never a good thing.

"Gigi? When are you coming home?"

"I don't know if I'll make the race, Ryder." She shushes me when I groan into the phone. "Trust me, I'm trying but I'm overloaded with work."

"You quit. As of Friday you're done."

"I feel bad for the patients. They're having a hard time with my resignation."

With an aggravated grunt, I stroll onto the patio, coffee in hand. "Well, *I'm* having a hard time with your absence, and I'm your husband. I win."

"I promise this is the last race I'll miss."

"I want you at this race." Am I being difficult? Yes, but I'm desperate for her to be in my arms again. Besides, the media will no doubt be looking for her at the race, wondering why my new wife is noticeably absent.

"How about I make it up to you with daily blowjobs for the rest of the circuit?"

Holy fuck, that got my attention. "I'm listening."

"Will you forgive me for missing the race?"

"You'll be here by Monday?" Glancing up, I see Greg

hovering at the far end of the patio, a stern expression coloring his face. Guess someone else read the tabloids.

"Promise."

"This is your one and only get out of jail free card. Call me later and be safe. Anyone bothers you, let me know and I'll hire security."

"No one cares about me, Ryder."

That's not entirely true, particularly not with my rabid fanbase, but there's no sense in upsetting her. "I care about you. A whole hell of a lot."

"You better." With a kiss into the phone, she ends the call and I mentally prepare for my discussion with Greg. Here's hoping I don't have to duck and cover. "Morning. Ready for the weekend?"

"Probably more nervous than you are."

"You'll do great."

Greg clears his throat, holding up a magazine. "You're married?"

With a sigh, I nod. "I am."

"Am I correct to assume your wife is my sister?"

"You are."

"Is this some sort of public relations thing? I know Greer mentioned some sort of deal between the two of you, but I thought that was just your way of keeping her close."

"There is no deal, except that she's my wife."

"Then why wasn't anyone told? You know, like us little people, also known as her family?"

Shit, this is taking a dangerous turn. "We eloped in Barbados. A quiet ceremony with just the two of us."

"Right, but Barbados ended weeks ago and I'm finding out from a rag mag."

"We planned on keeping it quiet until after the first race."

"Meaning *you* planned to keep it quiet?" He holds up his

hand when I try to interject. "Let me say my peace. So, you eloped. Fine. You're keeping it on the down low. Okay. But then, on the same rack of magazines that is crowing about your marriage to some mystery brunette, there's this."

He tosses two magazines my way and I cringe, reading the captions about Mandi and my imminent reconciliation. "Dude, it's tabloids. They're all bullshit."

"Normally, I'd agree. But this woman who claims you two are back together was at your house last night. I saw you drinking wine on the patio."

Mayday, mayday. "I didn't know you heard us."

"I live literally across the pool, Ryder. But that's the wrong response. Your ex was here and your wife—my sister —isn't. It's your life but if you hurt Greer, I'm going to hurt you."

"I'll never hurt her. You have my word. I absolutely adore Gigi."

"This looks bad, man. Dead this situation with Mandi because if Greer finds out there's truth to these claims, she'll run away faster than any F1."

∼

GREG'S WORDS stick with me until the second I slide behind the wheel for Friday's practice. I need my head in the game, tabloid fodder or no. Luckily, he's shelved any discussion of his sister, his sole focus on the safety and speed of the vehicle carrying me around the circuit.

Just like me, he has a one-track mind when it's go time.

My friend has also proven himself a valuable addition to the team. Hey, I don't just choose my crew willy-nilly.

I trust him with my life because that's what he holds in his hands.

Friday's practice went smooth as glass, even though I noticed Greg didn't give it twenty minutes before a beer was in his hand. When I pulled him aside, he downplayed it, promising me, much like his sister, that he doesn't mix business with pleasure. Let's hope that's the truth.

As soon as practice wraps, a hand claps around my shoulder. Glancing up, I catch Mick's amused smirk. "So, is there truth to this rumor, or are the magazines spouting shit again?" I chuckle, and Mick's grin widens. "Holy crap. You crossed to the dark side. Please tell me it isn't Mandi."

"Her name is Greer, and I've been in love with her since I was ten. We reconnected at her brother's wedding," I add, motioning in Greg's direction.

"That old Vegas adage doesn't hold true for you, does it?" Mick shoots me a light jab in the arm, toasting me with his water bottle. "Congratulations. Where is she?"

"Still in New York. She's a nurse practitioner and has to finish up with her patients."

"I get obligations. Does she have any idea about the world of crazy she just married into?"

"Likely not, but now she's trapped. Hell, my lawyer almost had a coronary when he discovered we didn't sign a prenup."

"Damn, you are in love." Mick gestures to where Greg stands with a few other crew members. "What crew did you steal him from?"

"None, but he's been around cars since birth. I came up racing with him. He was better than me, to be honest, but his family situation ended his chances of a career. He's been an excellent addition so far."

A frown creases Mick's brow. "I've no doubt, but this is the big league. Maybe he should function as a backup for a few races. Get his feet wet."

"He's good to go." Normally I don't question Mick's authority, but I know my friend.

He was born ready.

~

After finishing first in Saturday's timed trials, I'm on top of the world.

Now if only my wife would get her sexy ass down here.

Grabbing my phone, I dial her number. Christ, I miss her.

"Hi, handsome."

"I'm leaving you a ticket, just in case. I know you're busy and have obligations, but I need my cheerleader."

Greer stays silent a few beats, and I wonder if I'm pushing too hard. Let's admit it—I'm used to getting what I want. "You know, if a woman was trying to surprise you, you would kill it every time. Focus on the race, Mr. Gray. Even if I'm not there in person, I'll be there in spirit. I appreciate the ticket, though. Just in case."

"Be forewarned after you get back here, I'm supergluing you to my side."

I love her husky chuckle. The only thing better? That chuckle followed by her naked body straddling me. That's the thing with incredible sex. Once you experience it, it becomes the most potent addiction in the world.

It becomes all you can think about.

She's all I can think about.

Even my racing career dims next to her light. Greer has usurped racing in my heart, taking center stage and becoming the center of my world. The weirdest part is how fine I am with that concept.

Feeling for the small box in my pocket, a smile crosses my face. I had to pay a mint, but the jewelers worked overtime to get Gigi's ring finished by this weekend. It's a six-carat stunner, as flawless as the woman herself.

Time to slide this beauty on my beauty's hand, locking her down for life.

Unfortunately, my beautiful woman isn't here, and time is growing short for her to arrive before the race. As is custom for races held in Charlotte, the entire team shacks up for the weekend at a luxury hotel only a mile from the track. Such a hardship, I realize, but there is a method to our madness.

I may only live an hour from the track, but Charlotte is renowned for her snarling traffic jams. Not something you want to encounter when time is at a premium. Staying here allows us to hash out any last-minute issues and also be only moments from the track, should the need arise.

It's a win-win.

Mick, Rachel, and I enjoy an early dinner discussing the next day's race. She's been a part of the racing world for years now by her husband's side, but I see the relief in her face that he's no longer sliding behind the wheel.

I know there are days when Mick misses the feeling of flying. Hell, racing is as much in his blood as mine.

Having a kid changed his mind. To hear him tell it, he knew he wanted to be there to watch him grow up. So, his priorities and position changed.

This is the best of both worlds for him. He gets to live amongst the sport he worships while going home safe every night to his family.

I'm not there yet. I still crave that adrenaline rush, although I admit that being with Greer is its own form of speed. For the first time, I understand Mick's position.

After dinner, we stroll toward the elevator. Time to turn in and get some rest for tomorrow. I have a race to win.

Rachel, although disappointed Greer didn't make it, is

thrilled to learn I'm no longer a single man. Stepping into the elevator with Mick, she sends me a megawatt smile. "I can't wait to meet your wife. She must have superpowers to tame Ryder Gray."

With a chuckle, I watch the doors close. To be fair, Rachel isn't far off. Greer is my superwoman.

"She's not the only one who wants to know about your new wife."

Spinning on my heel, I release a noisy exhalation. "Mandi. What are you doing here?"

"Looking for answers." Her pale blue eyes fill with tears, a few escaping down her cheeks. "I think after everything, you at least owe me that. I asked you if it was serious, and you denied it."

"No, I wouldn't answer the question because I knew how you'd take it." Honestly, I knew she'd be pissed, but I figured she would key my car, not break down in tears, demanding answers. "I'm sorry if you're hurt because of this news."

"I'm hurt because of *you*," she huffs, her body shaking. "I deserved better than that."

To be fair, I don't think my ex deserves *any* explanation, aside from what I told her the other night. I moved on. She needs to do the same.

But I'd be a bastard to leave her in the lobby, sobbing out my name.

The least I can give her is an explanation. Wrapping an arm around her shoulders, I steer her toward the lobby restaurant, prepared to give her one.

CHAPTER 10
GREER

For once, I'm ahead of schedule.

Let me rephrase. I'm always on time. The airlines? Not so much.

But the universal forces seems to align, ensuring I make it to Ryder's side before the race. I know my husband is desperate for me to join him, even texting me the name of the hotel where he'll spend the weekend.

That was all I needed to solidify my decision to hop on a plane and surprise Ryder.

I'm shocked the man didn't see through my flimsy fib, but he's also got his mind on a million different things. Not the least of which is our recent marriage, even if the world doesn't yet know who snagged the king of racing.

Glancing down at the band on my finger, I smile. I know who snagged Ryder Gray, and I'm sure as hell not giving him up.

I'll admit that doubt did rear its ugly head several times during our separation. Part of me worried he would change his mind, wanting to walk out of the whirlwind courtship as quickly as he walked in. It didn't help to learn he wasn't wearing his ring nor disclosing his newly minted marital status.

Then there are the articles, not the ones about Ryder's mystery wife, but ones about his supposed reconciliation with Mandi.

Tabloids are the stuff of fairytales, right? But if they got the marriage rumor right, how far off are they about the ex-girlfriend one?

These are the thoughts vying for position in my brain, yet another reason I had to get my ass to Charlotte. I know once I see Ryder and he wraps his arms around me, that all will be right with the world.

Besides, I'm likely overreacting because I have zero experience in this celebrity arena. No one ever put anything about my life into print. Hell, it was never noteworthy enough for that nonsense. But Ryder? He drives down the street and the world clamors about, eager for a glimpse into his private life.

My husband swore his daily life is normal, even if life during the circuit is anything but. At least he's accident free and now, he has Greg on his crew. My brother would sooner die than let his friend down.

With a sigh, I release any niggling doubts as I pop out of the cab in front of the luxurious Charlotte hotel. Talk about swanky. No wonder the team doesn't mind spending a few nights here. It's practically palatial.

My phone buzzes in my purse. Another message from Mr. Givens. That makes the third one today, all equally cryptic but claiming that we need to sit down and talk as soon as possible. All I know is Mr. Givens works for Ryder in some capacity. Beyond that, it's a mystery.

Ryder also left me a message, telling me he has a plan for us. One I will want to know about immediately.

Knowing my man's romantic inclinations, it's likely some post-race soiree, celebrating his win and our marriage.

One thing I know for certain. After two weeks without him, I know being with Ryder is the right choice. The only choice. To hell with preconceived notions.

My heart wins.

I duck into the lobby bathroom to change into a sexy slip of a dress and apply fresh lipstick. I'm no fool. Ryder has his pick of women, but I'm going to drive home the point that he made the best choice, and a dress that hugs all my assets is just the ticket. Besides, the look on his face as his eyes travel the length of my body—I'm hot just envisioning it. It's been two weeks since the best sex of my life, and I'm ready for another helping.

Here's hoping Ryder doesn't have some weird belief about no sex before a race. I've heard stranger things before.

Ryder left his suite number and the code word to get me past the front desk staff, but I'm coy when they inquire who I am, claiming to be an old friend. It's true. We are old friends, along with being the hottest lovers on the planet. But these people don't need to know that bit of information. Unfortunately, he isn't answering the phone in his suite, so I flash the clerk a smile and head for the hotel lounge.

A glass of wine will do wonders to soothe my nerves while I track down my husband. Dialing his cell phone, I hear his phone ringing from inside the bar.

Isn't that a bit of luck?

Glancing to my left, my heart sinks.

Looks like my luck ran out.

So much for tabloids being bullshit.

Not ten feet away sits Ryder, his hands grasping Mandi across the table. With trembling fingers, I dial his number again, desperate to witness his reaction. Maybe it's that I don't want to believe what I'm seeing, or perhaps it's some leftover masochism from my youth, but I can't leave without knowing.

My heart shatters when he gives the phone a quick glance before silencing the call and returning to his conversation.

This is what it feels like for someone to make a complete fool of you. It was gut-wrenching to watch my mother endure this treatment. To be on the receiving end is far, far worse.

Breathing is increasingly difficult with each passing moment, but I jerk when the bartender inquires about my drink order. "Nothing, thank you," I manage before dashing toward the front entrance, my suitcase wobbling precariously behind me.

So much for surprising Ryder. I guess he figured since I wouldn't be arriving until Monday that he was free to do as he pleased. With whomever he pleased.

My phone rings and I answer it without looking. "Hello?"

"Ms. Hammond, this is Mr. Givens. I've been trying to reach you."

"Who are you?" I snap, in no mood to beat around the bush, especially where Ryder Gray is concerned.

"Mr. Gray's attorney."

I've heard enough. "I can't talk right now. I'll call you later." It's all I can manage, the tears bouncing off my phone's screen.

Suddenly, it all makes sense. His lawyer, desperate to speak with me. Ryder refusing to acknowledge our nuptials or wear his ring. The articles detailing Mandi and Ryder's reconciliation all culminating in what I just witnessed in the lobby restaurant.

Ryder didn't miss me. He needed me in Charlotte to discuss a quick annulment, softened by a cash payout, no doubt, if I go away quietly.

This is the stuff of television reality shows, only this time, it *is* my reality.

My terrible reality.

Thankfully, the valet is able to have a cab by the entrance within moments, and I hop into the back. My destination? The airport.

Less than ten minutes later, my phone rings.

Ryder.

How quaint. He must have decided it's bad form to ignore your wife, even if you only plan on keeping her on the docket for another few days.

I silence his call, but he phones again. Likely Mr. Givens told him about my frantic state and he's hoping to smooth over this mess.

To think I thought he was different from all the other men. What a fool I am. He dangled the idea of true love in front of me and, like a fish with a shiny lure, I jumped at the chance.

I knew better, but I did it anyway. This is absolutely the last time I believe anyone with a penis.

By the fourth call, I realize he isn't taking silence for an answer. "Hello, Ryder." Funny how calm my voice sounds, considering the tempest brewing in my heart.

"Hey, beautiful. Sorry I missed your call. I was in the shower."

Liar, liar. I chew my lip, uncertain how to proceed. I want

to scream at him, rail at his myriad of lies, and demand answers. Hear him admit the wicked truth and force him to explain why he would want to hurt me, of all the people in his life.

But what's the point? I got my answer, in no uncertain terms. I saw it with my own eyes. His additional fibs are just icing on the proverbial cake.

So, as I've done since I turned eighteen and my father destroyed my family, I slip on my mask, presenting a strong front to the world. Besides, Ryder doesn't deserve my tears. "How was qualifying?"

"Finished first," he boasts, and I picture his arrogant ass strutting around his suite like a peacock. Likely strutting around for Mandi's benefit as well.

I did not need that visual.

"Of course you did. Ryder Gray never loses."

"I won with you. So, is my cheerleader going to be here tomorrow, rooting me on?"

I almost inquire to which woman he is referring, but I bite my tongue. "Please be careful. I worry about your safety. I worry about you." My words are the truth. Despite everything, he's someone I've known the majority of my life. My brother's best friend. A man who thinks a car moving over 200 mph around a track is the definition of excitement.

What the hell was I thinking? Talk about opposites.

"I'll be fine. I've got an angel protecting me now."

Swallowing back the nausea, I pass the driver some cash as he pulls up to the airport terminal. I need to end this call, and fast, before Ryder realizes where I am. "Get some rest. I have to get back to work."

"You're still on Long Island?" His voice reeks of disappointment, but I know it's all a front.

"I am, but I'm trying to get there. Don't lose hope." It's a lie. I lost hope almost an hour ago.

Why don't I admit I'm in Charlotte? Because then he'll spend the night embroiled in a row with me, which is stupid, pointless, and highly unsafe. Regardless of if he gets ten hours or ten minutes of sleep, Ryder will race tomorrow.

I refuse to be responsible for him being anything less than perfect. We will talk, but not now. Right now, I'm a ball of emotions and none of them are pretty. Give me a day or two, and I'll be back to my rational self. My heartbroken, never trust a man again, rational self.

Then, I'll let him have it with both barrels.

"I wanted to discuss something with you before the race, but... I didn't want to do it over the phone."

Of course not. Divorce is such a sticky topic. Much better suited for an in-person discussion.

"Will it keep? Can it wait until I'm there?"

"Sure. Just know that I have plans for us, Gigi. Big plans."

I'll bet he does.

Swallowing back tears and forcing a smile for the aggravated cab driver, I push open the door, blasted by the cacophony of noise. "Good luck tomorrow. I'll see you soon, Ryder."

"Not if I see you first—"

I click off before he can finish his sentiment, and immediately regret my decision. I didn't tell him I loved him or that I cared. Even though I know what he did, I hate the idea of him racing without that knowledge. Something about working around life and death every day that sinks into your soul. You never know when the last time will be the last time and you'd better let people know how you feel.

Even if they don't feel the same.

I dial his number again, struggling with my suitcase as I head for the ticket counter.

"You hung up."

"The call got disconnected. I love you, Ryder. Promise me you'll be safe."

"I promise. Thank you. I needed to hear that."

Blinking back tears, I end the call.

I know this is the last time I'll see Ryder, save for any dates with his lawyer, but at least he'll know what was in my heart.

It's all I ever had to give him, but apparently, it wasn't enough.

Not by a long shot.

~

I PEEL my eyes open as the sun streams through my blinds, a headache blasting through my skull.

I rarely drink—a glass of wine here or there—but any plans for sobriety flew out the window last night, after discovering Ryder with Mandi.

To top off an already banner evening, there weren't any available seats back to New York, so here I am, in a somewhat seedy motel, a bottle of vodka by my side with a quarter of the contents missing.

No wonder my damn head feels like it's going to explode.

Unfortunately, I have to get my ass up and moving. I snagged a flight back to Long Island this afternoon, and at the rate I'm going, it will take until boarding for me to feel human again.

Never mind my aching heart. I'll deal with her later... or not at all, as is my modus operandi.

Stumbling into the shower, I scald my body into submission, before sucking down a cup of coffee that ranks right up there with hospital brew.

But I barely taste the acrid liquid, my eyes instead glued to the television set. It's almost race time, and the crowd is gearing up to cheer on their favorite hometown hero. When the cameras scan the packed stands, I wonder if Mandi is there, rooting for her man.

He doesn't need me as a cheerleader, he's got her. Besides, I'm far more tempted to shove a pom-pom up his ass than wish him well at this point. Nothing too severe, perhaps a case of noxious gas to liven up his rekindled romance with Mandi.

My thoughts drift back to our weekend in Vegas when Ryder first proposed this cockamamie idea. He needed the good press, or so he claimed. Seems the truth was, he wanted to spark Mandi's jealousy.

In that regard, I suppose I served my purpose. A few well-placed articles about Ryder with another woman and his ex is eating out of the palm of his hand.

Could he have hired the paparazzi to stand outside that restaurant? Was that why he kissed me so openly? The events muddle together, and I can't make truth of any of them, save one.

My deal with Ryder ended the moment Mandi walked back into his life.

I still don't know why he asked me to marry him. I wasn't going to pressure him into any sort of commitment. Not my style. I expected we would go our separate ways once our sojourn to Barbados ended. Instead, he dropped to one knee and asked me to spend my life with him. Have a ton of babies with him. Be with him.

Me, being the lovesick fool, saw hearts and rainbows and screamed yes. For me, it was the greatest moment of my life.

For Ryder, it was a well-executed plan, knowing that if him being with another woman raised Mandi's ire, him marrying one would send her into a tailspin.

Finding out the marriage wasn't real has certainly sent *me* into one.

What other reason could he have? Obviously not love, as evidenced by his recent rendezvous with Mandi.

So, instead of a few fond memories of incredible sex on a tropical island, I now get to finagle a deal with his lawyer to earn back my independence.

This is why I never fall in love.

Love stinks.

One thing is for certain, his rich ass is footing the bill for any legal costs related to this annulment. I've wasted enough time and tears on the man.

A tear slides down my cheek, cutting through my emotional armor and revealing the caustic pain simmering under the surface. I hate what he did to me—the mind games, making me believe in him, making me believe in love. But what I hate most is how real it felt. Every look, every touch, felt genuine.

I've never met a man like that. A talented player in every sense of the word, both on and off the track.

With a grunt, I turn off the television. No point in watching the race, watching his beautiful, lying face light up when he wins yet again.

I have my own business to attend to—namely to finish packing and then beg my boss to take me back in that hell-hole of a position I was so overjoyed to escape. I loved the patients but the mismanagement of the clinic made working there like the seventh level of hell, and that was on a *good* day.

Then I get the added fun of finding a place to live since I

sublet my apartment to a friend's cousin for the remainder of my lease.

Add another line on my to-do list.

The throbbing in my brain refuses to back down, so I fill the tub and soak for an hour, desperate to get warm. Desperate to feel anything but this gnawing in the pit of my stomach that reminds me how my world is upside down, and it's all my fault. Ryder may be an asshole, but I believed him.

That's on me.

When there are no more tears to cry, I hoist myself from the tub, staring at my reflection and looking for answers that aren't going to come. My reflection thinks I'm a blooming idiot, too.

Time to head for the airport and back to my reality, or whatever term we want to use for this funhouse of nightmares. My phone rings, and I grab it, fully expecting yet another call from Mr. Givens.

It isn't Mr. Givens. It's Greg, and he's called twenty times.

That means one of two things, possibly both. Ryder won the race and Greg is gearing up for one hell of a celebration tonight, or my brother has learned of my brief marriage and impending annulment all in one fell swoop.

No doubt he'll have some choice words for us both once that debacle hits the airwaves.

Dialing my brother, I fall back on the mattress, a loud whoosh sliding from my lips.

Greg answers on the first ring. "Gigi, where are you? I've been calling for an hour."

I've heard my brother upset before, but there's something in his tone that strikes fear into my heart. "Why? What's wrong?"

"You don't know? Gigi, where are you? You need to get to Charlotte. Now."

"I'm in Charlotte."

"Get to St. Luke Hospital immediately."

I bolt upright, my blood pounding in my ears. "Are you okay? What happened?"

My brother's sobs break through my hangover haze. "Don't turn on the television, Gigi. Ryder has been in an accident."

CHAPTER 11
GREER

An hour later, I dash through the front entrance of St. Luke. I'm shocked the cab driver could understand me through my rash of tears, but he gave my hand a squeeze before proceeding into the snarled mess of the Charlotte parkways.

Greg told me to avoid watching any replays of the accident, but he should know me better after all our years together. I've seen the video a minimum of fifty times, each time more devastating to my heart than the last.

Ryder was in the lead as he pulled into pit row and it looked as if he would win the race. Another trophy in his gilded case. But then, as he pulled out, everything went wrong. His car jerked, and he didn't pick up speed. Instead, another driver slammed into him, upending Ryder's car and tumbling him like a rag doll down the track.

I can't watch beyond the moment of impact. My professional training is both a blessing and a curse. I don't want to know how dire the prognosis is until I'm by his side. All I know is that he's alive, and right now, that's all that matters.

The anger I feel regarding Ryder's betrayal? That will keep until he's better. Then, I'm serving up the ass-kicking of a lifetime for breaking me.

The hospital staff directs me to the Neuro ICU, and my heart sinks. That unit is reserved for critically ill patients will all manner of head and spinal injuries. You don't need a medical degree to know it doesn't bode well.

I rush off the elevator, which moved at a snail's pace and hurry to the waiting room. Inside, I find Greg, his head buried in his hands. I haven't seen that posturing since the day he discovered he could no longer race.

"Greg."

His head shoots up hearing my voice, and I see the tears brimming in his dark depths. Then I'm in his arms, his embrace so tight it constricts my breathing. "Thank God you're here, Gigi."

I grasp his face, trying to calm him. "How is he?"

"I don't know. They don't know. It's all my fault."

My brother slumps back into the chair and I scan the room for a doctor or nurse—anyone with more information than Greg. He tends to fall apart during times of family stress and Ryder is as close to family as they come.

My gaze lands on a lithe blonde seated away from the group. Mandi. It's a knife in the gut to know she's here, but I can't spare her the time or energy right now. I need information about Ryder's condition. Once I know he's stable and on the mend, I can make myself scarce.

Mandi will just have to understand. Greg and I had dibs on Ryder's heart long before she came into the picture.

"Are you Greer?"

Turning, I gaze into a handsome, chiseled face; one I recognize from all those racing magazines my brother devoured. "Yes. You're Mick Marsh."

"Just Mick works. When you address me by my full name, I figure I'm in trouble. Trust me, Rachel uses that tactic." He clears his throat, averting his gaze. "The doctors are running some tests. They don't know the extent of his injuries. At least they won't tell me anything."

That's not a surprise. Unless you're family, a hospital is a vault, no matter if you're Joe from down the street or the President. "What happened? I saw the accident but—" Words fail me as my voice breaks and Mick wraps an arm around my shoulder, giving it a squeeze.

"His tire came off coming out of pit row. Before he could get off the track, another driver struck him."

My gaze flits over to my brother, still hunched in his chair. No wonder he's beating himself up. Something happened on his watch, and he's carrying the weight of that failed responsibility. I need more details, but first, I need to know about Ryder. If nothing else, I'm still his wife, and that gives me certain legal rights, including his health status. "I need to speak with a doctor. I'll get some information for you."

"I'm sorry we had to meet this way. Ryder won't shut up about you."

I narrow my eyes at his words, wondering what in the world Ryder *has* said, considering recent events. But I don't get the chance as a doctor enters the waiting area.

"I'm looking for Mrs. Gray."

So much for Ryder keeping his marriage under wraps. I'll sort that later. "I'm Mrs. Gray." My gaze flits to the far side of the room where Mandi sits, gaze locked on mine. She may hold his heart, but legally, I'm his next of kin. I can get them the answers they desperately seek.

"Come with me, please. Mr. Gray is requesting you."

A breath whooshes from my lips as relief washes over

me. If he's requesting me, he's awake and lucid. All steps in the right direction. I follow the doctor into the unit, sucking in a lungful of oxygen to steel myself for what lies beyond that door.

"Come on. He's waiting for you." The doctor forces a smile, nodding toward the room.

There, lying in the bed is Ryder. He's covered in bruises and scrapes, but he's alive.

That knowledge damn near brings me to my knees.

"Mr. Gray, there's someone here to see you."

Ryder turns his head in the direction of the doctor's voice, but he doesn't make eye contact. Odd. "Gigi?"

Rushing to his side, I grasp his hand, noting how he still isn't meeting my gaze. "Hey, speed racer. How are you feeling?"

Ryder swallows, an audible noise in the quiet descending over the room. It's the kind of quiet that suffocates you, the same quiet I felt when my mother told us about my father's abandonment. "I can't see, Gigi."

My throat constricts as I blink back the tears, willing every ounce of strength I possess to move me past that moment. "What's his diagnosis?"

"Traumatic optic neuropathy," the intensivist replies, stepping to Ryder's bedside. "He was unconscious when he arrived, so we didn't realize there was any visual deficit until he woke up. Your husband told me you're a doctor?"

"I'm a nurse practitioner and I told Ryder never to call me a doctor in front of a doctor." I squeeze Ryder's hand, desperate to provide him reassurance. "Neurology isn't my specialty. What's the plan?"

"Many times, it rectifies on its own, once the swelling impinging the nerve resolves. To be on the safe side, I've ordered some tests to ensure the retina is attached and blood flow isn't compromised."

"When will that happen?"

"As soon as possible. There's no time to waste. But, he wanted a few moments to speak with you, so I'll take my leave and tell the nurse to send up transport."

Once the intensivist leaves, I put on my proverbial nursing hat. Ryder doesn't need a wife; he needs a friend who understands medicine. Adjusting his pillow, I try in vain to make him more comfortable. "Are you in pain?"

His eyes, those beautiful bright blue eyes, gaze past me into the distance. "Everything hurts. What's going to happen to me, Gigi?"

I want to lie to him. I don't want to tell Ryder the brutal truth about his condition. He needs hope. That's the fine line medical personnel tread every day. "They're going to perform some tests and find out how extensive the damage is to your eyes. From there, they'll develop a treatment plan."

"I'm going to get better, right?"

"Of course you are. You're Ryder Gray."

"Your voice is trembling. Gigi, don't lie to me. It's bad, isn't it?"

Stroking my hand across his scalp, I press kisses to his forehead and tell him the only truth I know. "We don't know yet. But they're doing everything they can to find out."

"You'll stay, right? Don't leave me alone."

The undercurrent of fear in his voice breaks me. "I can't go with you to the procedure, but I'll be in the waiting room. I won't leave you."

"Promise?"

"I promise. I'm here." I mean it, too. There's no way I'll leave his side now, not as long as he needs my help. It doesn't matter who he's in love with. Ryder Gray is my childhood friend, and I'll be damned if he spends one second thinking he's alone in this world. "Transport is here to take you for the testing. What should I tell everyone in the waiting room? Greg and Mick are both worried sick."

I don't mention Mandi. Ryder must know she's there.

"Tell them the truth. I'm not done fighting, not by a long shot." His fingers tighten around mine, pulling me closer. "I wanted to win for you."

I lean my forehead against his; the tears dripping off my nose. "You're always a winner to me, Ryder."

His hands grip my face, his breath hot against my skin. "I want to see your beautiful face, Gigi. If I see nothing else, I want to see you. Just you."

The tears fall in earnest now, sliding over his hands. "You will. Don't you give up."

"Promise you'll be here when I'm done?"

Pressing a kiss to his palm, I nod against his hand. "I promise."

As they wheel him out, the apprehension lines his face. Gone is the superstar facade, replaced with a man terrified by the thought of his future.

I have one job now—to protect him at all costs.

The moment I enter the waiting area, his mother rushes over, pulling me into a tight embrace. She must have just arrived at the hospital. "How is he?"

"He's awake and talking. Moving all of his limbs." I pause as Mick, Greg, and Mandi edge closer. Might as well fill everyone in at the same time. Let them know Ryder has only begun to fight. "He's lucid but scared. When he woke up, he couldn't see."

A collective gasp rises from the group.

"It's what is known as traumatic optic neuropathy."

"Will he regain his vision?" Mandi inquires, her face drawn.

Under normal circumstances, I'd claw her eyes out, so she could experience blindness firsthand. But that was before. Now, I only want to care for the man we both love. He begged me to stay. I made him a promise, one I intend to keep.

"They aren't sure. They're running tests to determine the extent of the damage. We'll know more later. Often, this type of thing resolves on its own."

Ryder's mother dissolves into tears, and I stroke her back, trying to offer a modicum of reassurance. Better if everyone sheds their tears now, because Ryder will need all their strength in the coming days.

After what feels like an eternity, a new doctor, a neuro ophthalmologist, appears. The initial diagnosis stands, but they're hopeful he might regain partial vision over time.

At this point, it's anyone's guess. The awful waiting game where the reach of medicine is overruled by the laws of nature.

The plan is high-dose steroids, with the possibility of surgery in the next couple of days, if he shows no improvement.

The doctor's words bring about another rash of tears from the group, save for me, who's desperate to return to Ryder's side. It's not that the temptation to break down isn't there, but what good will that do him? Ryder needs me to keep it together so he can fall apart. Then I'll put him back together, piece by piece.

Rushing to his bedside, I press my lips to his cheek, noting the slight smile at my caress. I'll give it to the man. He's stoic in the face of the unknown, his features a sea of calm. It might also be the effects of the sedative. "You spoke with the doctor?" he inquires.

"I did. They're hopeful—"

"Are you going to leave now?" Ryder cuts me off with a grimace.

One look at his face and I know to what he's referring. "Of course not."

"Right," he mutters, his sightless eyes peering at the ceiling. "Because being stuck with a blind man is what you always wanted, right Gigi?"

I slide my hands along his jaw. I know he can't see me, but he needs to feel the determination in my touch. The reassurance that I'm not going anywhere. "Hey, you're going to get better. I'm here to ensure that happens."

"What if I don't?"

"Then we'll figure it out together. You're not getting rid of me, Ryder Gray. Nice try, but it's not happening."

Finally, the hardened mask slides from his features as he cracks a smile. "You were always stubborn."

"You don't know the half of it." Am I terrified? Absolutely, but he will never see that side of me. The logistics, the brutal truth of his injury—that he will probably only regain partial vision, if he's lucky—is not a story I'm allowing anywhere near Ryder. Hope is the most powerful drug in the world, and he needs a plethora of it right now.

Besides, if there's anyone on the planet who can overcome this obstacle, it's my husband.

My husband. A pang of sadness overtakes me when that thought enters my head, but I push it away. Now is not the time for *that* discussion, either.

Ryder huffs out a breath, shaking his head. "I was winning. Everything was going so smoothly... until it wasn't. I don't know what happened."

He's not the only one who wants to know what occurred in those fateful moments. A talk with my brother is imminent. He'll know the specifics of the accident, be able to shed some light on the subject. "Mick has an investigative team looking into everything."

"I can't be done. Not like this. Not like this." Ryder's voice cracks, his hand trembling in mine.

How do you reassure someone their life is going to continue, despite such a debilitating injury? How do you convince them that despite limitations, they will laugh again? Find joy in their days? Have a reason to live when the only reason they had has been stripped from them?

I wish I knew the answer to any of those questions.

Instead, I dig deep, letting my sarcastic sense of humor bubble to the surface. "You be quiet. You're not done. You are many things, Ryder Gray—arrogant and overly confident among them—but you are no quitter. I sure as hell won't let you quit now."

That does it. A chuckle slips past his full lips. "You had to list all my strengths, didn't you, Gigi?"

"Hey, I knew you when. Don't forget that." I lean over him, pressing a kiss to his forehead. "Get some sleep. Your body needs the rest. I'll be in the waiting room if you need me."

His hand darts out, catching at my forearm. "I always need you. Don't forget that."

With a final kiss on his cheek, I return to the waiting room. Mick has left, no doubt, to get a jumpstart on the investigation and bring another driver up to speed. He loves Ryder, but this is a business and the show must go on.

Mandi, too, is nowhere to be found. I find it odd that Ryder never asked for her, even to question if she was at the hospital. But I'm no masochist. Until he brings her up, I'm sure as hell not mentioning her name.

Greg, however, hasn't moved from his chair, his head still buried in his hands as the guilt wafts off him. Time to find out what really happened.

"Greggo, let's get some coffee."

Without a word, he falls into step behind me, trailing me to the hospital cafeteria.

After directing him to a table, I order us some food. I'm no fool. We need to keep our wits and strength about us, or we'll wind up in a hospital bed, too. That's the last thing Ryder needs.

"Here. Black and thick as mud. Just the way you like it."

He accepts the drink, his hands gripping the mug as he stares into the dank liquid.

"I doubt the answers are at the bottom of that cup."

"I let him down, Gigi."

Grasping his hand, I give it a reassuring squeeze. "It was an accident, Greg. Accidents happen."

"The tire was loose."

I nod, uncertain where he's headed. "Like I said, accidents happen."

"I was in charge of tightening the tires. I thought I got it on there, but the second the car hit the pavement, I knew something was off."

My heart skips a beat at his words. "Wait a minute, you knew before he drove off?"

Greg shakes his head, his eyes red-rimmed from crying. "By the time I realized, he was gone. Before I could utter a word, he was hit."

"It's still an accident. You never meant for this to happen."

"It doesn't matter. He's blind, and it's all my fault. Do

you think a simple apology is going to fix this situation? It won't. Once he learns the truth, Ryder will hate me, and he has every right."

Kneeling by Greg's chair, I clasp his hands, forcing him to meet my gaze. "Ryder will never hate you. He trusts you. That's why he hired you."

Greg wrenches his hands from my grip, pushing himself to a standing position. "He almost died because of me. His racing career is likely over because of me. Trust me, Gigi, I'm no good to anyone."

My brother storms out the door, but I'm too exhausted to follow. Besides, it's fairly obvious Greg is in a self-destructive mode, blaming himself for Ryder's current predicament. His next stop? Likely the nearest pub, where he can drown his sorrows. After Dad left, that became his coping mechanism, his escape from reality.

The only saving grace is his drinking never interfered with his work, but it's still spiraling out of control. Once Ryder is on his way to recovery, I'll chat with Greg about reining in his habit and finding one a little less lethal to the body and soul.

Trudging back to the ICU, I check on Ryder. He's sleeping. Good. He'll need every ounce of strength. I collapse into a waiting room chair with a blanket offered by one of the nurses. Ryder's mother is asleep a few chairs down, her gentle snores echoing the exhaustion of the last twelve hours.

My eyes drift closed, but I can't relax enough to rest. Instead, Ryder's accident plays over and over in my head, the fear constricting my throat when I saw that mangled pile of metal and carbon fiber. I never want to experience that feeling again.

Even if Ryder never regains his sight, at least he's alive.

The idea of that man—that cocky, self-assured, gorgeous man—not on this planet is more than I can bear. Every fear I discussed with Ryder on our vacation screeches to the forefront of my brain, and I can't help but wonder if I somehow breathed it into creation by uttering my fears aloud.

Shaking off the notion and chalking it up to lack of sleep, I jump when my phone buzzes in my pocket. "Hello?"

"Greer? This is Mick. I'm sorry I didn't get a chance to say goodbye earlier."

"I understand. He's sleeping now."

"He needs the rest." Mick clears his throat, and a sense of foreboding drifts over me. "Look, I hate to lay this on you, considering the day we've all had, but I think you should know before the media gets hold of it."

Rubbing a hand over my brow, I wonder if he's going to mention my spur-of-the-moment nuptials. Bad timing, certainly, but the last thing Ryder needs on top of everything else is bad press. "You mean our marriage?"

"No," Mick scoffs, "although he knocked my ass sideways with that one. It's about the accident. It's standard to run a toxicology screen on the driver and pit crew after something of this magnitude occurs."

"Ryder was on something?"

"Not Ryder, but certain members of the pit crew tested positive for cocaine and alcohol. It's a hard and fast rule you don't imbibe before a race. That's just common sense, but a few members of the crew opted to toss that rule out the window, and here we are."

"Which members?" I barely manage the question as the blood pounds in my ears and my anger careens into the red.

The people hired to keep Ryder safe were working under the effects of drugs and alcohol. They held his life in their hands and didn't respect it enough to be sober.

"I can't disclose their identities yet, since there are legalities involved. But I wanted you to be prepared for the fallout when Ryder finds out. This is going to devastate him."

"Which is why you can't tell him," I argue, pacing lines into the waiting room carpet. "Mick, he does need to know, but not now. This news will only increase his stress level and impede healing. I'm begging you, don't tell him yet."

"Greer, the media is going to have a field day with this story. There's no way he won't find out."

"I can monitor what information he receives. I want him to have the truth, but not until he's stabilized. Please, can you hold them off for a few days?"

Silence echoes from the other end of the line before Mick releases an audible sigh. "I'll do my best. I understand your perspective and you're right, he doesn't need more stress."

"If he gets mad when you tell him, just blame me. He can't hate me forever. I won't let him."

Mick chuckles. "Now you sound like *my* wife. I'll be by tomorrow to check on him. Any changes, you can reach me at this number."

I collapse into the chair, my mind reeling from the news. This accident was likely preventable if Ryder's staff had only taken their damn jobs seriously. My thoughts flicker over to Greg and his earlier statements. He was certain Ryder would hate him.

What if Greg was one of the people who imbibed before the race? What if the alcohol clouded his brain, even for a second, resulting in Ryder's injury?

If my brother was involved, I'll never forgive him.

Worse, he'll never forgive himself.

CHAPTER 12
RYDER

I awaken with a scream stuck in my throat as I try in vain to claw my way out of the darkness enveloping me. But despite every effort, the blackness remains, even when I pat my eyes to ensure they're actually open.

When I realize they are, the memory of the crash floods back into my brain—the sudden jerk of the vehicle, followed by a sickening crack as my car tumbled end over end.

Then it all went black.

Permanently, it seems.

Voices edge closer, some of the medical staff reassuring me I'm safe, but I know that's a load of garbage.

I'm not safe. I'm blind. For how long, I don't know.

When I turn my head, I notice a slight demarcation between light and dark. That must be the window—another sunny Charlotte day. Beyond that graduated blur, there's nothing.

I'm no quitter, but this is one hell of a daunting challenge. This dark reality makes the Monaco Grand Prix look like a walk in the park.

A hand squeezes my shoulder, making me jump. "Sorry to startle you, Mr. Gray. My name is Nicole and I'll be your nurse today. Are you hungry? I have a breakfast tray for you."

I manage a nod, although I learned from the many meals eaten by my father's bedside that hospital food isn't winning any gourmet awards. Still, beggars can't be choosers, and for the first time since I can remember, I'm very much a beggar.

The nurse raises the head of my bed as I shift on the mattress, attempting to locate a comfortable spot.

No such luck.

With a sigh, I squint, struggling to identify anything when she places the food on my bedside table. But it's no use. I'm staring into a void, an endless black sea. Doesn't help that the aroma wafting off the tray is none too appetizing.

"I'll send in someone to help you," she offers, shattering my last vestiges of confidence with her words.

Twenty-four hours ago, I was Ryder Gray, king of F1 racing, with legions of fans clamoring for a moment of my time. Now, I'm being treated like a toddler who can't feed myself.

"I'll manage," I grit out.

"Are you sure? It's no trouble."

"I said, I'll manage." I sense her hesitation about leaving me, certain I'm incapable of performing this mundane task. My temper flares at the knowledge. "Can you leave me alone?"

"Here's the call bell, should you need us." She presses the cord into my hand before leaving me with my first task of the day.

I've been feeding myself for decades.

How hard can it be?

Five minutes later, as I'm covered in orange juice and

scrambled eggs, I have my answer. Tossing down my fork in disgust, I give up, having only managed to get two bites of food to my mouth in the melee.

"Hey," a familiar voice sounds out, "let me help."

Gigi. Just the sound of her voice soothes my frazzled nerves, even if I'm embarrassed as hell for her to see me in this state. "I told them I could do it."

"You sure showed them." I can hear her smirk, but I'm not in the mood for levity. Her hands pull away the bedside table and I feel her collecting the pieces of food I've tossed around my bed.

Mortification at its finest.

"That's better. I'll see if we can't get you a shower after breakfast." She dabs my face with a napkin, and I'm torn between laughing and screaming.

Is this what my life has become?

"I can't wait to see how I do in the shower."

"I'll be right there with you. You'll be fine."

"I'm pretty fucking far from fine, Greer." She doesn't deserve my anger, but my emotions are vacillating wildly with one constant—abject terror.

The man who's never known fear is absolutely terrified.

My wife seems undeterred by my emotional wall. Typical Greer. "It will take time, but you are going to be fine. Besides, hospital food isn't the cure for what ails you. So, I brought you something better. A spinach and tomato omelet, just the way you like it."

"Might as well toss it on me, like my first breakfast."

"I have a better idea." The mattress sinks next to me, only a moment before my nostrils are assuaged by two scents, both indelibly better than hospital chow. One is the subtle undertone of gourmet food. The other? The spicy amber scent Gigi wears.

The one that drives me wild in the best possible way.

"Open," she demands, and the mental image of my wife riding my cock slips away, replaced by the reality that she's not fucking me. She's feeding me.

"You don't have to do this."

"Your choice. You can keep going the way you were and waste three-quarters of this ridiculously expensive omelet, I can straddle your waist and force-feed you, or you can open your mouth and cooperate."

"Thanks, Nurse Ratched," I mutter, opening my mouth and releasing a groan when the flavors mingle on my tongue. "This is so much better than that hospital crap."

Ten minutes later, my belly is full and my mind calm. Calmer, anyway. Greer does that for me, and she's the only one who can.

"Better?"

"Much. Thank you."

Her lips dust across my cheek, and I'm tempted to request that she keep moving down. I may be blind, but I still have needs.

I need her in every possible way.

"I'm going to speak with the staff about getting you a shower. You still have dried blood on you from the crash. I'm also fairly certain there will be a line of nurses eager to assist with that task."

"I've got a nurse already."

"Damn straight." Her footsteps fade away and I fall back against the pillow, turning my face toward the only light in my world.

Well, the only light besides Greer.

She returns a few minutes later, triumphant in her quest, and within an hour, I'm feeling almost human again.

Emphasis on almost.

The blindness is a bitch. The myriad of scrapes and bruises? A bonus in this shit show.

Gigi took her time with me in the shower, her hands so gentle as they washed away the debris of the day before. Still, she seems to be holding back her affections, and I need them now more than ever.

I'm likely paranoid. It's less than twenty-four hours since I was involved in a massive wreck. Per the doctors, I'm lucky to be alive. Add in the fact that I can't see and my entire world is upside down.

Besides, she's here. That's all that matters. Over the top affections will come, all in good time.

"Feel better?" Greer asks, perching next to me in the bed. Thankfully, they changed the sheets while I was in the shower. The only thing worse than hospital food? Cold hospital food stuck to your bare ass. Trust me on this one.

Raising my hand in the direction of her voice, I sigh when her fingers close around it. "What am I going to do, Gigi?"

"Get better so you can go home."

"What then? I can't feed myself. How am I supposed to do this?"

"I told you. I'm here. I'll take care of you. Besides, I'm a nurse, so it's a lucky coincidence."

"When I mentioned that you're a sexy nurse, this is not what I had in mind."

Greer giggles, leaning over to steal a kiss. Hey, at least this time it's on the mouth. But before my hand can tangle in her dark locks, she pulls back, giving my hand an awkward pat.

What the fuck?

"Your doctor is here," Gigi murmurs. "Good morning, Dr. Levine."

Please let him have some positive news. "Hey Doc, what's the good word?"

"Are you okay with me speaking in front of your wife?"

"Obviously. She can translate what you're saying into English."

He chuckles, but I detect something else in his voice—hesitation.

Shit.

"The good news is that there doesn't appear to be any bleeds or swelling in the brain, beyond the optic nerve. That being said, I had hoped the steroids we started last night would relieve some of the pressure, but it's still too early to tell."

"Tell what?"

"How much vision you can expect to regain."

"I can detect brightness this morning." My words fly like bullets from my mouth as I flounder to escape the sinking feeling surrounding me.

"That's a step in the right direction, and I believe there's a good chance you'll regain more vision in the coming days or weeks."

I hold up my hand, cutting him off as my world crumbles around me. "I need all my vision back."

"One step at a time, Mr. Gray. At this point, we're cautiously optimistic that you should regain partial vision. What that means exactly, we can't be sure. But we will continue the steroids while observing you for the next couple of days. Precautionary measure. Since you're stable, you'll be moved to a regular room, where you can begin working with occupational therapy."

"What the hell does that mean?" These terms fly at me, but I'm unable to wrap my mind around anything beyond the idea that this dark hell might last forever.

"The occupational therapist has special training to help people learn to navigate—"

"Without sight." I spit out the words, hating the taste of them. Hating the sound of them even more. "I can't live without my eyes, doctor. We need to do more."

"They're doing everything they can." Greer strokes my forearm, but I shake her off. The last thing I need is her coddling.

"No, they aren't, or I'd have my sight back. There has to be more we can do."

Dr. Levine clears his throat, no doubt aggravated by my staunch stance. "Surgical intervention is an option, but not one we take lightly, Mr. Gray. I don't think you're a good candidate for it, regardless."

My heart pounds as his words sink in. I can't wrap my mind around what they mean for my career, my life, and my future. "I can't race if I can't see. I don't want to live if I can't race."

A soft cry escapes Greer's lips as she wraps her arms around me. But I don't need pity. What I need is a damn cure. "If this is about money, I have plenty. I'll pay for whatever experimental treatment you have in your bag of tricks."

"I wish money were the only obstacle, but it's not that simple, Mr. Gray. Let me worry about your treatment plan. You need to focus on rest and recovery. The stress isn't helping your situation."

Now the bastard tells me.

Dr. Levine continues on a few minutes more, but I've tuned out. I'm tired of half-truths and unknowns.

The tension is palpable in the room after the doctor leaves, my anger rising with each passing minute.

"Do you want to listen to some music? I can annoy you with Elvis tunes."

I know she's trying, but every cheery word out of Greer's mouth only makes me angrier. "I want you to leave."

"Ryder, I know this is scary, but you need to stay positive. It's so important."

With that, my anger breaks free of its chains as I hurl my call button off the bed. "Am I bothering you with my negativity, Greer? Putting a crimp in your day?" Punching the side rail, I release a string of obscenities. "I don't want to live like this."

"Please don't say that. You could have died yesterday."

"If this is what my life looks like now, I wish I had."

Her hands wrap around mine, but it does nothing to soothe the beast raging inside me, and her muffled sobs only increase my angst. I don't have the bandwidth to take on Greer's pain.

I have enough of my own.

"Get out, Greer. Don't worry, I won't hold it against you. This is not what you signed up for."

"I'm not leaving you, Ryder. I told you that yesterday and I'll keep telling you until you believe me."

"Get out," I bellow, my voice sounding off the walls. Within moments, footsteps enter the room. No doubt it's the nursing staff, wondering what the hell is transpiring. "Leave me alone, Greer. I beg of you." It's all I can manage, my words catching in my throat as I turn my face toward the wall.

I hold back the agony until the door closes and I have my wish.

I'm alone with the darkness. My own impenetrable fortress of solitude.

∼

I AWAKEN A FEW HOURS LATER. At least that's my guess by the lack of light surrounding me. It must be evening, or close to it. Through my hazy memories, I recall being moved to a different room because I was stable, as the doctor termed it. After the emotional breakdown earlier today, that might not be the most appropriate term.

At least I feel a bit better, although it might be the lingering effects of the sedative. Yep, I'm that guy.

Shifting in the bed, I fumble for the call bell. I need to speak with Greer, apologize for biting her head off earlier. She's only trying to help, and I know this is hell for her, too. If I'm not careful, she'll race out of my life permanently.

I'd hate that more than the blindness.

"May I help you, Mr. Gray?" a voice asks through the call system.

"Can you see if my wife is around, please?"

"Certainly, sir."

"I guess I'm not good enough anymore."

My head jerks at the unexpected female voice to my right. "Mandi?"

My first thought? Why the hell is she here? The second? How different her voice is from Greer's. My wife's voice washes over me like the warm Caribbean ocean—enticing and beckoning. Mandi's voice slices through my thoughts like a cheese grater.

Heels clack across the floor, and I flinch when her hand strokes my scalp. "You didn't think I could leave here without checking on you, did you?"

Leaning away from her touch, I grimace. What I think is she's intent on making waves, particularly after our chat the other night. Let's just say Mandi was none too thrilled to learn how invested I am in my marriage or how much I adore my wife.

I thought she got the hint.

I thought wrong.

"I'm doing swell, as you can tell by the hospital bed I'm in." With each and every word, my volume increases, and I stop myself, not wanting a repeat of earlier. At this rate, they'll throw my ass in the loony bin before the end of the day.

"I'm only trying to help, Ryder. You don't need to be so hateful."

"Everyone is trying to help," I mutter, releasing a heated sigh. "I'm sorry for my temper. It's been a rough twenty-four hours."

"I know, and I feel awful for you. I wish I could make it better, make you better, but I can't handle this situation."

A bark of laughter flies from my mouth. She's joking, right? What the hell does *she* have to handle? Time to break out the big guns and kill her with sarcasm. "Consider yourself lucky we broke up. Otherwise, you'd be stuck in this situation."

I expect her to retort with a biting comment, but instead, she dusts a kiss across my forehead. "Maybe when you're all better, we *can* revisit the idea of reconciliation. The whole shebang—marriage, kids."

Once again, I jerk my head from her grasp, wishing she would grant me some space. I have two choices, continuing this inane discussion or smile and nod my agreement as I usher her out the door. "Good to know."

"I'll be in Europe for the next couple of weeks, doing that promotional tour, but I'll call you. Check on your progress."

Biting my tongue to keep from biting her head off, I offer a stiff jerk of my chin. "Have fun."

"Bye, Ryder," Mandi coos, pressing her mouth against

mine in an unwarranted and unwelcome advance. Mandi's heels click across the room but pause. "Hello, Greer."

My heart sinks, wondering what my poor wife heard, or worse, what she witnessed. "Gigi?"

It's the longest seconds of my life, waiting with outstretched hand until I feel Gigi's warm fingers enclose mine. Then I can breathe again.

"I'm here, Ryder. Mandi has gone." Although Greer's voice is even, there's a lack of feeling to her words, as if she's holding back all emotion.

"I wasn't expecting her. She surprised me."

"That makes two of us."

Okay, my wife is definitely not happy. Time to make amends. "I'm sorry you had to see Mandi. I know how it looks—"

"Doesn't concern me," she grinds out, her voice low. "What concerns me is you getting well. That's what I'm here for, considering she's too busy."

The last part of her statement is whispered, barely audible, but I hear every word. My hearing is highly acute, a damn miracle after all my years of racing. And those words make my entire body tense. "Are you angry? I'm sorry for before. I shouldn't have yelled at you—"

Greer fluffs my pillow but makes no move to touch me further. "It's fine. You have a ton to process. Besides, do you honestly think you're the first patient to yell at me?"

Now my back is really up. I'm her husband, not her patient. "What is that supposed to mean?"

"Only that you can't scare me off. I told you that before."

But that isn't what she means. I feel the emotion pulsating behind her calm facade, as palpable as a heartbeat. "Gigi—"

Once again, she cuts me off. "There's a cafe across the

street. I thought I'd grab us some dinner. Does that sound good?"

A knock sounds at the door, only a moment before a familiar voice breaks into my and Greer's moment. "Hi, I dropped by for a visit. Am I interrupting anything?"

Yes, Mick, you actually are.

But my wife is all too happy to dead our conversation. "Hi, Mick. I'm heading to the cafe for some food. Would you like anything?"

"I'm good, thanks." The chair legs scrape against the floor as Mick plops down by my bedside. "How are you feeling?"

"Blind as a fucking bat."

"Greer said they're considering upping your medication to see if there's any effect. I like her, Ryder. Hold on to her."

"I'm trying," I mutter, my mind focused on my earlier conversation with Greer. It's so tricky to distinguish emotions when I've always relied on visual cues. "She's been distant since the accident. Likely rethinking her decision to marry me."

"That's a load of bullshit. Greer isn't the type to cut and run. I can see it in her face. She'll roll up her sleeves and get down in the mud with you."

Despite Mick's reassurances, I'm not so certain. Greer is highly affectionate, as evidenced by our ridiculous displays of loved-up PDA in Barbados, but since her arrival in Charlotte, she's held me at arm's length.

Stop with the paranoia, Ryder. She's here, and that's all that matters.

Time to change the topic. Besides, I have questions, and Mick may have the answers I seek. "Any leads in the investigation? Do we know what the fuck happened out there?"

The silence rings out like a church bell, save for the

tapping of Mick's foot against the linoleum. I know the man well enough to pick up on the agitation. "Man, I don't want to have this conversation. Greer asked me to wait—"

"What?" I interrupt, sitting up in the bed. "What the hell are you talking about? What do you know? What does Greer know?"

The chair grates against the floor, and I can tell by the change in volume that Mick is now pacing the room. Wonderful.

"Mick, don't you dare hide information from me. This is my career on the line. My life."

"Shit," Mick swears, falling down into the chair again. "I suspended the pit crew."

What the hell? The hair on the back of my neck stands on end as I mutter one word. "Why?"

"It seems certain members of the pit crew decided it would be a good idea to go out partying the night before the race. A few of them tested positive for cocaine and alcohol. They all swore it wasn't a factor, and they were on their game, but I don't give a crap what excuses they have, considering my star driver is now blind because of an accident on their watch."

I grab my head with my hands, trying to make sense of the situation. Why the hell would they do this? Why take this chance? Why risk my life? "Was Greg with them?"

"He was, although he tested clean."

"Doesn't matter. He broke the damn rules and risked my life in the process."

"Greg says he was there to usher everyone back to their rooms. Claims he gave them all hell, but as the new guy, they weren't listening to him. I'm sorry, Ryder. Greer wanted me to wait to tell you because she worried the stress would make your condition worse."

My blood boils in my veins as the situation becomes clear. I might be a blind bastard, but I'm not a dumb one. Even I can see what's happening here. "You fired everyone?"

"They're suspended, but they know they won't be asked back. I also let them know that there's a good chance of a lawsuit."

"Good. Make sure their lives are as fucked as mine," I seethe, jerking my arm away when Mick squeezes my shoulder. "And as for my *wife*," I spit out the words, "you can send her back in. I want to speak to her. Alone."

"Don't be angry at Greer. She was only trying to protect you."

"Not hardly. She's protecting Greg. Do me a favor? Open that drawer and take out the jewelry box."

Mick clears his throat but obliges my request. "Is this her ring?"

With a final lock, my emotional wall cements. "Not anymore. Hold on to that until I can sell it. Please send Greer in."

"Ryder, I know you're mad, but—"

"Send. Her. In."

"I love you, man. You know that, right? Greer loves you, too." Another squeeze of my shoulder, a show of brotherly camaraderie, but I say nothing.

I'm saving my energy and my anger for my wife.

∽

A DELICIOUS AROMA fills my nostrils, but I'm like a bull in front of a red flag—furious and ready to charge the moment Greer enters the room.

"I got you a pastrami sandwich. You always liked those when we were kids."

"Put it down and leave."

"What? Don't you want dinner?"

"What I want, is you gone. You think you're so clever, don't you Greer? Even got me to marry you without a prenup. Smart move. I should have known you were just like the rest of them."

"What the fuck are you talking about?" Her voice is a strangled whisper, the emotion evident. "I don't want your money, Ryder. I never did."

"Why are you really here?" I hold up my hand, cutting her off before she can answer. "Don't lie, either. Mick told me all about your bastard brother and the rest of the pit crew trying to kill me. He also mentioned how you begged him to stay silent on the matter. He claims you were trying to protect *me*—"

"I was. I knew the stress would be detrimental to your healing."

"But lies and false sympathy were going to help? That's all this is, right?" I motion blindly around the room. "That's why you're here, doting on me, isn't it? Trying to save your brother from the ramifications he damn well deserves? Well, you can take your sweet nurse act and shove it up your ass. I want you gone. We're done."

Her fingers close around my hand, but I jerk away as if I've been burned. "I'm sorry I didn't tell you. I thought it would be better if we waited until *you* were better. But that's not why I'm here, Ryder. I love you and I want to help you, but you keep shutting me out."

"If you loved me, you wouldn't have lied to me. Now, you're shut out for good. Get out."

Her sobs are like bullets, but my anger shields me from her emotional onslaught. All I can feel, all I can process, is the bottomless fury that the love I thought I found is nothing more than a lie. An act of pity for a broken man and a last-ditch effort to protect her family.

Fuck pity and fuck Greer. I'll be damned if I become a charity case.

"I'll be in the waiting room," Greer manages between sniffles. "I'll leave your food here."

The bag crinkles next to me, but I reach for it, tossing it across the room. "Get out, and don't ever come back."

After what seems forever, I hear the door close.

She's gone.

One down, one to go.

Paging the nurse, I request three things—clean up the food now littering the floor, ban Greer from stepping onto the unit, and dial Greg's number.

Then I request privacy, although I'm certain to get loud enough for patients in the next unit to hear.

"Hey brother, how are you?"

"Blind, thanks to you and my pathetic excuse for a pit crew. Was it worth it? Those fucking beers you can't live without? Were they worth ruining my life?"

"I didn't drink that night, Ryder. I swear. My test was clean."

"There hasn't been a day when you've said no to alcohol."

Greg is silent for a few beats, and the darkness threatens to suffocate me. "You're right. I have a problem, and your accident made me realize I need to deal with it. I signed myself into rehab and I leave in the morning, but I swear on my life, I was stone-cold sober during the race."

"What you are is jealous. You couldn't stand it. I made it and you didn't."

I expect him to fly off the handle, but he's calm. Achingly calm. "I am jealous, but I would never—*never*—put you in danger. I've always been proud of you and I hate that this happened. I feel responsible—"

"You are responsible," I bellow, my fist making contact with the side rail. "Mick told me he put the crew on indefinite suspension. You need to leave my house immediately. I never want to speak to you again."

Ending the call, I chuck my phone across the room, the agony of silence now an unbearable roar.

I'm alone in the dark and the thoughts swirl, blacker by the second. I believed in Greer. I believed in her love. The one woman I thought would save me, the woman I thought would love me for a lifetime, never loved me at all.

Oh, she would have stayed, but only out of a sense of obligation to tend to me since her brother had broken me. That's the way Greer is, always cleaning up Greg's messes.

Now, I'm just another mess.

That explains her lack of affection since my accident. The emotional distance. Greer no longer wants me, but she'll play the part, knowing how bad it would look if she left me at my lowest.

I saved her the trouble. I kicked her out before she could leave.

Before she *did* leave.

CHAPTER 13
GREER

I stare at the number on my caller ID. I don't recognize it, but with a Long Island area code, it's likely one of my former patients. A patient I don't have patience for right now.

I've been in Charlotte for two weeks, trying to figure out my next move after Ryder chucked me from his life. It might seem pathetic, but I won't leave him.

How can I? Despite his terrible treatment of me, I love him and I know he's hurting. I know he's terrified. I also know if he'll take down the wall of anger for one damn minute, he'll realize I only want to help him.

Ryder is currently at rehabilitation, learning to live unsighted in a sighted world. He's banned me from having any access to him, but I left my name and address with the nursing staff, in case he changes his mind.

I'm not even sure what I've done, save for withholding information about the pit crew until we had *all* the information. I didn't do it out of any malicious intent. I just wanted to protect him. Everyone in the world wants a piece of Ryder Gray, and all I want to do is shield him from the onslaught.

I thought that's what I was doing.

I thought wrong.

Meanwhile, I'm the one who should be livid. He's the one carousing with his ex, not me. Yet, somehow, I'm the bad guy.

Perhaps I should take the hint and leave. Call it a day. But I'm nothing if not stubborn, so here I sit, waiting in a cheap motel room for a phone call that isn't coming. Waiting for a man to love me who told me, in no uncertain terms, that he didn't.

Perhaps I'm more stupid than stubborn.

A knock sounds at the motel door, and I swing it open with a sigh, expecting to see housekeeping with clean linen. Instead, Lorna, Ryder's mother, stands on the stoop, a bag of food in her hand and a rueful expression on her lips. "May I come in?"

Wonderful. Now I'm going to hear it from her, as well. Waving her into the room, I direct her to the sad excuse for a dining area. Then I sit, feeling a bit like a prisoner awaiting her fate.

"You look like you could use this," she murmurs, sliding the cup of coffee across the table. "What happened, Greer? Why aren't you with Ryder? Why are you here in this, forgive me for putting it this way, seedy motel when Ryder's house sits empty? Well, I'm there, but there's more than enough room. The place is gigantic."

"Trust me, he wouldn't want me there. How is he?"

"Ryder is many things right now—belligerent and angry among them. The rehab nurses assure me this is normal behavior."

My heart clenches at the thought of his fear about this

unknown, and unwelcome, new world. "It is normal. He's scared about his recovery and what life looks like for him now. The anger will subside, not at me, but toward the world in general."

"That's why I'm here, to get to the bottom of this mess and get you two patched up."

"Trust me, that won't happen," I groan, planting my head on the table. "I'm sorry he involved you in our mess. My mess, I suppose. I know what I did was wrong, but I did it to protect him. That's all I want to do, Mrs. Gray."

"Call me Mom. What exactly did you do?"

"Mick discovered some of the pit crew was inebriated during the race, and he told me while Ryder was still in ICU. He wanted to tell Ryder then, but I asked him to wait until he was stable and knew for certain what happened. Why upset him without all the facts, right? So very, very wrong. He thinks I'm trying to protect Greg, which is not true. If Greg was involved, then he needs to be punished."

"He's calmed down about that, especially after his doctor agreed with your take on the situation. That's not why he's angry, though."

Wiping my eyes, I take another swig of my coffee. "There's another reason? Wonderful."

"Call it a mother's intuition, but I think he fears the only reason you planned to stay by his side is because you feel sorry for him."

Sputtering my drink, I grab a napkin to mop up the mess. "What in the world? I *do* feel sorry for him, but that has nothing to do with why I wanted to stay. I adore that man, with every breath in my body. But it doesn't matter. Ryder won't speak to me or see me. He's banned me from the rehab."

"So he informed me. He's being petulant, but that's

because he's so desperately hurt by the idea that what you had wasn't real."

For the first time during the conversation, my anger flares. I'm tired of taking it on the chin for Ryder. He's hardly innocent. "Trust me, it wasn't. I caught him and Mandi together. Twice."

Lorna's brow furrows. "When was this?"

"The night before the accident, I flew in to surprise him. When I got to the hotel, I saw them together. They were holding hands and talking. Then in the hospital, I walked in on them kissing." The tears stream down my cheeks, no matter how often I wipe them away.

Lorna leans back, a sigh escaping her lips. "I'm certain there's more to that story, but I agree it looks bad. I know Ryder adores you. Mandi never came close and once he had a chance with you, that was it for him."

"Doesn't look that way from my end."

"Did you confront him about what you saw?"

Sighing, I down another sip. "I planned on it, but I needed a few minutes to gather my thoughts. I was so out of sorts after walking in and seeing her lean over him, their lips pressed together. So, I decided to get us dinner and give me a chance to calm down and try to rationalize everything. I'm a really rational person. Then I got back, and he chucked his sandwich at me and told me to get out of his life. The worst part? Even after *everything* I saw, I never planned on leaving. At least not until she got her scrawny ass back here to take care of her man. I promised him I wouldn't leave. I keep my promises."

"He's not her man. He's always been yours, Greer."

"But he's not. Don't you see? He kicked me out of his life. Somehow, I became the bad guy and I'm supposed to know why. So trust me when I say he doesn't love me. Not now, not ever."

I adore Ryder's mom, but I need her to go. An emotional breakdown is imminent, and every passing second leads me one step closer to the meltdown.

"Something happened last night, which solidifies his true feelings. In my opinion, at least. I was at his bedside, and he awoke from a nightmare. He has so many of them now."

"Nightmares are common after a traumatic injury, particularly one involving the eyes."

"So the nurses said, but that's not my point. He called out for you, Greer. Kept calling out for Gigi, and it took everything in me to calm him down. Once he was fully awake, he still asked for you. I had to remind him he told you to leave. The look on his face, the realization that you were gone, it broke my heart." Lorna reaches across the table, grasping my hands. "Will you do me a favor?"

"Anything." I mean it, too. I'll help this woman in any way possible, especially if it will be of benefit to Ryder.

She grabs a pen and paper, jotting down an address. "Meet me here tomorrow afternoon."

"Where is this?"

"Ryder's house. He's coming home tomorrow."

Sliding the paper back across the table, I shake my head. "That's a bad idea. He hates me."

"He loves you and he needs you now, more than ever. Greer Hammond, I mean Greer Gray, you've always been fearless. Don't quit on me now."

Perhaps I'm looking for a reason to be near him, but something in Lorna's eyes forces me to believe in myself again. Believe in my ability to help Ryder, even if he's too embarrassed to ask. "I'll stop by to help get him settled."

"Settled? No dear, you're moving into your new home."

I launch away from the table as if it's on fire. That is *not* part of the plan. "He definitely won't go for that idea."

"He needs a nurse. I'm hiring you. That way, you two can work through this nonsense and get busy giving me a grandchild."

"Great. Another job," I mutter under my breath.

She skews her mouth, staring at me. "Whatever do you mean?"

"Nothing." No point in getting into it with his mother. No doubt she'll have both our heads for acting on such a ridiculous proposition. "Just the second time I've been offered a... unique assignment."

"Well, it's my way of interfering in my son's life and ensuring he's reunited with the woman he loves. A woman who, judging by the tears she's crying, loves him just as much. Besides, I'm his mother. He can't disown me."

"What about Mandi?"

Lorna smirks, shaking her head. "Trust me, he doesn't want Mandi. Her name has never come up. Unlike yours." She grasps my hands, and I feel the energy coursing beneath her skin. The determination to repair what Ryder and I have driven asunder. "My son swore off marriage, and believe me, I bugged him enough about the idea. He told me he would only get married for true love. True, unquenchable love were his exact words. He married *you*. He doesn't want Mandi."

God, I want to believe her.

With a sigh, I weigh my options. I can continue to sulk here or I can risk Ryder's wrath. At least with the latter option, I'll be of some use. If he doesn't kill me first. "I'm still not convinced. I've never seen Ryder so angry before. But, if it will help him, how can I say no?"

"So, you're in?"

Lorna opens her arms to me, and I don't waste a second falling into her embrace. She's right. I'm no quitter, especially when someone I love needs me. And Ryder, even if he'd rather spit nails than admit it, needs me more than ever. "I'm in, but I'm warning you. He's going to be furious with us both now."

"I'll handle my son. See you tomorrow."

∼

Lorna called last night to verify the plan was still in place. She mentioned how Ryder had spoken about me again during dinner and our recent trip to Barbados. In particular, a beach we loved frolicking on during our stay.

Thankfully, she couldn't see the flush crawling up my cheeks, because we did a hell of a lot more than frolic on that beach.

Now, I'm a bundle of nerves as the limousine pulls up Ryder's driveway. I arrived early at his palatial home, but it took me fifteen minutes to will up the courage to enter the gate code and drive onto the premises.

To say I'm a bit out of my element is an understatement. The sprawling Mediterranean mansion more closely resembles a resort than a home, complete with manicured gardens, walking paths and a lagoon-style pool just visible from the front entrance.

I beat the limousine driver to the rear door, pulling it open and steeling myself for the inevitable argument with my husband. As soon as Lorna helps Ryder from the car, I place my hand on his forearm in an effort to lessen the shock. "Hi, Ryder."

So much for that idea. His nose scrunches before a

grimace crosses his handsome face. "What are you doing here, Greer?"

"She's here to help," Lorna replies, shooting me a grin brimming with confidence I don't feel. "I have to fly home, so she's resuming her role as your wife."

"I don't need her," he mutters, those brilliant blue orbs aimed toward the ground.

Taking a step back, I throw up my hands with a helpless shrug. See? I knew he didn't want me here. Absence has definitely not made his heart grow any fonder—at least not where I'm concerned.

"Don't let him get to you. His bark is worse than his bite. He's being difficult, but he knows he needs your help." Lorna maintains a low tone, aimed for me, but her son and his acute hearing catch every word.

"You can leave too, Mom."

"I plan on it. In less than an hour, in fact."

We can stand on the driveway all day, arguing over nonsense, or we can focus on getting the man settled into his home. Suddenly, determination overtakes uncertainty. His mother is right. Ryder is terrified. Angry that his world has been stripped from him with no guarantee of what that means for his future.

From his point of view, he no longer *has* a future.

It's my job to prove that he does.

Ryder jerks away from his mother's steadying hand but doesn't make it three steps before tripping over the edge of the stair.

In a flash, I catch him, pulling his arm around my shoulder and setting him back to rights. But instead of appreciation, he glowers at me. "I can do it, Greer."

"I know you can. Just think of me as a backup." Giving his hand a squeeze, I will a smile from him, but it's not happening. "I know you're angry, but could you let me explain before you hurl yourself onto the steps?" Part of me wonders if he'll recall his sarcastic comment to me that New Year's Eve, as he grabbed me from tumbling to my death on a Manhattan sidewalk.

The realization flashes across his face, complete with the hint of a smile, before the scowl takes over once again, and he grunts out a reply. At least he isn't fighting me as I direct him inside, settling him on the couch.

Glancing around, the unease sinks in. I'm way out of my element. This is by far the most expensive home I've ever been in, every inch screaming luxury, from the frescoed ceilings to the high-end leather couches.

I'd be ill at ease on a good day as a welcome guest. That Ryder doesn't want me anywhere near him only ups the ante on the discomfort.

Lorna pulls me into the kitchen, handing over Ryder's medications and therapy schedule. "They're coming tomorrow at ten. He likely won't cooperate, but they said this isn't their first rodeo with difficult patients."

"I promise I'll take care of him, even though he doesn't want me to. He doesn't want me," I manage, those damn tears backing up again.

Grasping my chin, she forces me to meet her gaze. "Love him with that fierce love I know you feel. Take care of my son. No one can do it like you."

With a final goodbye, she walks out the door, suitcases in tow.

The woman just deserted me with a man who can't stand me. Let the good times roll.

Then again, maybe she's right. Maybe all Ryder needs is some time to calm down.

"You can leave, too," Ryder mutters from the couch.

Maybe not.

"I'm not leaving."

"Why are you still in Charlotte? I told you to leave over a week ago."

"And I told you over a week ago that I wasn't leaving. It's not happening, Ryder. You're not the boss of me." I cross my arms over my chest and although he can't see the gesture, I know he can feel the energy. I'm an immovable mountain. "Are you hungry?"

Ryder stands, his hands stretched out in front of him, desperately searching for anything familiar. "I'm going to bed."

"It's two in the afternoon."

"Does it matter? Not like I have a life anymore." He steps forward, knocking his shin against the coffee table, a hissed curse flying from his mouth.

With a resigned huff, I realize I have two options: continue fighting him or let him win this round and focus on the long game. Moving to his side, I grab his arm, feeling him tense against my touch. "Come on. I'll help you to bed."

∼

IT'S BEEN A WEEK. In that week, Ryder hasn't said more than ten words to me, with the exception of a variety of grunts and growls.

He also hasn't left the bedroom, nor has he showered. His beard and hair are grown out and unkempt and his clothing can stand up on its own.

The only saving grace is that he's learned to navigate his master suite, so at least he isn't shitting in a box by the bed.

I've stayed out of his way, at his behest, only daring to check on him when I'm delivering his food tray or the stray moments when exhaustion overtakes him, and he sleeps. Then, I slip to his side, quiet as a mouse, the helplessness squeezing my heart as I gaze upon him, desperate to be of value but feeling more useless with each passing day.

He's refused every therapy visit, but they promise they'll continue to drop by in the hopes he changes his mind. Hell, at this point they're bringing me coffee and words of encouragement.

God knows I need both.

I know Ryder is hurting. He's scared. He's also built a wall a mile thick around himself, blocking out everyone, including the people who love him. Especially the people who love him.

But I soldier on, though I'm not sure if it's stubbornness or stupidity at this point.

In the evenings, I sit by Ryder's pool, though I don't dare swim. I know I'm not welcome, and the last thing I need is him hearing me having any semblance of fun. That's why the television has remained off, as well. I fill my downtime researching everything I can find about his condition or cleaning his house from top to bottom.

Hell, even his housekeeper commented on how the place sparkled during her last visit.

Jillian gives me updates every few days on Greg's progress through rehab. Ryder's accident threw my brother for a loop, along with his childhood friend cutting him from his life. Apparently, Ryder now detests the entire Hammond clan.

Mick has also stopped by a couple of times, although Ryder refuses his visits, as well. But he's offered me support, which I desperately need. I've worn down over the last week. I'm exhausted and sick to my stomach most days, no doubt because of the enormous stress.

That's also likely why my period is late.

Stress.

In one of my two jaunts out of the house, I grabbed a test on impulse. Now, if I could only find the guts to use it.

After staring at the box for the better part of an hour, I snatch up the test and rush to the bathroom. I'm still on the toilet when a resounding crash sounds upstairs, and I chuck down the test, taking the stairs two at a time to Ryder's room.

Bounding inside, I note the glass of water I set on the bedside table is now in a million pieces on the other side of the room.

Wonderful.

"What in the world happened?" I ask the question aloud, although I don't expect an answer, since Ryder hasn't spoken directly to me in the last several days.

"I'll tell you what happened. Mick and the team are headed for Europe. Continuing the circuit without me. My life is over."

Willing my breath and mind to settle, I attempt to think of something—*anything*—that won't further agitate him. "I'm sorry."

"For what, Greer? Using me? Lying to me? Being here? So many choices, aren't there?"

So much for not agitating him. With a huff, I walk over to the pile of shattered glass. Best to focus on my task and stay out of his way. Glancing over my shoulder, I see his sightless gaze locked in my direction; the anger wafting off him.

My finger rips across a shard, and I drop it with a yelp. "Ouch. Shit."

"What happened?"

"I cut myself," I mumble as I assess the damage. Thankfully, it won't need stitches, but the sucker sure is bleeding.

"Don't move from the bed, please. There's still broken glass but I need to bandage my finger."

"Gigi?" For the first time since he kicked me out of his life, he uses my nickname, and his voice is softer, lacking the harsh edge.

"Yes?"

"I wasn't thinking when I threw the glass. Are you okay?"

"I'll be fine. Nothing a bandage won't fix. I'll be back in a minute."

A small smile crosses my face as I descend the stairs and head for the first aid kit tucked into the main floor bathroom. It's hardly a declaration of romance, but I'll take it.

Then my gaze falls on the pregnancy test, tossed aside in my haste, and my breath catches, the cut on my finger long forgotten.

Grabbing up the test, I stare at the results in disbelief.

I'm not stressed.

I'm pregnant.

CHAPTER 14
GREER

I'm keeping my wits about me.

To be fair, I'm falling apart on the inside, but externally, everything appears dandy.

I returned to Ryder's room last night with his dinner tray before cleaning up the remaining glass, but I never uttered a word about my recent discovery.

Why would I? Ryder can't stand me, so there's no chance in hell he'll be anything but furious that I'm pregnant.

Mick called again this morning, the concern clear in his voice when he learned Ryder refused yet another therapy session. "Go be his wife, Greer. He doesn't want to listen? Make him. Force his hand. He needs you, despite what he claims, but he's stubborn and scared."

"He needs a lot of things, but I'm damn sure I'm not one of them."

"Ryder is in love with you."

A scoff flies from my lips at his words. "Trust me, he's not."

"Trust *me*, he is."

"What makes you think that?" Better question, do I want to know?

"Ryder and I met for a drink. I'd heard through the grapevine he'd gotten married, so of course, I had to bust his balls a bit. But it didn't matter, because the man was so excited to show you off to the world. He said he'd loved you since he was a kid."

My mind reels, sure that Mick heard him wrong. "If that were the case, why was he with Mandi at the hotel the night before the race?"

A surprised huff escapes Mick. "Shit, I didn't know he was, and he certainly never mentioned her being there to me. I remember seeing her at the hospital, though. Found it odd she was there, but I was too focused on everything else to speak to her. Trust me, I avoid speaking to that woman at all costs."

"I take it you're not a fan?"

"That's one way to put it. I don't know what happened with Mandi, although I suspect nothing. But I do know one thing. You two need to talk and clear the air, using full sentences. Grunting doesn't count. I know you're tough, Greer. Go show him who's boss. Believe it or not, he'll listen."

I doubt that sentiment highly but agree to give it a shot. I'm not sure why Mick and Lorna are convinced Ryder loves me or will even consider listening to me at this point. They haven't spent the last week living in a house where the tension pervades every square inch.

I have, and much more of this, I'll be signing myself into the nuthouse. Hey, it would be a far more relaxing environment.

Still, I promised to pull out all the stops. My mission for the day? Get Ryder's ass out of bed.

How hard can it be?

HOOK UP

Balancing Ryder's lunch tray in one arm and an ice bucket in the other, I climb the stairs, praying he's in a decent mood. He needs to return to the world of the living, although I know he won't go quietly. That would be far too easy.

With a sigh, I ready myself for the inevitable argument.

Please God, give me a break. Just a twenty-four-hour ceasefire.

Since I know God and his warped sense of humor lately, I'm not relying on prayers. I've got my armor on and sword drawn, ready for the inevitable verbal spar.

Come at me, Ryder.

I knock on his door before swinging it open. Ryder shakes his head in aggravation, tossing down the television remote. "Which part of leaving me alone don't you understand?"

Oh well, so much for civility.

"You don't really want me to go. Your bark is worse than your bite." Thanks for that gem, Mrs. Gray.

"I've been telling you to leave for the last two weeks. You won't listen."

I plant my hands on my hips, certain that despite his lack of sight, he can feel the energy pervading from my petite frame. "Call the cops, then. Have me escorted off the property."

Ryder groans, burying his face in the pillow. "Just go, Greer."

"No can do. You need to rejoin the human race, and that starts with a shower and a change of clothes."

"Go away," he reiterates, his voice muffled into the pillow.

"If you don't get out of this bed—"

"You'll what?" he counters, a muscle jumping in his jaw.

"Make you regret your decision."

"Doubtful."

Can't say I didn't warn him. Setting down the food tray in a safe location, I hoist the ice bucket over his bed, dumping the entire thing onto his body.

Now I have his full attention.

Shocked curses fly from his mouth as he scrambles to escape the cold cubes. "What the fuck is wrong with you?"

So glad you asked, Ryder.

"You don't even want to know. There are *so* many things wrong with me these past couple of weeks."

Ryder thrusts out his hand, his face curled into an angry snarl. "Don't do that again."

"Or what? You'll ignore me? Spout more lies? Treat me with disdain? I'm getting used to it, Ryder. Do your worst."

He pulls the shirt from his body, tossing it on the bed. "You expect me to feel sorry for you? That's rich, Greer."

My mobile buzzes in my pocket just as I'm about to release a verbal tirade on my husband. Pulling it out, I groan at the caller ID.

Here we go again. Normally, I take any calls away from Ryder, but I'm done tiptoeing around his wildly vacilating emotions.

"Hello, Mr. Givens. What can I do for you?"

Ryder turns his head toward me, his expression curious.

"Ms. Hammond, I hate to bother you, but we really need to sit down and talk."

Releasing a deep sigh, I realize there's no point in fighting it anymore. The decision has been made. "I'm giving Ryder his lunch and a shower. Can I call you in an hour to set up an appointment?"

"That's fine. Send Ryder my best."

Clicking off the call, I turn back toward my husband, noting the confused look crossing his features. I shake my head in disgust as I glance over at his disheveled appearance. Don't get me wrong, the man is still gorgeous, but he needs a date with some soap and a shower head.

As soon as possible.

"Was that my lawyer?"

Oh, boy, here we go. Round two, and this time, I'm out of ice. "Yep."

"What did he want?"

A scoff flies from my mouth. "What do you think?"

"Just ignore him."

"Do you want your lunch before or after your shower?"

"Didn't I just get a shower?" Ryder snorts, and I have to bite back a laugh. This situation is ridiculous, and now I'm knee-deep in the muck with him.

"I can get some more ice if you like."

"Pass." He fumbles to the armchair, reaching for the tray.

"Your chicken is at twelve o'clock. Pasta is at six." Taking a step back, I watch as he spears a noodle, making it to his mouth.

Hey, it's progress.

Now, the real question is, do I proceed with our current conversation? I've already poked the bear once today. Why would I continue down this path?

One good answer—because I'm damn aggravated with said bear.

"Why would you want me to ignore your lawyer?"

"It's not important to me," Ryder mumbles, a noodle falling back to the plate.

"Seems our annulment is *really* important to him," I fire off, my sauciness at the ready. I've been a modest mouse for the last week. Today, I'm swinging back.

Ryder turns in my direction, his brow furrowing. "Our what? You had Mr. Givens draw up annulment papers?"

With that question, the gloves come off as I pace brisk strides around his room. "You can stop pretending, Ryder. At least now I know why you refused to wear your ring and didn't want to announce our marriage. It makes perfect sense when you see it from a distance."

Ryder tosses down his fork, pushing the tray aside. "What the hell are you babbling about?"

The last vestiges of restraint holding back my temper release as I storm to my husband's side. "I saw you and Mandi in Charlotte. I flew in to surprise you, to stand by your side and cheer you on. Instead, I found you and your ex-girlfriend together in the lobby bar. You wouldn't even pick up your phone. Then I get to the hospital and who's there? Mandi. But I said nothing, because your health was my only concern. Besides, you seemed to want me there, and you never mentioned her. I thought I'd misread the situation until I walked into your room and saw you two kissing. Maybe this was only a public relations stunt to you, but this is my *life*." I swipe at the tears rolling down my cheeks, the emotional dam busted all to hell.

The mask of anger slides from Ryder's face. "Shit. Gigi, why didn't you tell me what you saw?"

"Tell you what? That you hurt me? Broke me? You turned my life upside down and spit on my dreams, but I'm still here. Unlike your precious Mandi."

Ryder opens his mouth to speak, but I cut him off. I've been silent for days. Time to let it *all* hang out.

Go big or go home.

With a deep breath, I open my heart to the man, even if I'm certain he'll destroy it. "I want you, Ryder—for the good days, the bad days, and the in-between days. When I spoke those vows in Barbados, I meant them. Even if you didn't. You're my perfect in an imperfect world. The man who made me believe in all the trappings of love. So even if you don't feel the same way, it doesn't detract from my feelings. My love has the power to heal you, and that's what I plan on doing. Once you're better, you can go back to hating me. Until then, can't we work together? We're on the same team."

"Hate you? Are you crazy?" Ryder shakes his head as if to clear it. "I've loved you from the second I laid eyes on you. You're more than a perfect woman. You're perfection itself."

My knees threaten to give out from his words, but I have to slog through all the anger and distrust. Ryder deserves it. We both do.

"If I'm so perfect, why did you push me away?"

Ryder's body tenses, and I can see him rebuilding that emotional wall. "You know the reason."

"I have no idea, actually. You claim I have this ulterior motive, but it was me whose heart shattered seeing you with Mandi. She may be beautiful, but she doesn't deserve you or your love. Instead of being here to help you, she hopped on an international flight."

Ryder scoots forward in his chair, and for the first time, I see he's doing his best to traverse the muck of miscommunication with me. "I don't want Mandi."

"Sure you don't." Hello sarcasm, good of you to show up.

"All I've ever wanted is you. Do you think I would mess that up? I married you, Gigi. I meant those vows as much as you did."

My heart leaps at his admission, but my head is far warier. The eyes will reveal what the lips can conceal. "Then why did you kiss her? Why were you holding her hands? Why is your lawyer barraging me with phone calls?"

The questions fly from my lips with the speed of a bullet

train, all the anger and frustration from the last week finally catching up to me.

"She kissed me. I wasn't expecting it. I didn't want it. That night at the hotel, she confronted me about our marriage. She was so upset, or so she claimed, crying and inconsolable. I held her hands in a desperate bid to make her understand. As for my lawyer? Give me the phone and I'll tell Mr. Givens to fuck off personally."

"Why is he calling? The man is worse than a bill collector."

Ryder chuckles, a foreign but entirely welcome sound to my ears. "He's pissed I didn't have you sign a prenup. I already told him to dead the issue, but he never was very good at listening. Although, I should call him. Tell him about the horrible abuse I'm suffering at your hands in the form of ice baths."

"You're out of bed, aren't you? I consider it a win."

"You would." His words are harsh, but the faint glimpse of a smile colors his face.

We're moving in the right direction, but I still have a boatload of unanswered questions. Time for Ryder to spill the beans.

"You don't want an annulment?"

"Greer, I told you on the phone that we are never getting divorced."

"You make no sense. You won't divorce me, but you've been hateful toward me. Tell me why." The words barely make it past my throat, the emotions clogging my airway, and I'm wholly uncertain I want to hear his answer.

"You know—"

"Don't you dare tell me I know the reason," I bellow, startling the man with the volume of my voice. I rarely yell, unless screams of passion count. Those, Ryder is *all* too familiar with.

Ryder sighs, running a hand over his unkempt beard. "I figured you were only here out of obligation. That you felt bad because of Greg's involvement and in typical Greer fashion, were trying to make it better." A resigned sigh echoes from his chest. "You were so distant after the accident. You barely touched me, and I needed that affection. I needed you. I thought you didn't want me anymore. Sucks, but I get it. I hate it, but I get it."

That's it. Wiping the tears from my eyes, I kneel in front of him, grasping his hands. "You get nothing. Your injury sucks. Your attitude these past weeks *really* sucks. Our miscommunication sucks. But despite everything, I love you even more than I did. So deal with it."

Ryder's hand tangles in my hair, pulling me close. "Deal with this."

He's aiming for my lips, but our noses bump and I fall back, laughing.

Thank God, so is Ryder. "Sorry," he mumbles, rubbing his nose. "Maybe we try that again?"

"Absolutely, but first, you are taking a shower. A real, honest to God shower. Then, I expect hours of make-up kisses from you."

I don't give him an opportunity to argue as I lead him to the bathroom.

"I'm pretty damn ripe," Ryder concedes, taking a whiff under his arm as we wait for the shower to heat.

"To say the least. Promise me I can burn these clothes, along with your sheets."

Guiding him under the spray, Ryder releases a low groan as he leans against the tile. I'm by his side in a flash, my clothes in a heap outside the shower door. I can coach him through the shower and offer him some privacy, but he's been alone in this dark hell for weeks. Time for him to share the burden.

I grab the sponge and soap, working across his skin with gentle strokes as he collapses on the built-in shower bench. Have to hand it to the architect, this bathroom is a thing of beauty with its three shower heads and Mediterranean-style tile. It's also half the size of my last apartment, but that's hardly a surprise.

Returning my gaze to the man in front of me, I offer up thanks to another architect, because when God designed Ryder Gray, he went all out. The man is the perfect male specimen.

With or without sight.

"Admit it, you feel better."

"Being near you feels better. It's been hell these last weeks without you, Gigi." His voice is thick with emotion, the fear and loneliness he hid behind the stern facade bubbling to the surface.

"I was right here. As close as you'd let me." Standing in between his legs, I work the shampoo across his scalp, earning a moan of approval.

"You don't have to do this," Ryder murmurs, but he makes no move to stop me.

"I'm your wife and I want to do it. I missed touching you. These past few weeks have been pretty damn lonely."

"Tell me about it. What am I going to do?"

"Stop being mean to me, for a start." My fingers work the muscles of his neck, trying to loosen the tension he's been carrying since the accident upended his world.

"It broke me even more than not being able to see," Ryder whispers, his voice laced with pain. "The idea that you didn't want me anymore."

"Let's promise to stop making assumptions about each other since we've proven we're terrible at it. I really suck at disliking you, Ryder, but I'm pretty damn good at loving you."

"You're amazing at loving me, even when I don't deserve it. Thank you for the last week. I didn't want you to go."

"Could have fooled me," I giggle, stealing a kiss from his full lips before returning to the task at hand.

But Ryder has other ideas as his hands drift up my back, his lips dusting kisses across my abdomen. When his tongue flicks against my breast, swirling around my nipple, I release a sated groan.

"You keep making those sexy sounds and I'm going to take you right here in the shower."

"Promise?"

His teeth nibble along my tender skin before his head collapses against my stomach, his grip tightening around my body. "I love you, Gigi. Please don't leave me."

Straddling him, I tip his chin up, kissing away his doubts. "If I haven't left by now, you'll have to pry me from your side with a crowbar."

Cupping my face, Ryder claims my mouth, his tongue tangling with mine in a provocative dance. But it isn't hurried or rushed. He takes his time, exploring every inch and reclaiming what he thought he lost.

We pull back, our foreheads touching, our hearts once again one.

"I don't want to sleep alone tonight. The nightmares—"

"No nightmares tonight. I'll be right by your side."

After washing away the physical and emotional remnants of the last week, we settle in the guest room, our exhaustion evident as we collapse on the bed.

Ryder pulls me tight to his side, his arms wrapped around me like a vise, his lips pressed against my hair.

For the first time since the accident stole his vision, he sleeps without incident. Every time the nightmares threaten, I curl closer to him, whispering words of love until he quiets.

Then, when he's settled, I allow myself the same luxury, my eyes drifting closed as the blackness takes hold.

∼

It's dark outside when I blink my eyes open, pressing a kiss to Ryder's chest as I glance at the bedside clock.

It's after eight. No wonder my stomach is rumbling.

With a sigh, I run a hand over my abdomen, wondering how to tell Ryder the news. Wondering *when* to tell him the news.

Ryder stirs next to me, gliding his hand along my spine. "You're really here."

Snuggling against him, I tease his lips with my tongue, unable to keep the smile from my face. Despite everything, at least I'm back in his arms again.

I need to celebrate that fact.

My husband strokes his hands along my arms, his face unreadable.

"What is it? What's wrong?" The nurse in me worries about his condition. After all, the man has a head injury and anything is possible, even weeks after the crash.

"Will you answer me honestly? Not tell me what I want to hear?"

"Don't I always? I am the one who dumped a bucket of ice over you a few hours ago. Trust me, I always speak the truth."

Ryder chuckles, tightening his grip. "Please don't do that again."

"No promises. What's on your mind?" Part of me wonders if he might ask about the pregnancy, although there's no way he could know. Until this afternoon, we barely spoke.

"Are you sure you're not staying out of pity?" There's no anger in his voice, just a hint of resignation regarding his current limitations.

So, to counteract that emotion, I toss sarcasm into the mix. Propping my chin on his chest, I skew up my mouth in a pout. "Are you sure you're not still in love with Mandi?"

A harsh laugh breaks from Ryder's mouth. "If you ask that question one more time—"

"Ditto."

The energy changes then, the last of the walls we erected crumbling away. "I've only ever loved one woman. There's you, Gigi, and then there's everybody else."

"You and those incredible one-liners, they get me every time. How in the world did little old me win Ryder Gray's heart?"

"You're seriously lucky?"

I snort out a laugh, giving his chest a light slap. "There's the egomaniac I know and love. I knew he was in there somewhere."

"Now, if I can only get my sight back..."

We need to stay positive. As a nurse practitioner, I know faith is half the battle. "What's the first thing you'll do when you regain your sight?"

"Stare at you."

"Be serious."

"Okay, fine. Stare at you while I'm balls deep inside you."

"Much better. But, do we have to wait?"

"I'm sure you can convince me." His hands slide along my sides, under the edge of my silk tank. "Tell me more."

"Uh uh uh. I want *you* to tell me. What do you want me to do?" I slip off his shirt, my fingers gliding along Ryder's firm chest, his muscles flexing under my palm.

"I wish I could see you." The pain and fear have etched lines into his visage. But I won't give them room to grow.

Not anymore.

"You don't need to see me. Just feel me. Feel me touch you." I trail kisses down the planes of his abdomen, smiling when his breath hitches. His entire body clenches in anticipation when I deliver a series of gentle nips along his hip. "Tell me what you want, Ryder. You'll know I'll give you anything."

"I want your gorgeous lips around my cock."

Ryder arches his hips, groaning as I wrap my fist around his length, stroking him. When I circle my tongue around the tip of his cock, he bucks against me, but I'm not caving to his whims. Not yet. I want to tease him. Push his limits until he's desperate.

I spend the next few minutes driving him out of his mind, my tongue gliding along his shaft, until his hands knot in my hair, holding me in place. "Suck me."

With a smile, I take him deep, earning a growl of pleasure as my mouth works him over. His fingers tighten their grip as his hips buck against me, both of us losing ourselves to the moment as I coax him closer to the edge.

"I need inside you. Now." Pulling me up the length of his body, his fingers shove my g-string aside as he sinks inside me, a hum of satisfaction escaping us both. Ryder wraps his hands around my hips, bottoming out as he grinds against me. "Ride me, Gigi."

I circle my hips slowly around his cock, whimpering as

the feelings threaten to explode. He's so deep inside me, his fingers bruising my hips as they hold me flush against him. "I want to feel you come, Ryder."

"Ladies first." Ryder flips me over, his thrusts strong and hard. "You're amazing."

"Tell me how I feel."

He grunts, teetering on the brink of control. "You're so wet. So tight."

"What else?"

"The way you smell. It drives me mad. One whiff and all I can think about is being inside you. Taking you. Claiming you. Showing you who you belong to."

Scratching my nails down his chest, I squeeze around him, earning another low moan. Twining my hand in his, I press my wedding band against his fingers. "I never took it off. I know who I belong to."

That realization is enough to push my man over the edge, a shout breaking from his lips as he pours himself into me. His broad body collapses onto the mattress as our breathing returns to normal.

"Better?" I tease, tracing my fingers through his beard.

"So much better," he concurs, as sleep catches hold again.

~

Lorna is thrilled Ryder and I have patched up our marriage, but her happiness is tempered by the fact that her son is still only able to see shadows, and it's nearly six weeks since the crash.

The past several weeks have been a rollercoaster of emotions, with the highs of our playful banter dulled by the knowledge that Ryder may never regain his sight. The sadness cutting through his features eats at my soul.

The man was on top of the world. Now, we have to figure out how to get him back there again.

The doctor has started injections in a valiant effort to relieve the pressure, and Ryder is a trooper for each visit. My role never changes. I'm his constant companion and cheerleader, reassuring him that together we can conquer the world.

I think he's finally starting to believe me, even if he's brokenhearted by his disability.

I'm also having an increasingly tough time hiding my pregnancy, considering how often I lose my breakfast. And lunch. And dinner. At the rate I'm going, I'll be skinnier than I was before I became pregnant.

There are moments I'm positive Ryder knows about the pregnancy, but he never asks, and I'm still garnering the courage to tell him. He's been through so much, but I'm hopeful the news of our baby will bring some much needed joy to his world.

Ryder has made great strides toward his independence. It doesn't hurt that he's now allowing the therapists through the door, but we also moved downstairs, and being on the main level gives him access to the kitchen and pool area. Suffice it to say that his neighbors are now well aware of our voracious sexual appetites.

Not that it ever stops us.

I plop down onto the outdoor lounger, smiling when Ryder drops his head into my lap.

My husband snuggles closer, pressing a kiss to my stomach. "You make all this worth it, Gigi. This whole crazy ride. Losing my sight. My career. I'd have given up if it weren't for you."

"I wasn't about to let you."

"I have to face facts, though. This might be it for me. As good as it gets. Do you really want a blind guy long-term?"

"No, I don't want some random blind guy. I want you." Leaning over, I steal a kiss, earning a small smile. "But you will regain your sight. Do you think you'll race again?"

My question is two-fold. I need him to stay positive and I'm also desperate to know his plans when—not if—he regains his vision.

"Screw racing. I don't care if I ever race again. Would you be okay being married to a *former* F1 racer?"

"As long as he's you. I just want you safe and happy, Ryder. That's all that matters." What I don't mention is the relief flooding my body at his decision to leave the world of racing. Don't get me wrong, I've stared at the trophies lining his shelves, the photos of his many podium finishes, and his talent is legendary. I'll forever be proud of him and what he accomplished in thirty years.

I know his fans want him back. He's a hero in the world of F1 racing, but I see his future through a different lens.

I almost lost him.

There's no way I could go through that agony and uncertainty again.

And again.

"All that matters is me being able to see something. Anything. Your beautiful face. Our baby's smile."

I hold my breath at his words, certain he can feel my heart racing. This wasn't the way I planned to break the news, but it's a good segue. "Our baby?"

"Not that there will be any children now. Not with my condition."

The bottom of my world falls out with his words. "You've

always wanted kids, Ryder. I think we'd have beautiful children."

A harsh bark of laughter sounds from his chest. "Kids I can't see. I couldn't do that to them, or to you. It's bad enough you're saddled with me, but a child, too? That's a dream for another lifetime." He squeezes my arm, his beautiful blue eyes staring off into space. "Looks like it's just you and me for the long haul."

Willing the tears away, I take slow and measured breaths. It's easy to understand his stance—his world has been turned upside down and there might not be an easy fix. Hell, there might not be *any* fix for his vision. I get it. He doesn't want to be a burden, and that's all he feels like since the accident.

How do you tell someone they're the light in your darkness when their world is literally without light?

"I hope you'll change your mind one day, because I want children with you."

"I love kids, Gigi, but that's one path we can't traverse. I need you to understand."

My answer is most definitely no, but I let the situation lie. Ryder is already on edge about his future, the trepidation coursing through him like blood in his veins. Pulsing with its own life.

Pulsing like the life in my belly.

The life he doesn't want.

The child he no longer desires.

What will happen when he learns the truth? Will he change his mind or push me away again?

CHAPTER 15
RYDER

Six weeks. It's been forty-five days since the world went dark around me. Losing my sight was something I never considered. Sure, I read stories about people suffering from glaucoma or cataracts, but they were older. I'm in my prime.

My entire world hangs in the balance, dependent on these needles they're now injecting into my eyeballs.

Let me tell you, I've always hated needles, but this is an entirely new level of hell. Still, if there's a 0.00001% chance I might regain my sight, count me in.

Thank God for my Gigi. The woman is tireless, always at my side, showering me with love and positivity.

I know two things: Gigi is the greatest thing in my life and I don't deserve her. Not that I'm ever letting her go. No chance in hell of that happening, particularly not after she put up with my ornery ass those first couple of weeks.

Talk about devotion.

The world still doesn't know who Greer is. After the accident, the media focused solely on my injuries and my return to racing. When it would happen. If it would happen. Any digging into my recent nuptials fell by the wayside.

Then, as is the norm in the world of celebrity, the media moved on to new topics. I can't say I blame them.

Now their sights are set on how our F1 team has yet to secure another podium finish. Fucking barracudas. Don't they realize they're working not only with new drivers but a new crew?

Yes, I'm protective of the team. It's still my team.

Mick tries to keep me in the loop, but he's a busy man with a racing empire to run. Me? I'm running out of options.

My wife informed me that Greg just completed a stint in rehab and seems like a changed man, but I'm not ready to speak to him. It doesn't matter that Mick verified Greg tested clean, or that Greg wanted none of this to happen.

None of them wanted this to happen, but that's not the point. Life as I knew it is over, and their haphazard skills while nursing a hangover are at least partly to blame.

The real fear that creeps into my mind, the one that plagues me, is that Greer is only here out of pity. A morbid sense of obligation to stand by her man. She's gorgeous and smart as a whip. She could have any guy she wants.

She didn't sign up to marry a blind man, no matter what vows we said in Barbados. Hell, she never even got the chance to live the high life by my side. I planned to wine and dine her as we toured the circuit together, showing her the world.

Showing her off to the world.

Instead, she's stuck here, day in and day out, catering to my needs. Not that she complains. She's never once said a cross word, save for when she dumped the bucket of ice on me, and let's be honest, I had that one coming.

She's the epitome of the perfect wife, along with being

the sexiest woman I've ever known. That I can grab her luscious curves anytime I want and sink inside her warmth is one hell of a wonderful concept. A concept I take full advantage daily.

I hear Greer dash out of the room, but I don't ask. I know where she's headed. She claims the stress is messing with her stomach, but I'm certain she's lying.

Call it male intuition, but there have been changes in the way she smells and feels; changes so slight I'd never have noticed them if I could see, since her tits and ass would have stolen the show. But in my world of shadows, all my other senses have kicked into high gear.

Greer is pregnant. Not that she's said a word to me.

I'm positive our conversation regarding children that one night is a large part of why she's refusing to disclose her current condition, and I could kick myself for opening my big mouth. I was trying to ease her mind, assure her I don't expect her to take on any additional burdens in our marriage. Instead, Gigi now thinks I don't want a baby with her, but nothing could be further from the truth. If I had to choose between us having a child and regaining my sight, I'd choose the baby every time.

In fact, once my feeble brain realized she wasn't nursing a stomach virus, the idea of her carrying my child re-energized my quest to find a cure for my condition. I have a goal now—to see my baby's face when he's born.

"You okay?" I ask when she returns to the living room.

"I'm fine. Sorry about that."

"I think you need a doctor."

"I told you, it's just stress."

"Or it's something else."

"We have to get going. You have your doctor's appointment in less than an hour."

Nothing like avoidance, Greer.

Every time I hint at her pregnancy, she changes the topic. Looks like I'm going to have to hold her down and force the truth out of her.

Not a bad idea, actually.

∼

ANOTHER DOCTOR VISIT and more injections in my eyeballs. Let the good times roll.

Greer, as always, sits at my side, clasping my hand. The woman deserves a medal for all the crap she's endured. "What's the latest, Doctor?"

"He's making progress. I'm still hopeful the injections will relieve the pressure and restore his vision."

"Anything at this point," I mutter. It's ironic. Two months ago, I wanted back all my vision. My life back as it was. Now? I'll settle for being legally blind, so long as I don't have to remain in this world of darkness.

"Usually," the doctor continues, "the return of vision is spontaneous. Let's hope this time is the charm. Unless there are any changes, I'll see you in two weeks."

Greer leads me to the car. But instead of settling into the driver's seat, she straddles my lap, twining her hands around my neck.

"This is new," I murmur, my mouth seeking hers.

"You've never had sex in a car?"

"I've never had sex with you in a car."

"Well, we both know that sex with me is superior to anyone else," Greer giggles, burying her face against my neck.

She's not lying. The woman is incredible in bed. I nudge her face up, capturing her lips and tangling my tongue with hers, as I fumble to free myself, eager to sink inside her heat.

Greer, always the temptress, teases me, rubbing her slick folds along the head of my cock. But this time, I'm taking the lead, holding her hips in place as I bury myself inside her, earning a low moan of approval.

"I'm glad your stomach bug hasn't killed your sexual appetite," I murmur against her mouth.

"Nothing can kill my appetite for you."

It's now or never. "We both know you don't have a stomach bug."

She stills on top of me, her breathing shallow. "We don't not know it, either."

Tangling my hand in her hair, I nip along the column of her throat. "Are you having my baby, Gigi?"

"Ryder—"

"You are, aren't you?" I arch my hips upward, earning another moan from my wife. Fuck, but the idea of her pregnant makes her even hotter somehow. Not that I thought it was possible.

The buzzing of her phone jerks us from our intimate moment.

"Ignore it," I murmur, intent on getting the truth out of Greer *before* giving her the best orgasm of her life.

"We can't. It's Mick. He says he's at your house and it's urgent."

∽

MICK IS by my side the second the car pulls into the garage, clapping me around the shoulder and startling the hell out of me. "Sorry to scare you, man, but we need to talk. How's your vision?"

"Not much change, but the doctor isn't giving up yet."

"Neither should you."

We settle onto the patio, Greer leaving us with some wine and a plate of cheese and crackers.

"Ryder, you scored a hell of a woman with Greer."

"Don't I know it. She puts up with me, and we both know I'm not an easy bastard to deal with."

"You're not that bad... most of the time," Greer calls from the kitchen, earning a chuckle from Mick.

"You have your moments, too, beautiful," I retort, smiling when her snort of laughter reaches my ears.

She knows she's magnificent.

"All I can say is I like you a hell of a lot more when you and Greer are talking. And fucking."

I can't deny the truth.

"Hey," I whisper, leaning forward, "you still have the ring, right?"

"I don't have it with me, but I'll get it to you in the next few days. When do you plan on announcing your marriage?"

"As soon as possible."

"Mandi called the other day. No clue how she finagled my phone number," Mick states, the disgust evident in his voice. "Wanted to know if you'd regained your sight yet. What did you ever see in that woman?"

"Not a damn clue. She might have tried to call me, but I had Greer block her number. I don't need my past mucking up my future."

"Smart man." He clears his throat, his shift into the official reason for his visit. "They finished the investigation, and it turns out that although a few of the crew were nursing hangovers, their actions weren't the cause of the crash. A couple of the bolts sheared off. An issue with the metal alloy.

The company has issued a recall and a public apology, likely trying their damnedest to avoid a lawsuit."

Sinking back into my chair, a feeling of relief washes over me. Yes, I'm blind, but not because of my pit crew.

Not because of Greg. With a grimace, I recall the fury I spewed in his direction during our last phone call, so certain of his involvement in my wreck.

The guilt is compounded by the way I treated Greer for that first couple of weeks, assuming she and her brother were in cahoots and trying to placate me.

Talk about being way off.

"What about the crew?"

"Well, I put them all on leave, pending the investigation, but those who tested positive are well aware there's a snowball's chance in hell of getting their job back."

"What about Greg?"

"He actually helped us solve the mystery of what happened. He swore he heard something pop right before your car dropped. Turns out, he was right. You know his test was clean, Ryder."

"He went to rehab over this situation."

"Not quite," my wife's voice interrupts the conversation. "Greg knew he had a drinking problem, and he wanted to get it under control. Turns out, he has a good reason. Jillian is pregnant."

I stroke my chin, a grin lighting up my features. "Holy shit. Greggo is going to be a dad. I need to speak with your brother and apologize for accusing him of trying to hurt me."

Gigi's arms twine around my neck, and I feel the dampness of her tears against my skin. "I knew he would never be that careless with your life. He loves you too much."

"I'll fix it, Gigi. Promise." I mean it, too. Greg deserves an apology and I'm not too big a man to admit it.

"Damn Greer, you must be starving. Quite a sandwich you've got there," Mick remarks, and I bite back a grin at Gigi's snort of indignation.

"What can I say? I'm not one of those salad chicks. I'll be inside, if either of you needs me."

"It's amazing. She has quite the appetite for someone who keeps throwing up."

Mick sputters his drink, chuckling. "Is she pregnant?"

"She hasn't admitted anything, but I'm pretty positive she is."

"Ryder Gray is going to be a dad. Damn, you've had a busy couple of months."

"That's one way of putting it, although the timing couldn't be worse. I can't see my hand in front of my face, Mick. I can barely take care of myself. How the hell am I supposed to be a dad, too? I'm totally overwhelmed at the idea."

Mick squeezes my shoulder. "You'd be totally overwhelmed even if you weren't blind. Trust me, it's a good thing. I've seen you with kids. You'll be an amazing father."

I nod at my friend's words, but deep down, I have my doubts.

So far, I feel like an utter failure at being a husband. Now there's the added pressure of figuring out life as a blind man, a newlywed, and a father, all in one fell swoop.

Mick leaves a short time later, and I settle down for a difficult discussion. I'm not sure Greg will forgive me, but I have to try. He's worth it.

"Ryder, man, how are you? I wanted to call, but—"

"I need to say something, Greg." With a deep exhalation, I release the anger that's been building in my body since the accident. "I'm so sorry I thought, for one second, that you had anything to do with the crash. Mick told me it was you who helped solve the mystery."

I expect my friend to be jovial that I'm no longer angry, but his sigh is heavy with regret. "I solved it, but it was too late. I should have noticed something sooner."

"How? None of us did."

"Doesn't matter, Ryder. I let you down, after I swore I'd protect you. I can't blame you for thinking I drank that night with the guys, but I didn't have a drop. In fact, it damn near came to blows when I caught three of the crew in the bar the night before the race, hanging all over your ex."

That got my attention. "Whoa, whoa, whoa. What?"

"Mandi. I got a text from one of the crew members, saying they were having a drink and I should join them. My only intention was to drag their asses back to their rooms after I shoved some water down their throats to ensure they were sober. When I walked into the bar, Mandi was all snuggled up with three of the guys." Greg releases a mirthless laugh. "She even tried buttering me up until she discovered I was Greer's brother. Then she turned into an ice queen. Told me she was going to have an orgy with your pit crew, just to piss you off. I told her you wouldn't care who she fucked, so long as it wasn't on the company dime. I also may have mentioned how much you adored your wife, just to twist the knife."

"Good man," I concur, taking another sip of my wine. Funny, but the shadows seem sharper tonight, not the fuzzy blur I've grown accustomed to these past weeks.

Likely wishful thinking.

"Just so you know, she was full of shit. The guys were all back in their rooms before midnight."

"How do you know?"

"I played hall monitor and checked on them. I told you,

Ryder, I've always looked out for you. I had a bad feeling that I couldn't shake, but I figured it was nerves. I should have listened to my gut. Maybe then, this wouldn't have happened."

"You and I both know you had nothing to do with the crash. Let's not talk about the damn accident anymore. I'm sick of hearing about it. Besides, I hear someone knocked up their old lady."

"Yeah. Jillian and I are having a kid. Crazy, right?"

"In the best way." It *is* amazing news and it's also time to make amends. "You still have a job with the team, if you want it. Mick doesn't plan to bring back the guys who were drinking, but he absolutely wants you as part of the crew."

"That's just it, Ryder. I want to be part of your crew. It's not the same without my brother."

"Then we have to make sure I come back, don't we?"

〜

THE MATTRESS SETTLES NEXT to me as Greer slides under the covers. She's been unusually quiet since Mick left, which is surprising. I figured she'd be ecstatic that Greg and I reconciled.

"You okay, Gigi?" Something about her energy makes me nervous, like she's pulling away, but I'm not sure of the reason.

I really hope she didn't hear me mention her engagement ring to Mick. I want to surprise her with the six-carat solitaire. If anyone deserves the royal treatment, it's my wife.

"Just tired." Her standard response this evening.

"Too bad I don't believe you." Pulling her close, I wrap my hand around her waist, resting my forehead against hers.

Greer's delicate fingers trace the planes of my face, and I

lean into her touch, desperate for more. Who the hell am I kidding? I'm always craving this woman's caress. "I've been thinking, about Greg and Jillian. About my Mom."

"Your Mom? Is she okay?" My brow furrows, realizing I haven't inquired about her family in weeks.

"Greg says she's fine, but I worry about her. She's getting older."

Smiling, I run my fingers along her arm, cupping her breast and giving her luscious nipple a squeeze. "What did she say when you told her we got married? Was she angry we didn't have a big wedding?"

I can only imagine Mrs. Hammond's reaction to the news —a mixture of disbelief and surprise, followed by a shake of her head as she recalls a ten-year-old boy proclaiming that one day, Greer Hammond would be his.

And she is, only her name is Greer Gray.

But my wife's response knocks me askew. "She doesn't know, Ryder."

I pull back as the confusion sets in. "Why not?"

"You didn't want anyone to know, remember? You wanted to keep it quiet, so I did. I never said a word to anyone."

Holy shit, I'm such an asshole.

I roll onto my back, realizing how awful the last several weeks have been for Greer. Not only is she a newlywed taking care of a newly blind husband, she didn't get any of the festivities most brides take for granted. No parties or cooing over gifts and rings. She still doesn't have her engagement ring. Hell, she didn't even feel she could tell her mother.

"Can you hand me my phone? Actually, dial Francine Juarez, please. She's in my contacts."

"Is everything okay?"

"It will be." Sitting up, I fumble my way to the bedside chair as my publicist answers her phone.

"Ryder Gray, as I live and breathe. How the hell are you?"

"Still blind, but I hope that will change soon. I need a favor. Can you set up a press release for tomorrow?"

"Sure. What are we announcing?"

Even though all I can detect is Greer's shadowy movement, I feel her dark eyes upon me. "My marriage. I want to tell the world about my wife."

Surprised gasps fly from both Francine and Greer's mouths—in stereo, no less.

"Congratulations. I'd heard the rumor, but it was never confirmed. I'm thrilled to help spread some happy news."

"Call me in the morning with the details. Nice chatting with you." I hang up the phone, making a beeline for my wife's side.

"Why did you do that?" Under my hands, I feel Greer trembling, the emotion threatening to get the better of her.

"I should have done that weeks ago. I never should have kept our marriage quiet. Makes no sense, because I married the woman of my dreams, and I want the world to know."

Her lips claim me, her tongue sliding against mine in a most sensual dance. "Are you sure?"

"I've been sure since I was ten. Go into the nightstand drawer and grab out my ring. It's about damn time I started wearing it."

Her throaty giggle warms my heart as she slides the heavy band over my knuckle. "Much better."

I wind a hand into her hair as I nuzzle her neck, littering her skin with kisses. "Told you, you're stuck with me, Greer Gray."

"How about I make us a celebratory dinner tomorrow, like the one we had on our wedding night?"

"Anything else we have to celebrate?" Yes, I'm pressing. It's about time my wife told me we're expecting a baby.

"Maybe," she whispers, her lips against mine. "You'll have to wait until tomorrow to find out."

With a chuckle, I roll on top of her, the need to claim her body growing by the second. "What if I don't want to wait?"

"Good things come to those who wait."

"Better things come to those who don't," I reply as I bury myself deep in her body. "Of course, I can always stop, if I'm putting you out."

Her only response? A purr escaping her mouth as I own every inch of her body.

After coaxing her over the edge several times, I collapse next to her, panting in her ear and pulling her flush against my frame. "You're my life, Gigi. My only reason for being."

She presses a kiss to my arm, snuggling every closer. "I wish you'd never been hurt, but I'm so grateful for this time with you."

"I'll always make time for you."

Greer turns in my arms, her fingers tickling my jaw. "Normally, you belong to the world. Right now, you belong to me. But one day soon, your sight will return and I'll have to give you back."

Suddenly it's clear, the distance I felt earlier. She's afraid there isn't space in my world for her, and so far, all I've done is compound that fear by hiding our marriage and any mention of my wife.

That changes tomorrow.

Tomorrow is about Greer Gray, the most perfect woman on the planet.

"Sweet dreams, my prince," she whispers, her mouth dancing along my skin. "I love you."

"I love you more." With a final yawn, I allow my brain to settle as I drift to sleep.

∼

THE BRIGHTNESS STREAMING through the windows jerks me awake, and I blink as my eyes adjust to the light. "Crap, it's sunny today," I mutter before time slows to a crawl.

My heart races like a junkie on a speedball as I gaze around the room.

It is bright, the colors so vivid they hurt my eyes.

Eyes that can see.

I can see.

CHAPTER 16
GREER

There's a certain hush in the early morning, and I need to find some peace before this evening. Tonight, I tell Ryder the big news about our baby. I'm still nervous, but the call to his publicist the night before eased my mind a bit.

He's ready to tell the world about us. I'm ready to tell him he's going to be a father. Despite overhearing his discussion with Mick and his claim that the timing is terrible, I have to believe he'll be excited.

Please, God, let him be excited.

"Beautiful, what's wrong?"

I look up, my gaze meeting Ryder's azure stare. "Deep in thought."

Ryder strolls over to me, that effortless grace on full display, as he pulls me into his arms and swings me around.

It only takes a few seconds for me to connect the dots—how easily he's maneuvering around his home, the exuberance I haven't seen in weeks—his vision is back and his excited whoop solidifies my hunch.

"You are so beautiful," Ryder exclaims, his hands framing my face.

Grasping his hands, I pull back, my heart racing. "You can see."

His smile is a thing of beauty. "I can see, Gigi. I'm back."

I jump into his arms, squeezing him tight. "I told you it wasn't over."

"I have to call Mick and let him know."

"First things first. Let's call the doctor and ensure everything is copacetic."

A grimace crosses his features. "You think it might not be permanent?"

"I'm fairly certain it is, but we'll let the expert make the final determination. Then, feel free to call whoever you like. I, for one, am retiring as your nurse."

His fingers tangle in my hair, those full lips drifting across mine. "Might be fun to play nurse and patient later. Just saying."

With a smack on the chest, I watch Ryder dash into the other room.

His enthusiasm is contagious.

Ryder Gray is back.

∽

It's been a flurry of activity for the last few hours, with the doctor in as much of a celebratory mood as Ryder about the return of his eyesight. He wants Ryder to take it easy for a while, but joked he knew that wasn't likely to happen.

The phone has been ringing off the hook, no doubt all manner of media eager for the latest scoop. His publicist, Francine, has been squirreled away in Ryder's office for the last few hours as they plan a press release to quiet the masses.

Ryder Gray is a big damn deal.

I've holed myself away in the upstairs lounge, taking advantage of the sun warming my face and the relative quiet. I tried to be of assistance, but my complete lack of knowledge about racing and celebrity made me more of a hindrance.

When I realized I was in the way, I told Ryder I was headed upstairs, but he was so involved in an animated discussion with his sponsor that I doubt he heard me.

My phone buzzes, and a smile cuts across my features. "How excited are you, Greg?"

"Is it true?"

"The doctor says his eyes are as good as new."

"It's a damn miracle. How are you holding up, Gigi? Don't lie, either. I always know when you're lying." That's my baby brother for you. Somehow, he always sees through my calm facade.

"A bit overwhelmed. It's just been Ryder and me for the last couple of months, but now, everyone wants a piece of him. I'm not sure where I fit into this life, or if I fit at all."

"Stop that shit right now. It's crazy, like before a race, filled with excitement and nerves and jitters. But it's not permanent. The world is thrilled that Ryder Gray is back, but he's still Ryder."

I mumble my agreement, but I'm not so certain. The truth is that Ryder and I existed in our own world, away from the spotlight. Hell, I can count on one hand the number of people, excluding therapists, who dropped by to visit him during his injury. Now, the house is bursting at the seams with strangers flowing in and out the door.

Perhaps I'm being petty, but where were they when he

needed them most? Hell, *I* could have used their help when he wouldn't budge from his bed.

"What's your plan, Greg? Are you going to work with Mick?"

"My hope is I get to work with Ryder."

My mouth goes dry at his blasé statement. "Ryder told me he had no plans to race again."

A guffaw echoes through the phone. "I'm putting money on the fact that he'll be in the next race, so long as he's cleared. That's who he is. That's what he does."

"Greg, he almost died." Shaking my head, I refuse to let that idea set up shop. "I'm sure he'll come back to F1 in some capacity, but not as a driver."

"I'll guess we'll find out. In the interim, go give my brother-in-law a hug and spend some time with your man. Trust me, you're still his number one priority. Talk soon."

Taking a few extra moments to bathe in the sunlight, I suck in some steadying breaths before heading downstairs. Greg's right. I'm being silly and jumping to conclusions—a nasty habit left over from my teenage years that never quite went away.

This is Ryder's time to shine. He's earned it.

Slipping downstairs, I knock softly on his office door. Ryder glances up, a smile crossing his face as he waves me over. "I wondered where you were. Come here. I'm sorry things are so crazy." He wraps me in a hug, pulling me onto his lap.

"Understandable. How are you feeling?"

"Fucking perfect." Grasping my chin, Ryder traces a finger along my lower lip. "I could stare at you all day."

With a smirk, I let a bit of my sass out to play. "Take a picture. It lasts longer."

A chuckle flies from his lips. "You're still using that line."

"Only with you."

Francine offers a smile, stretching her hand across the desk. "You must be Greer. A pleasure to meet you." She glances at the clock, clearing her throat. "Ryder, we need to get going. The press release is in an hour."

Ryder nods, helping me to my feet. "I'll be back soon, okay?"

"Isn't she coming?" Francine questions, her eyes wide. "You said you were announcing your marriage today."

A cloud crosses Ryder's features at his publicist's words. "Not today. That's too much information. We can save our announcement for another time." Turning to me, he shoots me a rueful smile. "Are you okay with that, Gigi?"

My honest answer? No, but I refuse to dissolve into a puddle of tears in front of him, even though the sympathetic glances Francine is shooting my way aren't helping matters.

Slipping on the emotional mask I've worn since childhood, I force a bright smile. "Sure. This is far more important."

"Thank you for understanding."

Averting my gaze, I feel the overwhelming emotions threatening to overtake me. I expected him to negate my statement. It is a big deal that he regained his sight, but so is our marriage. At least to me. "Should I postpone our dinner plans for tonight?"

Dropping a kiss on my forehead, he shakes his head as his phone buzzes for the umpteenth time today. "I'll be back way before dinner. Besides, no one can cook as well as you. I'll be here by six. Not a minute later." With that, he's out the door, leaving me to feel a bit of nowhere.

Again.

"You did a really amazing thing, taking care of him like

that. Few women would have done what you did, or put up with what you did."

Glancing up, I catch Francine's gentle smile. "I was happy to help him."

"Men," she sighs, shaking her head. "Let him get over his giddiness, and he'll come back to rights. I'll remind him about your dinner and make sure his ass is here before six."

∽

So much for reminders.

I shoot a quick glance at the clock when the house alarm sounds. It's almost three in the morning. Not only did Ryder miss the dinner, he never called me, either. The food I spent three hours preparing as a tasty treat before telling him about our baby now sits in the refrigerator.

My own hopes and dreams are just about as cold at this point.

Ryder leans over me, his lips caressing my cheek. The smell of alcohol is overwhelming, and I turn my head away. "You missed dinner."

"I know. I'm sorry. The guys wanted to celebrate and time got away from me."

Blinking back tears, I pull the sheet tight around my body in a futile effort to stave off the chill in my heart. "I hope none of you drove drunk." Now I sound like a parent. Come to think of it, I feel a bit like one at the moment.

I imagine this is how my mother felt when my father crept into bed at ungodly hours of the night, claiming he'd lost track of time.

"A car service dropped us all home."

How nice. A car service requires planning, meaning there

was time to arrange transportation but not enough minutes to send his wife a text message.

My temper flares, but I talk myself down. It's the middle of the night, and Ryder is drunk. No good can come out of a fight now.

"Hey, you okay?" Ryder slides his hand under the cover, cupping my breast, but I'm in no mood for playtime.

"I'm tired. I was asleep."

"Can I wake you up?"

"You already did."

His hand halts its movements, no doubt attributable to my flat tone. "Are you angry?"

"We'll talk about it tomorrow."

I feel him watching me in the dark, and I know he's weighing whether to push the issue or leave it alone. When he moves from the bed to the bathroom, I relax.

He'll leave me be for the rest of the night.

∽

"Shit, my head hurts." Ryder stumbles into the kitchen, shooting me a smile.

I don't smile back. In fact, I'm tempted to chuck my laptop at his handsome head after seeing all the photos of him floating around the internet. There are oodles of them from the night before—Ryder and his celebrity racing pals at some upscale Charlotte nightclub, women hanging off them.

One woman, in particular, catches my attention.

"How's Mandi?" I snap, sliding the aspirin bottle in his direction with far more force than necessary.

Ryder's brow furrows as he shakes his head. Sorry, bud, pictures really are worth a thousand words. "Why are you asking about Mandi? Beautiful, I'm so sorry about last night." He wraps his arms around my waist, but I shove him off, motioning toward the laptop.

"How nice that Mandi knew where you were. How sweet that you had time to flirt with countless women, but no time to call me and cancel our plans."

His face drops when he sees the photos. "Shit. They were fans, excited about the news."

"Their breasts look very excited. I suppose that's why they needed to shove them in your face. Are you always this up and personal with your fans? With your ex?"

Ryder throws up his hands to ward off my verbal onslaught. "I didn't touch my ex. I was shocked when she showed up. Greer, it looks bad, but nothing happened. You know me."

"Do I?" His face falls when I utter the question that's been spinning in my brain for the last day. "You've had your sight back for less than twenty-four hours and in that time you've stood me up, called off our wedding announcement, stayed out all hours drinking and openly flirted with"—I poke the screen, my nail clicking against the glass—"at least four women. Excuse me, *fans*. So no, Ryder, I don't think I know you at all."

He leans against the counter, a muscle jumping in his jaw. "We were celebrating. I know it got out of hand and I never meant to hurt you, but this is a big deal. I would hope you'd understand."

Good, now it's my fault. I know this trick. My father played it on my mother for months before he left.

"I know it's a big deal. It's huge. But it's sadly amusing how you regain your sight and lose sight of me. Where were all your fancy friends these last several weeks? No one, save for Mick, came to check on you."

"I didn't want them around. I didn't want anyone around."

"You didn't want me around, either, but I wasn't going to let you go through that alone. When someone you love is hurting, you help them. When they're down, you pick them up. Even when they push you away, you push back. That's love, Ryder." Swiping the tears from my eyes, I stand, not wanting to go any further down this conversation path.

That he celebrated, and it wasn't with me, speaks volumes. But unlike my mother, I won't stick around and be played as a fool again and again. I have my pride.

Ryder pulls me to him, setting me on his lap, his gaze soft. "I was an asshole. Don't think, for one second, that I've forgotten who was there for me every single day."

"You already have."

He presses kisses to my hair, holding me fast against him. "Give me one more chance? I want to take you somewhere tonight, somewhere really special. We'll have our celebration."

I'm fairly certain he didn't cheat on me and that he is remorseful for his actions the night before. But Ryder's behavior—his egocentric, devil may care attitude—wounds me. To him, it's an oversight. One I should forgive.

To me, it's three strikes in less than twenty-four hours, each one proving I don't have a place in his world.

"I don't know, Ryder. I didn't sleep well last night."

That smile of his. I hate how endearingly sheepish it makes him. "Don't say no. Trust me, I'm making it up to you."

He's not lying about the restaurant. It screams money—money I don't have—not that Ryder would ever let me pay, regardless.

I'll give it to the man, he's generous with his funds. I witnessed that in Vegas and it hasn't changed.

We're seated at a private table, and Ryder is intent on ordering us everything on the menu.

"The food here is amazing. Gives Manhattan restaurants a run for their money." Ryder leans forward, stroking a lock of hair behind my ear. "You look gorgeous. I can't believe I missed seeing your face all these weeks. Missed seeing this killer body, too." His gaze sweeps down my length, a flirtatious wink and smile at the ready. "But not anymore."

"Now you get to see all the imperfections, too," I respond with a smile.

"You don't have any. Trust me, after twenty years, I'd know." His phone buzzes, and he shoots me a rueful glance. "It's Mick. Do you mind if I take this?"

Shaking my head, I wave him off. Look, I get it. Ryder Gray is the biggest name in racing and as I told him the other night, the entire world wants a piece of him. I just pray there's enough left over for me and the baby.

Sucking in a breath, I wonder if I should broach the topic of my pregnancy tonight. I've waffled on it all day, uncertain how much more I should pile onto his plate.

All things considered, perhaps I need to let it lie for a few more days.

Ryder strolls back to the table, an exuberant smile on his face. "Great news."

"What's that?"

"I'm cleared for the next race."

With those words, the bottom of my world drops out.

"What?" It's all I can manage and to be honest, even that is an effort.

"The doctor cleared me to race next week. He wasn't thrilled, but he understands I need to get back out there. I'll be back on the circuit and you are going to see the world by my side, Gigi."

I slump against my chair, releasing a slow exhalation as I try not to lose my appetizer. "You're really going back to racing?"

"Of course. It's what I do, Gigi. It's who I am. You'll finally get to see me in action."

"I saw you damn near die, Ryder." My hands shake as I wrap them around my water glass. "I know you don't see it, but you're so much more than racing. The doctor said another accident could kill you. How can you take that chance?"

Ryder leans across the table, grasping my hands. "Do you know how many races I've been in over the course of my life? Hundreds. I've only ever been hurt in one. Granted, the timing sucked, considering we were just married, but how lucky am I? I had this gorgeous nurse taking care of me. You wouldn't let me quit then. I can't quit now."

My head pounds at his admission, so expected and yet still a surprise. "What if there's another accident?"

"I can't predict the future."

"Racing a piece of carbon fiber around a track at two-hundred miles per hour doesn't help your odds any."

Ryder leans back in his chair, his mouth turning down in a frown. "You knew what I did for a living. Racing affords us this lifestyle."

His cold temperament unleashes my anger but I maintain a low tone. We don't need to give the tabloids any fodder for an expose. Ryder is big enough news already. "I don't give a shit about this lifestyle. I'm talking about you and me. About you taking unnecessary risks. About you not surviving the next crash. I'm scared, Ryder."

He's next to me in a flash, pulling me close as he tries to soothe my fears. "It's always you and me, Gigi. I know this has been a rough ride, but let me show you how much fun we're going to have." Tipping my chin up, he steals a kiss. "Give me a smile, beautiful. Please."

Blotting my tears with a napkin, I offer a tremulous smile, but inside, my heart is shattered. He's right. He's an F1 racer, and I knew that going in. What kind of woman would I be, asking him to change his life for me? The fact that I changed my life and plans for him is irrelevant. I did it willingly.

My mistake was expecting him to do the same. Expecting that the statements he made while blind would hold up once his vision was restored. But the real Ryder Gray is back, eager to reclaim his place in the history books. That another accident would almost certainly be fatal is secondary to his need to win.

I'm secondary to his need to win.

"Hey, I said I would show you the world. It's about time I made good on that promise. It's a bit crazy on the circuit, but we'll have time for the best restaurants, the fanciest hotels. You'll love it."

Kissing away my tears, Ryder scoots his chair against mine, but I feel the acres of space between us. Space that will continue to grow with each passing day.

I force myself to eat, even though the consommé tastes like prime rib and the prime rib tastes like cheesecake. It's all a gray blur, but he's spent a small fortune, and I refuse to appear ungrateful.

Plus, we're out together, which hasn't happened since

our marriage. Save for the doctor visits, which I'm happy to never revisit. At least he isn't out with Mandi again.

Stop it, Greer. Deep breath. Relax.

He promised he did nothing with Mandi or with any of those women, and I'm trying hard to believe him. It looks bad, but that's what the media does. They're shit stirrers. They love making things look more dramatic than they are.

I'm a rational woman and I won't buy into their crap. Instead, I'll rely on Ryder's words and actions.

"Did you enjoy the food?" Ryder asks, pressing a kiss to my palm.

"Very good," I lie, forcing yet another artificial smile. "Do you really need me with you on the circuit? Won't I be in the way?"

The smile fades from his face, his grip tightening. "You're never in the way. I need you by my side during the race. You're my cheerleader. You're my wife."

Ryder has a plethora of people at his beck and call, both on and off the track. Still, his words warm my heart until I glance down at our entwined fingers and the chill immediately returns.

"Where's your ring?" The band he slipped on last night, promising me he wanted the world to know the truth, is no longer on his hand.

Ryder clears his throat, averting his gaze. "I took it off earlier today. I didn't want the press hounding me with questions—"

"About your wife." A fat tear rolls down my cheek as reality sinks in. I'm not even an afterthought. I'm a secret.

"It's not like that. I promise, I'm going to tell them soon. Right after—"

"The next race. I've heard that one before." Rolling my shoulders, I call upon all my strength to present a strong front. Facade, don't fail me now. "You don't have to tell them anything. You don't owe them an explanation of your private life. It's probably better you don't say a word. I'm not much for the limelight, anyway."

"Gigi, I know how it looks but I swear, I'm not hiding you."

"I never said you were, but you just did." Slipping my fingers from his, I fold them in my lap.

Strike four, and this time, it's the final out.

CHAPTER 17
RYDER

I stretch out, my hand drifting to the opposite side of the bed, but instead of Greer's soft curves, all I feel are the cool cotton sheets.

The woman is always awake before the sun. Likely on her third cup of coffee by now.

Sitting up, I rub the sleep from my eyes and grab my phone. Half-past seven. Time to get moving.

First order of the day? Driving to Mick's house and getting Greer's ring. Then I need to get on my damn knees and beg the woman to give my sorry ass another pass.

I've screwed up royally the last couple of days. It's not intentional, but what does that matter? My actions have hurt the woman I love, and it's time to make amends.

The last few days blur together, a whirlwind of frenetic activity as I plan my comeback to my former life. Before Greer, I only had myself to worry about—my needs and desires sat shotgun—a perk of being single. But now, my life is about more than just me. When I married Greer, we became a package deal. A team. The only issue is I've kept my teammate in the dark since regaining my sight.

I'm one hell of a lucky guy to have a woman like Greer by my side, and I'll be damned if I let my stupidity drive a wedge between us.

With a sigh, I dial Francine. Time for another press release, and this time, I'm ensuring the world knows about my wife. The look on her face last night when she noted I wasn't wearing my wedding ring gutted me, as did the distance between us for the rest of the evening.

I know a press release won't fix things, but it's a start.

But the phone slips from my grip as I notice something lying on Greer's bedside table.

Her wedding band.

It sits atop a folded piece of paper, and I know what it's going to say without opening it.

"No, no, no," I mutter, my heart pounding as I snatch the note.

I HAVE TWO REQUESTS. *The first is that you continue to be your amazing, remarkable self. The second is that you'd better not die on me, Ryder Gray.*

Do you know how hard it is to leave you? To step away from the only man I've ever loved? I would never ask you to choose between me and racing, but I can't stand idly by and worry if this race will be your last. That this time, luck might not be on your side.

I leave all my luck with you because the world needs you. You might not realize it, but you're a hero. The ultimate comeback king.

But the truth of the last few days is that there isn't room in your life for me. I've never been one for parties and late-night festivities. In some weird way, I'm grateful for the accident, because it allowed me those months where it was just us. You and me against the world.

Now, you're on top of the world again, and I'd like to think I played some small role in that. After all, I wouldn't let you quit. Sometimes, stubbornness pays off.

Thank you for showing me how to love. Deep down, I always knew it would be you who could unlock my heart, and you'll forever hold it.

Be safe, my prince.

All my love,
 Gigi

"Ryder," a voice booms out from the phone. "Did you butt dial me?"

Grabbing up my phone, I realize with a start that I never ended the call to Francine. "Sorry, I—"

"Are you okay?"

The paper slips from my fingers, drifting back to the mattress as my mind attempts to comprehend what's happened. Am I okay? Not even remotely close. "Greer left me." I'm not sure why I'm disclosing this news to Francine. We aren't terribly close, but right now, my shock outweighs any need for discretion.

I expect words of comfort, but I'm met with silence.

"Francine, are you there?"

"I'm here, Ryder, and I'm sorry it came to this, but what did you expect to happen? You refused to publicly acknowledge her as your wife and then you gallivant with some random bimbos at the club."

"Whose side are you on?" I bellow, my anger careening into the red.

"You don't want to know." Francine releases a loud sigh into the receiver. "I'm simply offering you a different perspective. You didn't notice Greer's face that day when you called off your announcement, but I did. You devastated her, but she kept quiet. Tried to be supportive. I promised her you would make it home for the dinner she had planned, the one you swore you wouldn't be late for, but then I find out the next morning that the guys took you out to get shit-faced."

"We were celebrating." I bite out the words, unable to fathom that Francine is siding with Greer.

"Wasn't that what the dinner was supposed to be? A celebration of your recovery with the woman who took care of you these last couple of months? A great way to thank her, Ryder. Blowing her off in lieu of dancing the night away with other women. I won't tell you that your behavior is acceptable, because it isn't, although I hope you can patch things up. Greer seems like a very kind woman, from the few moments we spent together. She deserved better than what got from you."

"A kind woman who left me a Dear John letter and snuck out in the middle of the night. She's a real winner, Francine." I click off the call, unable to listen to her—my hired help—tout Greer's attributes.

Time to find a new publicist.

∽

My anger carries me through the next couple of days. That, and a few glasses of whiskey. For a brief moment, I consider calling one of my former bed buddies, but I can't stomach the idea of sleeping with another woman.

HOOK UP

Greg arrives this afternoon, but first, I have to meet with Mr. Givens. He called yesterday, with an urgent request that we sit down for a serious chat. No doubt he'll have some choice words for me and my current financial predicament.

Strolling into the granite building, I throw up a wave to his receptionist before heading back to his office.

Mr. Givens, Marty to his friends, glances up from his coffee, motioning to a chair. "Have a seat. How are you feeling?"

"I can see, but my wife left me."

"I know." He clears his throat, sliding some paperwork across the desk. "Greer asked me to draw up annulment papers."

My breath catches at his words as the severity of the situation settles over me. This isn't some passing grievance or tantrum. Greer is serious. And because I didn't sign a prenup, I'm now in serious trouble. "She asked *my* lawyer to draft annulment papers? That's fantastic. How good of her," I hiss, unable to control my rising fury. "Can't wait to see her list of demands. How much is she asking for?"

"Nothing."

My head flies up at his reply, and I snatch the papers, scanning over them. "Nothing?"

"No alimony, no payout, no claim to any real estate or cars. Nothing." He shifts back in his chair, studying me. "Trust me, Greer didn't want me to draw up the agreement, but she couldn't afford an attorney. Asked if I might consider the request as a favor. She thought I might help this go away quietly for you, so you would never have to let the world know you were married. I must admit I pegged her all wrong. She was never after your money."

Just like that, the anger slides away, and the grief takes hold. Dropping my head into my hands, I realize I'm more blind now than I was before. Suddenly, it's so clear. All Gigi wanted was reassurance she had a place in my life. In my world.

What did I do? Showed her all the ways she didn't. Inadvertently playing on her fears of abandonment by leaving her alone when she needed me most. In the last couple of months, she never asked for anything except my love. But in my rush to reclaim my former glory, I forgot about the one woman who ensured I got there.

"Are you okay?"

"No," I admit, scrubbing my face with my hands. "I screwed up and lost the most important thing in my life."

"She loves you very much, that was clear. After she refused any type of settlement, I inquired if she had a nest egg, considering she's been caring for you for the last couple of months. To quote Greer, she has neither a nest nor an egg, but assured me she would get back on her feet. She's in the process of setting up interviews and mentioned she's staying with her Mom until she can afford her own apartment. I offered her a settlement that I considered fair, but she unequivocally denied it, stating you don't pay someone to love you. That woman has a great deal of pride and an enormous heart. She's a class act, Ryder."

Every statement slams into me like a fist. My life, to the outsider at least, is picture-perfect again. I'm on top of the world, complete with new endorsements, pending interviews, and television slots. The money is pouring in. Not that I had any financial woes before the accident.

But Greer? Her life is upside down. She gave up everything to be by my side and now she's worse off than before. Yet, she still asked for nothing.

Mr. Givens slides a pen across the desk. "All I need is your signature, and I'll get the paperwork filed."

I snap from my thoughts, shaking my head at his request. "Not so fast. I have a few changes to make first. I'll see that Greer gets my list of demands."

My lawyer's eyes widen as he sits forward, resting his elbows on the desk. "What are you doing, Ryder? The woman has a boatload of debt, a crap car, and nowhere to live. She has nothing to give you."

"Yes, she does. The only thing I've ever wanted. Her." Standing up, I suck in a deep breath, feeling my resolve strengthen. "I'm not annulling my marriage. I'm saving it."

For the first time since I've known the man, Mr. Givens cracks a smile. An honest to God, genuine smile. "I like the sound of that. Keep me posted."

After leaving his office, I drive to the local watering hole, intent on discussing my plans with the one man who can understand my plight.

Mick.

Slipping onto the barstool, I motion to the bartender for a drink, managing a smile for my friend and mentor. "Hey, Mick."

"Damn, it's good to see you back again," Mick remarks, offering a toast.

"It's good to see everything." The words are true, although the one thing I want to see most in this world is once again several hundred miles from my side, and it's all my fault.

"Ready for the race?"

Drumming my fingers against the bar, I consider how to best answer his question. "I am, but I think this may be it for me."

To my surprise, Mick looks anything *but* surprised. "I had a feeling you might say that."

"Really?" Here I figured he would flip the script, coming

up with a list of reasons I should stay firmly planted in the driver's seat.

"That was no fender bender, buddy. You almost died, Ryder. Plus, you're married now, with a wife who no doubt is terrified you *will* die. I've been where you are. That exact same spot, with all the crazy fucked up emotions about what to do with my life. I thought I couldn't live without racing, but when it came down to it, I couldn't live without Rachel. Once I got that idea through my thick skull, it was a no-brainer."

"Greer left me," I spit out, staring down at my half-empty glass. As if anyone ever found answers there. "I messed up, Mick."

Mick swivels in my direction, clicking his tongue against his teeth. "Does this have anything to do with those photos circling the internet? Please tell me you didn't screw any of those women."

"Of course not. I would never do that to Gigi. The photos sure as hell didn't help, but it was more than that. She is scared I'm going to die, and I can't promise her I won't. Plus, I never announced our marriage and wasn't wearing my ring. So she feels like a dirty secret, but one who was good enough to take care of me when no one else would. Just an all-around cluster fuck, compliments of yours truly."

Mick swigs back his drink. But I know him. He's buying time, searching his brain for the right answer. A fix to this mess I've created. "It's no guarantee, but if Greer loved you enough to put up with your array of bullshit these past few months, she'll likely give you another chance. Do us all a favor, though, and stop screwing shit up. Rachel is going to have your head for this one."

"Don't I know it." It's true. Rachel has been my confidante for years, the big sister I never knew I wanted. She knows all about Greer, and she's going to kick my ass into the next county when she hears the news.

"Are we going to announce your retirement, or are you still weighing your options?"

"Let me get through this race first." Am I stalling? Yes, but right now, I'm so mixed up I don't know what I want. That's not true. I know I want my wife back, and I'll do whatever is necessary to ensure it happens.

"Fair enough. Keep your head in the game."

"Eye on the prize." Only difference? This time, I'm eying a different prize.

~

A SMILE SPLITS my face as I spy the beat-up van with New York plates parked in my driveway.

Greg has arrived.

Just in time.

Strolling across the pool area, I knock on his door, enveloping Greg in a bear hug the moment it opens. Sometimes you don't realize how much you miss a person until they're no longer in your life. It's like that with Greg.

With Greer, it's agony.

Now, I have to plead my case and pray Greg will help me salvage my marriage.

We settle onto the patio with glasses of lemonade instead of beer. Greg insists that it's fine if I want to crack open a cold one, but why risk it? My friend just completed rehab. I refuse to dangle that carrot in front of his nose.

Leaning back in my seat, I cross one booted leg over my knee, considering my approach to this conversation.

Greg beats me to it.

"I visited my mom before I left New York. Imagine my surprise when Greer opened the door."

"Did she tell you she left me?" I struggle to speak the words aloud, as if every time I give them breath, I'm also giving them strength.

Greg nods but doesn't offer any further information. Looks like he's waiting for me to spill my guts.

Here goes nothing.

"I didn't do anything with those women, Greg. I swear."

His eyes widen as he sucks down half the contents of his glass. "What women? Do I even want to know? Don't forget, she's my sister. Job or not, I will kick your ass if you cheated on her."

Raising my hands, I attempt to ward off his growing fervor. "Some overly exuberant and handsy fans got close one night at the club. The media got a few shots and went to town with it. It looked bad, but it really wasn't. Then Mandi showed up, and of course, they snapped a photo before security showed her the door." Running a hand over my beard, I shake my head. Time to own my shit. "It looked bad. Greer was so upset when she saw the photos. She had every right. If our roles were reversed, I'd be furious."

"Jillian would have my balls in a vise, are you kidding? Greer let you off easy."

Huffing out a breath, I swing my gaze to meet Greg's. "She left me, remember? What did she tell you? What reason did she give?"

"Honestly? She didn't, simply mumbled something about not fitting into your world and promptly changed the subject. Typical Greer."

"She is my world, Greg."

He fixes me with his dark stare, mouth pursed in a thin line. "You sure about that? It doesn't look good from where

I'm sitting. I'm sure you didn't mess around with those women, but the whole secret wedding and keeping everything on the down-low, it stinks."

"She wants an annulment, but I'm not giving her one. I'll fight her for years if that's what it takes. I want another chance to make her happy. Put her first. Everything got so screwy after the accident. I never treated her the way she deserves and now, she thinks I'm like every other man."

"She knows you're not like every other man. I think that's messing her up even more." Greg huffs out a breath, his eyes skyward. "She's had hangups since Dad left Mom, and they often get the better of her."

"Gigi told me years ago she wasn't built for relationships or love. I set out to prove her wrong, but I mucked it up then, too. I had her, Greg, and I let her slip through my fingers. I lost her."

"I doubt it."

"She's gone, isn't she?" I snap, my emotions getting the better of me.

"You know, Greer didn't want to come to Vegas after discovering you'd be there. Not because she hated you, but because she was in love with you. She thought she was slick, but I'm her brother. She was way too interested in where you were and how you were and what gorgeous women you were dating. I knew she had a thing for you. I also knew you had a thing for her, back in the day." He stands up, pacing the stonework floor. "Do you know the two of you lit up Vegas the second you saw each other? It was like a fucking movie, the way you gravitated to one another. I knew it then, that you two were meant to be together. I also worried if Gigi loved someone that much, it would scare the shit out of her."

I stroke my beard, smiling despite the pain. "Glad to know I wasn't the only one all those years."

"All these years, you've had a thing for Greer?"

With a chuckle, I nod, letting her brother in on all my secrets. "Since I was ten. I dated women and screwed plenty more, but it wasn't like that with Gigi. I wanted to give her three things: my ring, my last name, and my baby in her belly." Holding up my hands, I wait for Greg's inevitable wrath. "Too much information? Likely, but it's the truth. It's always been the truth."

"Well, two out of three ain't bad," Greg jokes, dodging the napkin I lob at his head. "Maybe after the season, you two can talk."

"Pfft."

"I'm serious. If you love her that much, don't walk away without a fight."

"You think I'm waiting until after the season ends? No way, man. I can barely make it through a day without her. I'd never survive the next few months." Sitting forward, I pull the annulment paperwork from my pocket. "Which is why I have a job for you."

Greg shakes his head, a grin coloring his features. "Does this involve a plane ride back to New York?"

Smiling, I down the rest of my glass with a flourish. "It sure as hell does."

CHAPTER 18
GREER

Staring at my reflection, I barely recognize the woman looking back at me. The light went out when I left Ryder, leaving a shell in its stead. With a sigh, I run my hand over my abdomen, wondering how I got into this mess and how in the world I'll ever get out.

Step one, get a job. Or three. I'm broke and having to borrow a few hundred dollars off my mother while crashing on her couch is an all-time low for me. Thankfully, I have an interview later today, although I doubt I'll be able to concentrate. Ryder's race, his inaugural run after his life-threatening injury, is tomorrow afternoon in California.

Every sporting channel is aflutter with excitement over his return. My heart is filled with anticipatory dread that the man I love will get hurt again. Such different priorities between fans and family.

Then there are the photos of Ryder with his arms around adoring fans, basking in the glory he's rightfully earned. It's ironic, but the photos somewhat soothe the pain of our separation.

Ryder bounced right back, as if nothing ever happened.

My heart will take a lot longer to recover.

Walking into the living room, I stop dead in my tracks. There, with coffee and a shit-eating grin, stands my brother.

"Greg? What are you doing here?"

"Visiting my sad sop of a sister," he replies, handing me a coffee. "Here's some caffeine to soothe the savage beast."

With a shake of my head, I decline his offering. "Thanks, but I'm off caffeine."

The grin widens, complete with Greg's infamous head tilt. "Jillian quit caffeine when she found out she was pregnant."

"Good to know." I'm not having this conversation. Not here and definitely not now.

Apparently, Greg has other ideas. "You're pregnant." It's not a question, rather a declaration. One I can't deny.

My mother joins us in the living room, pulling her son into a hug. "She is, but she won't admit it."

With a grunt, I throw up my hands in resignation. "Fine. I'm pregnant, okay? Are you two happy now? Can I return to being a sad sop?"

Greg shakes his head. He's not letting me off that easily. "No can do. Does Ryder know?"

I groan, flopping back against the couch. "Not yet."

"Gigi—"

"Don't Gigi me. I'm going to tell him, Greg. I figured I'd wait until after the season ends."

"That's not for a few months. You'll pop out the kid before then." Greg sits next to me, a stern expression coloring his face. "He deserves to know."

"Relax. I would never keep this information—or his child—from him. I don't even know how he'll take the news, considering our current situation." It figures. For most people, discovering you're pregnant is the greatest news on the planet, complete with elation and celebration. For me, it's yet another situation I have to figure out, with limited funds and an uncertain future.

Like I told Ryder, I knew I'd wake up from the fairytale and find it all to be a dream.

"About that." Greg pulls a manila envelope from his bag, tossing it on my lap.

"Is this what I think it is? I've been served by my own brother. How quaint." Picking up the envelope, I chuck it on the coffee table. "At least Ryder took the news well, judging by all the photos of him with gorgeous women decorating the internet."

"Those are stupid promo shots. Trust me, he's not in a good way, which concerns the hell out of me, considering he's about to race. But he's hopeful his list of demands in response to your annulment will help the situation."

"His list of demands? Greg, I'm broke. I'm living on Mom's couch. Let me guess, he's billing me for room and board?" Despite my internal mantra that I won't crack, the tears roll down my cheeks. "I can't pay it."

Greg grabs me about the neck, pulling me to him. "Open the damn envelope."

Why delay the inevitable, right? Doesn't matter how long I wait, the contents will remain the same.

With a grunt, I pull it open, scanning the first page. "It's the agreement Mr. Givens drew up. Doesn't look like anything is out of order—what the hell?"

It *is* the agreement Mr. Givens drew up, except that my husband has written all over the damn thing. He's crossed out paragraphs, changed every instance of Greer Hammond to Greer Gray, scribbled no way in hell by the sections where I requested nothing—it's a mess.

It's also the most illegal legal document I've ever seen.

Flipping to the last page, I see a note from Ryder, penned in his neat hand.

Are you done being mad at me? I told you before, Gigi, I'm not divorcing you. I'll fight you until the end of our lives and I know I have more money than you do, although you are now debt-free. Yes, I paid off everything.

No way was my wife going to worry over something as trivial as money. Not when she has me to worry about. And I know you do.

I also know you love me, so if you're willing to give me one last chance, here's a ticket to California.

I need my cheerleader. I need my wife.

P.S. Tell Greg to give you the other package. Figured I'd sweeten the deal a bit.

"He's not divorcing me," I remark with a dry laugh, tears dripping down my nose. "What else do you have?"

With great ceremony, Greg pulls a small box from his pocket. The aquamarine color is unmistakable—Tiffany's.

I've never been inside the store. What was the point? I couldn't afford anything in there, although I did plan that one day, I'd walk inside and order some grand piece of jewelry, nary a care to the cost.

My heart pounds as I take the box and peek inside.

It's empty, save for a piece of paper.

If you want it, come get it. Get your gorgeous ass on the plane next to your brother.

HOOK UP

. . .

"This is Ryder's idea of romance?"

Greg and my mother exchange a smirk before bursting into laughter.

"I think it's pretty good, all things considered," my mother adds, her eyes twinkling. "How can you say no to Ryder Gray? That man has loved you his entire life. Besides, I'm champing at the bit to see that ring."

"Might not be a ring," I manage, although I'm right there with her. I'd love to know what was originally in that box, too.

"I think we all know it's a ring. One so gigantic you won't be able to lift your hand."

My mother is trying to maintain a lighthearted atmosphere, but those niggling fears still circle in my head. I was forgotten once before when Ryder got caught up in the glory of his former life. What if second-fiddle is the best I can ever hope for? The little woman at home, waiting for her celebrity husband to grace her with his presence.

That's not what I had in mind when I said yes to Ryder's proposal. But maybe the man in Barbados and the man who lost his sight isn't the real Ryder Gray. Perhaps I envisioned a man who doesn't exist, created by my fanciful imagination.

"I don't know what to do."

"You don't?" Wonderful, now they're speaking in stereo.

"Mom, I'm so afraid of ending up..." I struggle for the right words, if there are any.

She wraps an arm around my shoulder, pulling me close. "Like me? I don't want you to end up like me, either. But honey, with the path you're on, you'll wind up far lonelier than I ever was. Your father was wrong for leaving the way he did, but he's paid a hefty price."

"He hasn't paid at all," I snap, my anger flashing at the mention of the man.

"He lost his family. His only daughter won't speak to him. He's spent the last several holidays alone."

"He deserves it."

"When is it enough, Greer? You're not only punishing him, but you're punishing yourself, and you have been for years. You keep everyone at a distance, thinking it keeps you safe. It keeps you alone and you deserve all the love in the world, but you have to let it in. Let Ryder love you the way he's always wanted. He messed up, but he's not giving up. Doesn't that say something?"

Her words turn on the waterworks, the sobs racking my body. My mother is right. I am alone, and I don't want to be anymore.

But that knowledge doesn't eradicate the fear holding my heart hostage.

The fear that I'll love Ryder and then I'll lose him.

"What if something terrible happens to Ryder? What if he dies?"

My Mom smooths my hair, sending me a soft smile. "You're going to pass on your soulmate because he might die? Spoiler alert—we're all going to die. Ryder is offering you a chance to live. Question is, will you take it?"

∼

Greg sleeps the entire flight to California, while I think—and rethink—my decision to drop everything and run to Ryder's side. I've done this once before and it didn't end well.

I'm not convinced there's room in his life for me, but at least I'll be there to root for him.

Be his cheerleader.

Then, I'll tell him about my pregnancy and take it from there.

There's also the worry that Ryder indulged with one, or several, of the half-naked beauties captured by his side, although Greg swears that isn't the case. My heart tells me my brother is correct.

Then again, my heart is an idiot.

By the time we land, Greg is raring to go and I'm halfway between nauseous and anxious. Not a fun place to be.

But I follow Greg through the myriad of buildings and trailers set up for the race, practically running to keep up with him. My heart pounds like a runaway train, and I only pray it doesn't infarct before I see Ryder.

Stepping into the team's trailer, I spot Mick, who lights up when he sees me.

"I'm sure as hell glad to see you," Mick says, pulling me into a hug. "Do you know that man never shuts up about you?"

Despite the nerves, I chuckle. "A woman likes to know she's missed."

"The man is lost without you. Don't repeat that, because he might want to kick my ass, but it's true." Mick nods at Greg, who's already by the vehicle, helping with last-minute tuneups.

"Where is the man of the hour?"

Mick jerks his thumb over his shoulder, motioning to a closed door. "Taking some time to himself. Get on in there."

Knocking the door with a trembling hand, I hear Ryder's familiar grunt from the other side. Pushing it open, I see him, his head in his hands.

"Mick, I really need some time, man."

"I'll let Mick know."

His head flies up, eyes wide as relief crosses his face.

"Gigi? You're here. Thank God you're here." He's across the space in two strides, enveloping me in his arms.

I melt into his embrace, those dang tears once again rolling down my face. "I had to respond to your demands regarding our annulment."

Ryder smiles, peppering my face with kisses. "I'm not divorcing you. You can fight me in court. Better yet, be my wife forever."

But despite his bravado and the electricity sparking through the air, my heart thuds at the unknown. "You're really doing this?"

"I have to, Gigi. I have to prove to myself that I'm still Ryder Gray." His lips seize mine, the desperation evident in his kiss. "But you were wrong. I've always loved you more than racing."

"Five minutes, Ryder," Mick's voice sounds from the other side of the door.

Cupping his face, I press a hard kiss to his mouth. "Stubborn ass."

Ryder's eyes—those beautiful blue eyes—are bright with emotion. "Will you stay?"

"Of course. I even brought my pompoms."

"I don't mean the race. Will you stay with me? I didn't wait twenty years to marry you, only to lose you a few months in. I love you, Gigi. My world is nothing without you."

All my insecurities race to the forefront of my brain, vying for position. But, with a deep breath, I kick them back where they belong. "I know it's terrible timing, and you said this wasn't a path you desired anymore, but I have something to tell you." Grabbing his hand, I place it on my stomach. "You're going to be a dad, Ryder. So, you'd better get out there and win."

I hold my breath, awaiting his reaction. Unsure if I should have said anything.

The brightness in Ryder's eyes increases as he tangles his fingers in my hair, resting his forehead against mine. "I was so afraid something happened to the baby."

Pulling back, my gaze widens in surprise. "You knew?"

He nods, dropping to his knees and wrapping his arms around my waist. "The way you smelled and tasted changed. It was so slight, but it was there. You were even more appealing than before and trust me, I already want to jump you twenty-four hours per day."

"You're not angry?"

Glancing up at me, I wish I could freeze Ryder's smile forever. "It's the greatest news in the world. You're having my baby. Three for three."

"What?"

"Inside joke with Greg and me." Popping to his feet, his mouth claims me again, his tongue demanding everything I have. "I love you, Greer Gray, and I'm going to win, for both of you."

With a final kiss, he walks out the door, my heart racing like a locomotive. All I can manage is a whisper of love and a prayer for his safety.

I stand toward the back of the crowd, my hands clenched as my eyes dart between the screen and everywhere else in the room. To say I'm a nervous wreck would be the understatement of the century.

Gazing to my right, I note a beautiful brunette. Even with her designer sunglasses covering her eyes, I feel her gaze upon me. No telling who she is or what her relationship is to Ryder, but that doesn't matter right now.

Returning my focus to the race, I realize Ryder is winning. Digging my nails into my palm, I can't breathe as he maneuvers around the track, seizing the inside corner. Within seconds, he crosses the line to the waving of the checkered flag.

Ryder Gray just won his first race back after a life-threatening injury. That crazy, insane, amazing man did it.

He's back on top of the world, and the crowd knows it, their cries drowning out even the roar of the motors. When the cameras focus on Ryder exiting his vehicle, the stands go insane. They all know he accomplished the unfathomable.

Talk about a comeback king.

When he takes his rightful place on the podium, I can see the giddiness on his face as he sprays his adoring public with champagne.

What a moment.

What a man.

I'm jostled from all sides as the crowd pushes closer, desperate for a piece of Ryder Gray.

He belongs to the world again. I always said one day I'd have to give him back.

After being bumped one too many times, I slip to the side, letting the throng of people pass.

Once again, that feeling of uncertainty settles over me, the nagging idea that I'm in the way, much as I am for the crowd of fans. It's been such a whirlwind romance, Ryder and I, that it's hard to know where my place is, or if I even have one.

Then my stomach rumbles, reminding me I need food, and I need it now.

I recall seeing a nacho stand across the way. Time to tame this beast of a belly.

A hand grabs my arm, and I whip around, staring at the same brunette from earlier. "Where do you think you're going?"

"I'm hungry." Not a lie, even if this strange woman did throw me with her direct question.

"Come on, the team has far better food." Without asking permission, she links her arm through mine, weaving through the crowd and flashing a smile at security guarding the team's trailers. "I've been waiting years to meet you. I damn near called you myself."

"Me?" After the events of the last couple of months, I feel like I've fallen down the rabbit hole, where nothing makes any sense.

"Yes, Greer Gray, you. I'm Rachel Marsh, Mick's wife."

I chuckle, my unease slipping away. "I've heard so much about you."

"Not as much as I've heard about you. Ryder and I have always talked. He's such a sensitive soul. One night after Mick went to bed, Ryder and I stayed up, chatting and finishing a bottle of wine. I wanted to know why he didn't consider settling down since he's such a catch. That's when he told me about you. His one great love."

My mind reels at her statement. "Ryder mentioned me? When was this?"

Rachel taps her chin, considering my question. "Hmm... the first time was five years ago? He'd often mention you, always with this wistful look on his face about the one who got away. But then he called me from Barbados. The man was giddy."

Now I know she's lying. "He did not."

But Rachel is not easily dissuaded as she pulls her phone from her bag. "Look."

She presses play on a video and there's Ryder, perched on the boulder right outside our villa, his tan skin glowing in the early morning sunlight. "Rach, you'll never believe it. I'm with Gigi. We've spent the last ten days together, and I was right, she's perfect." He produces the small pouch that I know contained our wedding rings, and that glorious crooked grin decorates his face. "I'm asking her to marry me tonight. I'm terrified she'll say no, so cross your fingers, toes, and any other damn body part for me, okay?"

Wiping the tears from my cheeks, I return Rachel's phone. "He's my first and only love, too."

"Then might I suggest you follow me? You're headed in the wrong direction. Plus, I'm under strict orders to bring you straight to his arms."

Digging in my heels, I grasp her hand. "Things are complicated right now. We're separated. I'm not sure how much I should be around today, in case the media inquires about who I am. His reputation is so important to him, and I don't want anything to detract from his win."

"Do you love him?"

"Yes, but—"

"Then there's no problem you two can't solve. Ryder asked me to ensure you were safe and stayed put, so I don't think he gives a damn what the media have to say. Come on, I know you're hungry."

Nothing like plying a pregnant woman with food. With a sigh, I follow her to where the team is gathered; the exuberance filling the space.

"Gigi," Greg lets loose with a whoop, racing to my side and swinging me around like a doll. The glow on my brother's face is contagious and I hug his neck, as the pride washes off him in waves.

"You did so good."

"Unhand my wife."

I swing my gaze to the right, offering a smile for Ryder, who's beaming from the race. I guess he's right. Nothing compares to a win.

I'm not on the ground for two seconds when Ryder scoops me into his arms, his mouth claiming mine. Once again, as is always the case with my husband's kisses, the world falls away as his tongue and fingers lay claim to me.

"I did it, Gigi," Ryder murmurs, his mouth refusing to leave mine.

"The indisputable king of racing."

"I won for you. I won for our baby." He pulls his head back, eyes wide. "I'm such a shit."

Holy hell, what did he do now?

"How are you feeling? Are you tired? Hungry? Do you need to sit? You should sit."

With each question firing from his mouth, my smile widens. "I'm fine. A bit hungry, but otherwise, I'm perfect."

"You are indeed perfect," he replies, pressing another kiss to my mouth. "But, let's get you some food."

"Are you going to be like this the whole pregnancy?" I joke, giggling at his pained expression. "Not that I mind. I appreciate your concern."

"Good, because I'll probably be worse. Fawning over you all the time. You okay with that?"

Grasping his chin, I direct his lips back to mine. "I think I can handle it."

"Hate to interrupt this reunion, but they're waiting to do an interview." Mick claps a hand on Ryder's shoulder.

With an embarrassed chuckle, I smooth a bit of gloss from my husband's lips. "You'd better go. Don't want to keep your public waiting."

"Not without you. We are blasting through this interview and then, I'm taking you somewhere private. I have needs, and you are the only cure."

My cheeks flush, certain that several people heard his provocative remark. "Are you going to put me down first?"

"No." That's all he offers as a response, save for a wink and another kiss. Within moments, we're surrounded by reporters, all desperate for a few moments with Ryder Gray.

Intimidating, to say the least, especially for this introvert. But I smile, wondering what in the world I'm doing in the middle of this throng.

"Congratulations, Ryder. That was one hell of a win."

"Thank you."

"Are you glad to be back in the driver's seat?"

Ryder's gaze locks with mine, a smile crossing that gorgeous mouth. "It felt amazing, but I'm considering retirement."

His statement shocks the media, but I'm floored. My jaw drops open, my eyes wide. "What?"

He ducks his head, his beard tickling my ear. "You need me safe. I need you. I told you, I've always loved you more than racing."

Turning to the crowd, he directs their attention to me. "See this gorgeous woman? This is my wife, Greer. I've loved her since I was ten. She stayed by my side during my injury and trust me, I was a bastard most days. Still, she never gave up. She never gave up on me." He pauses, and I see the tears backing up in his eyes. "Greer gave me the best news today. We're having a baby."

Cupping his face, I kiss him, nuzzling his nose. "You're not supposed to say anything yet."

"Oh well, it's not like the international media will print anything," Ryder jokes, but the smile softens, a look of intensity crossing his features. "She's my entire world. Racing is in my blood, but my wife and child are my heart. I don't work without them."

Any walls holding my heart from Ryder blast apart, and I wrap my arms around his neck, tears pouring down my cheeks. For the first time since my father walked out all those years ago, I'm sure of my place in this world. I'm also sure of the man who holds my heart—a man willing to give up his dream to pursue ours.

That's the quintessential definition of love, and if he's willing to go the distance, so am I.

The buzz around us grows ever louder as the reporters clamor on, desperate for details.

"Are you really retiring? Is this it?"

Ryder offers me a reassuring smile, but it's my turn to speak. "Not yet. He's got more winning to do."

His eyes widen, a look of confusion crossing his face. "I thought—"

"I was wrong. We'll all die one day. The important part is how you live. I want my life with you. Only with you."

This time, I meet Ryder's kiss more than halfway, but I feel the trembling under his skin, the bevy of emotions coursing through him. "Thank you. Once our child arrives, I'm done."

Somehow, I know he means it, and there's not a drop of hesitation in his tone.

"Anything to add, Mrs. Gray?" a reporter interjects, cutting into our moment.

"Take good care of my husband at the track. I've got him covered at home."

Ryder sets me down, and I leave his side with a final kiss, letting him bask in the glory of the moment. But I see his gaze flit my way every few seconds, and I know the truth. Between racing and me, there is no competition.

Our love wins every time.

∽

"I'm starving." Making a beeline for the catering table, I have one aim. Food.

Hey, I'm pregnant and my nerves wouldn't allow me to eat for the last week or so.

Now? I plan to eat my weight in food.

A hand snags my sandwich, and I swing my head up with a glare. "What the—oh, figures it's you. You win one little race and act like you're king of the world."

"I am king of the world, but it's got nothing to do with the race." Ryder wraps his arms around me, and I melt against him. "You threw me for a loop out there. Did you really mean what you said?"

"I did. Were you really going to retire?"

"It meant that much to you. You wanted me safe and after you told me we're having a baby, it was no question. But I'd love to finish the season."

Sending him a saucy wink, I grab another sandwich. "That's the spirit. You'd better win. Hammonds don't like losers."

"Well, you're not a Hammond anymore. You and my baby are both Grays. And Grays always win what really matters."

This man and his one-liners. Just when I think he can't do any better, he ups the ante. "You're pretty damn good at being romantic."

"Like that?"

"I do. Oh, I have a bone to pick with you." I pull the small box from my purse. "It's empty. Who does that?"

Ryder bursts out laughing. "I figured it would drive you nuts."

"To say the least. Was there anything good in here?" Truth is, I don't care. I won the ultimate prize—the man who holds my heart.

HOOK UP

But my knees buckle when Ryder sinks to one knee—in front of everyone—and pulls a ring from his pocket. Not just any ring. This beauty is flawless and absolutely gigantic. "I'm not sure. Does this seem good enough to you?"

"Oh, my God." It's all I can manage as Ryder slides the ring onto my finger, pressing a kiss to my palm. The stone is enormous and my mother was right; I can barely lift my hand under the weight. "It's so beautiful, but I didn't need this, Ryder."

"Yes, you did. I got a perfect stone. Perfect, like you. I love you, Gigi, forever and always. But I have a request. We need to get married again in front of everyone. Otherwise, my mom will never forgive me."

My smile stretches from ear to ear as I wrap my arms around him, taking in the whoops of excitement surrounding us. "What the hell. I think I like you well enough to marry you again. Can I have my wedding ring back, please?"

With a nod, Ryder slips it from his pocket and onto my finger. It's then I notice the band on his hand. He really wasn't going to let me go.

Willing back another onslaught of tears, I pepper his face with kisses. "Now, about that private time. Do you really have something planned?"

"It was supposed to be a surprise, but yes, I have a beautiful suite waiting for us."

"I ruined the surprise?"

"You did."

Biting back a grin, I let the laughter bubble up. "How about this? I have one of my own."

Ryder pulls me closer, his gaze curious. "Really?"

"You keep referring to the baby, but that's not entirely accurate."

"What do you mean?" A furrow creases his brow, concern evident. With a sly smile, I hold up two fingers, watching his eyes widen like saucers. "Twins?"

Nodding, I giggle as he sweeps me back into his arms, a look of joy and disbelief on his face. "I figure I'll keep you on your toes until the twins arrive. Then they'll be sure to keep their Daddy busy." Twining my hands around his neck, I bask in our glow. "Are you happy?"

"Beyond, and it has nothing to do with winning the race. I mean it, Gigi, you two—I mean three—are my entire world. You're the light. I never knew such darkness as when you left."

"I'll make you a deal. Let's never leave each other again."

"Best deal ever, and this one comes with a lifetime guarantee."

EPILOGUE
RYDER

"Where is she?" I ask Jillian, a permanent grin stretched across my face.

Hey, I earned this smile. After returning from my injury, I won six of ten races. Not too shabby.

But that's nothing compared to the real prize. Greer and our babies.

My wife was a trooper on the grueling race schedule, never once complaining, although I did often send her back to the suite to rest.

When the season ended, she flopped onto our bed and announced she wasn't moving for a week.

I fully supported that plan.

Now, we're making good on the promise to the parents—a wedding with all the trimmings, along with a bride who's five months pregnant.

With twins.

Like I said, total trooper.

Although, judging by the exasperated look on Jillian's face, Greer may be done playing nice. To be fair, Jillian is a week ahead of my wife, but Gigi claims it doesn't count because she's building two babies.

She wins.

In my book, she always does.

"She won't come out of the bedroom without speaking to you."

"On it." Chuckling, I duck into the guest quarters at my mother's house on Lake George, uncertain what to expect. Hopefully, I don't walk out with a shoe lodged in my head. "Beautiful, you okay?"

"I will be."

Turning, I let my gaze wander over Gigi's curves. If I thought she was gorgeous before, she's exponentially more so now. My wife stands before me, hands on hips, clothed in nothing but lace underwear and a sexy grin. "Look at you. Can you just stay like that?"

"I can, but we have to do something about you."

Glancing down at my suit, I shoot her a smirk. "I think I look pretty damn good."

"You do," she responds, her fingers undoing the buttons on my shirt, "but you'll look so much better naked."

See why I love my wife?

"Do we have time?"

"Seriously?" Greer pouts, intent on the task at hand. "They can't have a wedding without a bride and groom. And this bride needs servicing. Please." She purrs the last word in my ear, her tongue gliding along the rim. Just like that, I'm rock hard.

The tux that took me an hour to put on is draped over a chair in less than a minute, and I'm bending my wife over the dresser, her gorgeous ass on full display as I sink balls deep into her heat.

Greer is desperate, arching her hips and grinding against

me. But I maintain an easy rhythm, loving how her body quivers beneath my hands.

"You feel so good."

"Not nearly as good as you," I huff, as the spasms reverberating through her body trigger my own release. I press open-mouthed kisses to her nape, twitching as she squeezes around me, driving me, once again, to the brink. "That was the greatest wedding gift ever."

With a giggle, Greer turns, claiming my lips in a fierce kiss. "Took the words right out of my mouth." Glancing at the time, she sends me a wink. "Will you send Jillian back in? About time I put on my wedding gown."

Ten minutes later, I slip from the guest quarters, sending my sister-in-law back in to dress my now sexually sated wife.

Like I said, life couldn't get any sweeter.

～

ALL BRIDES ARE BEAUTIFUL. It's true. They glow, the thrill of a life next to the person they love shimmering through every pore. But Greer? She's next level as she walks toward me, escorted by her father.

Yep, her father. I forced my wife to sit down and hash things out with her old man because I know the feeling of not having that option. Turns out, they have a ton in common and although the scars remain, they're forging ahead on a new path.

Mr. Hammond hands off his daughter, and I steal a kiss from Greer, even though I know I'm now wearing some of her lip gloss. Totally worth it. It also gives me another opportunity to nip her neck, catching that amber scent I love so much. If it wouldn't be frowned upon for years to come, I'd strip Gigi down and have a replay of our earlier tryst. What can I say? Orgasms look good as hell on my woman.

After the ceremony, where we proclaim once again that forever really means forever, the festivities begin. I spared no expense on the party because you only get married once, or in our case, twice.

"Tell me again why you were late for your own ceremony?" Jillian asks, as Greer's cheeks flame.

"I... I..." Poor Greer, the woman can't lie to save her life.

"Don't tell me you two were having sex before the ceremony." Thank you, Jillian, for announcing that so loud the neighbors heard you—in the next county.

"What? He's my husband. It's pretty apparent"—Greer motions to her stomach—"that we've had sex."

"Too much information," Greg interjects, his face curled in a fake grimace. "I can't believe you married my sister. What are the odds?"

I chuckle, toasting my brother-in-law. Soda, of course. "Hey, I told you when I was ten that my dream was to make Gigi my wife. I'm just damn lucky it came true."

Greer wraps her hands around my neck, offering up a sweet kiss. "You are my dream come true."

"Why can't you say things like that?" Jillian demands of Greg, eliciting peals of laughter from the group.

"I know why," Greer whispers in my ear. "Because there's only one Ryder Gray, and he's mine."

Talk about perfect timing. As if on cue, the strains of our Otis Redding song fill the air, and tears mist in Greer's eyes.

"May I have this dance?"

"You can have every one of them," she replies, taking my hand as I lead her to the floor.

"How are you feeling?" Yes, I worry. Constantly. But it's a perfect balance to my wife, the medical professional, who is more laid back about this pregnancy than any woman I've ever known.

"Perfect. I—" her voice cuts off, her hands flying to her belly.

See? This is why I worry. "What is it, Gigi? What's wrong?"

A smile stretches across her face as she grabs my hands and places them against her stomach. "Looks like someone else is a fan of our song."

There, by the shores of Lake George, I feel the tiny tap from inside her belly, and I sink to my knees, pressing kisses to her skin. "My babies." Glancing up at Greer, I know the brightness in her eyes matches my own. "Thank you."

"For what?"

"Waiting for me. Believing in me. Loving me. Giving me the greatest gift in the world. Take your pick."

"You're not so bad yourself, Mr. Gray."

Popping back to my feet, I claim that gorgeous mouth in a kiss. "Gigi, you ain't seen nothing yet."

THE END

Hello Lovelies,

I hope you've enjoyed Ryder & Greer's story. I'll admit that I never thought I'd be a sucker for a brother's best friend story, but the fact that this man loved one woman since he was ten is too adorable. Plus, the fact that he's sexy as sin doesn't hurt.

Be sure to sign up for my mailing list so you never miss a release. Plus, I make sure to include a freebie or giveaway (or both) in every newsletter. You don't want to miss it!

Join My Mailing list here!

One last favor—if you loved **Hook Up**, tell everyone! Seriously though, lovelies, reviews are greatly appreciated. They're like gold to an author.

Best wishes for a life well-lived. Until we meet again.

M.L. Broome

Also by M.L. Broome

Make You Stay

Friends to Lovers / Opposites Attract / Single Dad

And Then Came You

Friends to Lovers / Slow Burn / Celebrity Romance

A Sinner's Memory (Lyrical Love Letters)

Rockstar Romance / Second Chance / Single Dad

Forgot to Tell You Something

High Angst / Surprise Pregnancy / Medical Romance

Alchemy Unfolding

Reverse Age Gap / Sexy Surfer / Medical Romance

A Series of Moments Trilogy Box Set

High Angst / Celebrity Romance / Medical Romance

Hook Up

Brother's Best Friend / Reverse Age Gap / Racing Romance

Baby Maker (Cocky Hero Club)

Young Widow / Forbidden Romance / Love After Loss

Yuletide Acres

Yule Holiday Romance / Second Chance / Single Dad

It Must Have Been the Mistletoe

Christmas Romance / Second Chance / Sexy Drummer

CONNECT WITH M.L. BROOME

Sign up for her newsletter
(Freebies, Giveaways & Subscriber Exclusives)
https://www.mlbroome.com/join-my-mailing-list

BookBub
https://www.bookbub.com/profile/m-l-broome

GoodReads
https://www.goodreads.com/author/show/19088931.M_L_Broome

TikTok
www.tiktok.com/@mlbroomeromance

Facebook
https://www.facebook.com/mlbroomeromance

Instagram
https://www.instagram.com/mlbroomeromance/

About the Author

I'm a bohemian spirit with a New York edge. I adore dressing up and kicking back, a nice glass of wine with an equally stunning view, and experiences that make the soul--and mouth--water.

When I'm not writing or holding one-sided arguments with my characters (spoiler alert—they always win), I love losing myself in nature on my North Carolina farm, one of my rescue buddies at my side.

Life is beautiful...so are you. Don't forget to look up. Peace, love, & magic.

"You'll climb as high as you dare believe you are capable. The stars are only as far as we imagine them to be, and time is neither friend nor foe. Magic is everywhere. Life is a thing of beauty."

Printed in Great Britain
by Amazon